LAS VEGAS TURNAROUND

ALSO BY KURT JOHNSON

The Outlaw Shuffle

The Barrens (with Ellie Johnson)

LAS VEGAS TURNAROUND

KURT JOHNSON

A Sin City Thriller

First Published by Street Level Press

This novel is entirely a work of fiction. The names, characters, and incidents portrayed in it are the work of the author's imagination. Any resemblance to actual persons, living or dead, events or localities is entirely coincidental.

ISBN: 9798218-347185

Street Level Press
www.StreetLevelPress.com

For Dolores, who waited years for her son to finally write a book.

CHAPTER ONE

What did she see? The bar glowed green from the sconce lights turned low and covered by library shades. The chocolate-brown carpet had a weird pattern with haphazard scarab-beetle figures—some color and design to mask the tracked-in desert dirt. She smoked a cigarette at the bar along with others so that the green, the brown, and the smoke combined into a forest-like haze that was, in a way, calming and mellow. The music was loud and drowned out the conversations in the booths and along the barstools beside her. The owner, Reuben, played seventies pop songs by guys like Hall & Oates, Neil Diamond, and Boz Scaggs. His favorite music was still the Rat Pack stuff, and he played Sinatra and those guys when he could, but it was the eighties now and at least he'd updated his soundtrack to the seventies. It wasn't like Reuben's was the hip place to be in Las Vegas, it wasn't, say, Tramps nightclub. His place was more of a relaxed bar where people came to just hang out, away from the high-energy spots, maybe wind down after a shift at the casinos, have a few drinks, then go home and sleep.

She ordered another tall Long Island iced tea that tasted sweet and summery. Her third. The bartender, Vin, lifted two bottles at a time, first the vodka and gin, then the tequila and rum. Something, something, then a splash of coke and a lemon wedge. Vin was cute in a Brooklyn sleazeball way, a movie character like Tony in *Saturday Night Fever*. Behind Vin was a huge fish tank with one small, lonely shark the length of a thigh-high boot. And sometimes, usually into her third Long Island, she imagined swimming—spreading her arms wide, spreading her fingers, and gliding through the shark-tank water and bar smoke. Claire felt like that now, relaxed and waiting. Waiting for a date.

Her best friend, Apple, was on a date already. Her beeper had gone off around ten, and she hadn't returned since. Claire was starting to feel like she'd rather not get a date. It was past midnight, and she was already three drinks into the evening. It would be another long night if she got one, probably back home after sunrise. She'd rather just skip it altogether. But then her beeper went off—not the sound part, just the vibration, startling like a rattlesnake.

At the bathroom pay phone, she held the side button on the beeper to see the displayed phone and room number. She dialed the phone number that she knew by heart—the Dunes switchboard. The operator transferred the call. After one ring, a man picked up. "Hello." The voice was deep, and she imagined a large man.

"Hi. This is Cher. You were looking for a date?" Her escort name was Cher, like Sonny and Cher. It was close enough to her real name, Claire, so she wouldn't confuse herself. And she had long dark hair like the real Cher and the same narrow Italian nose, so it was a thing—they'd hear her name, see her, and think Cher, *Bang Bang*, a fantasy. She wasn't

Italian, though, she was English and Mexican. Last name, Welch. Her mother's maiden name, De La Rosa.

"Yeah, a date. Can you meet me at the Dunes Hotel, room one-six-four-nine? Like soon?"

"They won't let me in the elevator without a room key." What she did was illegal in Clark County. If caught, Dunes Security would ban her from the premises and slap her around for good measure. "You got to meet me downstairs. Let's meet at the bar right outside the showroom, and then you can escort me to the room. You'll recognize me. I have long black hair and I'll be carrying a pink purse." That was another one of her things—a big pink purse that held all her stuff like wallet, keys, makeup, perfume, condoms, Summer's Eve, a miniature charge-card machine—really just a plastic tray and spoon for making an imprint—and Mace. The guy could always find the pink purse. It was big, like luggage.

"Okay, I'll find you. Can you be fast, twenty minutes?" He was anxious, but what date wasn't?

"Sure," she said, "I'm close."

She sat back at the bar, then looked up and motioned Vin with a smile. She asked for a to-go cup. Vin spilled the contents of her Long Island into a clear plastic cup with a top and straw. She slipped a twenty from her wallet, fifteen for the drinks and a five for Vin. She stood. He took the twenty and tapped his knuckles on the bar, "Have a good one, Claire."

Reuben's was in a strip mall on Maryland Parkway, just off Flamingo. The glass windows lined up along the parking lot were all tinted with acetate that let in zero sunlight, and each carried Reuben's signature in gold script like some Rat Pack autograph, like *Sammy* or *Dean*, or *Frank*. She stepped into her red Porsche 924. She'd bought the sports car used with ninety-thousand miles on it, but it was still a Porsche, and she knew she looked good behind the wheel, especially on a sunny, not-so-hot day with the windows rolled down and wearing her white Vuarnet cat-eye sunglasses. Crap littered the car—old to-go cups, shoes, and a pile of clothes—but she rarely saw those things at night. What she saw were the spread of gauges pulsing with the throaty engine, and the Porsche steering wheel badge that looked like some medieval coat of arms. She drove down Flamingo, took a left on the Strip, and a right into the Dunes self-parking lot. She parked farthest from the casino next to an RV and then finished her Long Island, sucking the last few syrupy drops like a milkshake.

She walked alongside tourists through a back entrance.

The guy spotted her pink purse right as she stepped up to the bar area.

And there he was, another date, another guy to fuck or whatever. But it wasn't like she was *totally* numb to sex. It could go either way. They could be old, like grandpa old. They could be fat with acne scars, with facial hair that smelled like rotting food. They could be all uptight, as though this was their first lay in ten years or their first time cheating on the wife. Sometimes, she took one look and just turned around and left (May, who ran the service she used, provided security if needed). Then there were those dates where she could have fun. Some of the guys were good-looking and casual, like this was no big deal, like just a fling—like *let's party.*

First and foremost, though, it was a job. She had to do her rules and negotiation thing. The guy needed to know that he'd paid the service for the date, but she would need to be tipped extra for anything else. Tips ranged in price based on the extra service: a hand job was forty, a blowjob eighty, and more for other stuff. She didn't do anal, she didn't do parties, and no rough stuff.

That night, the guy looked like he could be fun. He was maybe just over thirty, had shoulder-length hair, and was very muscular, like a body builder. He was clean-shaven. "Hey, Pink Purse," he said and smiled. There was a cute gap between his front teeth. He said his name was Rod (really?). He had a seat saved for her at the bar, and she ordered a fresh Long Island iced tea. He talked about himself—thought he was cool—single, from LA, sold Lamborghinis and Bentleys at a dealership on Wilshire Boulevard in Beverly Hills, and had a comped room at the Dunes because he spent so much at the tables—a real high-roller. Claire just assumed these were all lies. He paid the bar bill (not comped), and they walked toward the elevator with their drinks.

When he closed the room door, he took the Long Island from her hand and set it down on the dresser. He turned back and smiled. It was then she started her rules and negotiation thing. The whole pitch began with the word "So," the uncomfortable transition word that women could use to stop men—husbands, boyfriends, dates—in their tracks (So, where were you… So, you didn't get… So, this is what you need to do…). And that's when he swung his fist and broke her nose.

Claire did not remember hitting the floor but remembered what happened afterward.

With one eye open, she saw a dark-red pool spreading slowly and soaking into the carpet. He forced her head down, her other eye pressed into the warm blood. He gagged her with a bunched-up sock. He never said another word and kept her face turned away, pressed into the carpet or, later, the bed sheets. She went numb and lifeless, waiting. She smelled his heavy cologne and his sweat like Brie cheese. She cried, more scared than hurt, and wondered if she would get out of the hotel room alive. She'd used her Mace only once. That time, she'd been on her way to a date at the Stardust. A boy barely out of high school met her at the bar and escorted her up. He was staggering and slurring drunk. When he opened the door, she saw it was a party—eight or ten guys all sitting around drinking beer and watching porn on the television. She calmly excused herself to go to the bathroom, then came out spraying. Now, she couldn't see her pink purse or even move. She waited and felt the pain. It was an hour before the guy was spent and tired.

As he left the room, he said, "Hey, Pink Purse, thanks for the memories."

When it was done, when he was gone, she lay lifeless on the bed, staring at the spit-out blood-soaked sock inches from her face. She'd stopped crying long ago and just felt numb—asleep but not asleep. She thought about the aquarium at the bar and saw herself reaching in, climbing in, and touching the shark that would startle and slither away—or maybe turn to attack. And the more she lay there, the more she wanted the attack. She wanted to feel the bite of flesh, the rip of flesh, her whole body consumed—her entire body disintegrating in blood under the blanket of water. The thought held her and comforted her, and she tried to close her eyes and sleep. And then she did fall asleep.

She woke up with a knock on the door. "Housekeeping."

Her cramped lips moved slowly. "Not now."

She found her purse in a corner of the room. Everything was there. She pulled out the Mace can and held it tight, like the guy might return for more. The bleeding had stopped, but dried blood had caked around her mouth, chin, breasts, and thighs. Her dress was mostly intact but bloodstained, and her underpants were gone. The guy had taken his souvenir and wouldn't be returning. She pushed the Mace back into her purse.

She went into the bathroom, removed her dress, and let it fall to the floor. Her whole bottom was sore, and there would be bruising where the guy had planted a knee, elbow, or fist. She looked at her face in the mirror and touched her nose. It was tender, slightly swollen, and severely crooked. The once straight and narrow bridge was now a wide arc like a lemon wedge or a crescent moon. Small dark bruises spread from her tear ducts like bad mascara. She turned the tap on the shower and waited until steam rose and started to mist the mirror. She stepped under the hot stream and soaked until the skin of her palms puckered. Later, she cleaned the stains off her dress under the faucet as best she could and then passed the hair dryer back and forth over the fabric.

She avoided the elevators and took the stairs down the sixteen flights. She made it to her car with few looks from passing tourists, then drove her red Porsche to the two-bedroom luxury apartment she and Apple shared. Inside, Apple was still asleep with her door closed. She took off her dress in the kitchen and stuffed it into the trash. She ate two Valium and then lay in bed. The Valium eased the pain and almost made her smile. She slept the rest of the day and woke late after the sun had just gone down. She might have dreamt of sharks or water, or men on dates, but she woke with no memories and only the reality of pain.

———

That night, Apple took her to the emergency room at Sunrise Hospital. Claire had no insurance. They couldn't turn her away, but they could make her wait, and she sat among the snufflers, the semi-comatose, the cut, the stabbed and the gimpy, while the car-smashed, the gun-shot, and the bone-broken—really anyone on a gurney—moved right through to the front of the line. Claire told Apple just to go. Hours later, she was led to an exam room and sat waiting in a paper gown for a doctor to arrive. She looked at her nose in the mirror, deformed and ugly. Finally, a knock on the door, and Claire said, "Come in." The doctor, a man, was young, late twenties or early thirties. His nametag said Dr. Harold Meiser, but he introduced himself as Harry Meiser. Like hairy and cheap.

She told the doctor that she had been in a car accident and that her nose had hit the windshield. The bridge of her nose was still severely curved but now more swollen. Right up front, the doctor asked, "Can you move air through your nasal passages?"

"Do you mean, can I breathe?"

"Yes, can you breathe through the swelling?"

She hadn't tried earlier; she was scared that pushing air through the thing would somehow cause more damage and hurt like a motherfucker. She tried now, softly, and nothing moved. She tried again, pushing more air through the swollen and crushed passages. She felt the release of air, like a pop, and a clot of blood flipped out and onto her lip. The stab of pain *did* hurt like a motherfucker.

The doctor, Harry Meiser, had a tissue ready. "That's fine, that's good." Then he went through the procedure. "What I can do is called a closed reduction procedure. We'll numb up the nose so there's little discomfort. Then I'll use an instrument called an elevator—looks like a long butter knife—to move the bones back in place as best I can."

"As best you can?"

"Well, you're lucky in a way. I can tell that the injury was from a lateral impact. In most car accidents, the person hits the windshield head-on, and we see a frontal impact, we see more trauma to the nose. It's more flattened, crushed. Eighty percent of broken noses are lateral and usually from a sports injury, fall, or classic punch in the nose. In Las Vegas, we see a lot of punched noses." He looked at Claire. "But you said yours was a car accident?"

Claire looked up to the doctor. It was none of his business. What she did with her life was no one's business but her own. "Car accident on Maryland Parkway. Rear-ended." Then she added, "So you were saying? Move the bones back in place as best you can?"

"It's not like fixing a car dent. I'll be moving small, pliable bones and cartilage around that have already been twisted and bowed. To get the car looking like new again, so to speak, you'll need follow-up plastic surgery."

"Do what you can," she said. "Make it so I can breathe good."

The doctor injected Novocain both outside and inside her nose, small squirts each time. It stung at first, but then the constant throbbing pain eased into a numbness. He tested the nose with finger pokes—she couldn't feel a thing. He then inserted the long butter-knife elevator tool into her left nostril, probing for an open channel. He shifted the tip of the elevator, trying to move past the broken pieces, like trying to rethread a lost drawstring. She could tell that the whole nose was shifting back somewhat. And she could tell that the young doctor was getting frustrated; he winced like he was preparing for an inevitable slap. Then he said again, "You're going to need a plastic surgeon." He kept on tunneling, and at one point, she felt the instrument deep in her sinuses, felt it near her eyeball. Then Claire saw the doctor clutch the handle in a tight fist, and she felt pressure and pain as he forced the nose—bones and cartilage—back in place. A pop sound echoed in her head, and then shooting pain seemed to encompass her whole face. She made a deep-throated cry, and the doctor said, "Sorry, almost finished." And then he did the other nostril.

When he was nearly done, the doctor appraised his work. He said, "It's close," then tweaked the nose with pinched fingers like he was molding clay. "That's the best I can do," He smiled, a big toothy smile, and then winked. He left quickly afterward, after again reminding her that a plastic surgeon would be needed to fix the dent, so to speak, good as new. A nurse came to clean up the blood around her nose, but there was no bandage, splint, or mask to cover her damaged face. Claire signed the discharge papers and called Apple.

Apple picked her up thirty minutes later and tried to be chatty, but when Claire asked how it looked, Apple said simply, "Worse."

Claire waited until they were home, when she could close herself in the bathroom and see herself in the mirror above the vanity, a mirror the size of a kitchen table. Her nose was more swollen, and now her eyes were swollen and underlined with deep purple bruising. She wanted to cry, and then she wanted to laugh. She looked like some new evil villain—not Cat Woman, but maybe Coon Woman. She cry-laughed. Crazy. What the fuck was she going to do?

CHAPTER TWO

Wood got a hard-on every time he looked at his truck. He loved it best sitting in the driveway after being hand-washed down at Terrible Herbst. It was a bright orange 1981 Chevy K10 4×4 with a Rancho lift kit. The truck stood three feet off the ground, and even with step-rails, his wife needed a leg-up just to get in, like mounting a horse. He had thirty-four-inch extreme-country tires that could eat up mud—if he could find any mud in the desert. His plates said WOOD, and he wanted some custom graphics across the side of his truck, like a desert sunset or a cool word like ZONE or CHILL. He'd have the money soon, and he'd have the graphics and also headers and dual exhaust. What he didn't like about it was the ugly cooler mounted in the bed. It took away from the whole off-road vibe and made it look more like a work truck, which it was. He'd tried to find a cooler that didn't stick up over the bed's walls, but this one came with the business. His side job was hauling dead pet carcasses. Maybe once he had money, he'd get a second truck just for work, or maybe quit the whole dead–pet–

hauling business altogether. He was considering a scam to get rich.

He thought of himself as a go-getter; someone who saw an opportunity and did what it took to make it happen. Some people had big dreams and cool ideas but never got off their barstools. Just blah, blah, blah and I'll be rich. But he could go for it and make things happen. Wood had a bouncer gig at Tramps, and sometimes his ideas came from just talking to people at the door or at the bar—like the dead-pet gig. A guy at the bar was saying that he had this stupid side job. Lamar was a Mormon, but one who drank alcohol. Twice a week, he drove a route through town, stopping at veterinary clinics and picking up pets that owners had put down or had just died. The vets paid ten bucks plus two dollars a pound for the service, so a big dog could be worth close to a hundred dollars, while a cat was only worth twenty bucks. The pets were already stuffed in heavy plastic bags and closed with a tagged zip tie. They were already weighed. Lamar said the nearest crematorium that took pets was in Barstow, one hundred and fifty miles away. The Mortician owner there charged a dollar a pound, so if he could haul four hundred pounds in one run, his net was $500 before gas. But sometimes the load was less than two hundred pounds and barely worth Lamar's time. So right then, Wood offered to take the business off his hands for $200 a week cash. They shook on it. His plan, which he thought up right there on the spot, was to work the Mortician out of the deal. With his truck and extreme-country tires, he could take the bags deep into the desert and dump the carcasses where nobody would find them. Empty and keep the bags so there'd be no trace. Foolproof. He hoped someday to cut out Lamar in addition to the Mortician—keep the two hundred.

His other side job was security. He and his buddy, John,

had made the trip down to LA to handle the scumbag who'd beaten up Claire. She was his sister-in-law, and he knew she didn't like him. She'd told her sister, Sally, flat out not to marry him, and she didn't even come to the Chapel of the Bells for the wedding. But he wasn't working for Claire; he was working for Mae, and *she* wanted to send a message, maybe not to dates that might cross the line, but to her own girls and to the other escort services in town. The message, "Mae took care. Mae got even." So, he drove down to LA and staked out the scumbag whose name was Todd something-or-other. The alias he'd used was Rod—fucking ridiculous. He followed the guy from his apartment to Venice Beach and watched as he removed his Gold's Gym hoodie and sweatpants. Then, before he pumped iron with the others on the beach, Todd actually oiled up— either suntan or baby oil. Wood was a bodybuilder also, but not in this league. These guys were huge and on steroids. The year before, he'd looked into steroids, couldn't find any for sale, and just gave up.

Todd's routine wasn't hard to nail down. John watched the apartment while Wood followed him to his work, an Italian restaurant on Ocean Avenue. He figured the guy would probably come back to the apartment after his shift, so that's where he and John planned to take him.

John was a strange guy—big and balding and looked like Friar Tuck. Besides security work and bouncing with Wood at Tramps, he did semi-professional arm wrestling. He'd won local tournaments and had played a bit part in the movie *Over the Top* with Sly Stallone where the two arm-wrestled in the preliminaries to some championship. Then, even stranger, John was a religious freak, always talking about God-this and Jesus-that. But on a professional level, as a bouncer, he was a straight-up specialist. John knew how to knock a guy out with one easy punch—a one-punch artist. Wood had seen him do it countless times at the club, and he'd seen him afterward get down on one knee, bend over, and pray, his hands pressed together like a kid before bed. His trick was wearing sap gloves, fingerless leather gloves padded and weighted in the knuckles with lead sand-like granules. When Todd returned to his apartment, John had his sap gloves on and walked casually down the hallway as he slipped his key into the door lock. John popped him quickly, then knelt and did the prayer thing. Wood opened the apartment door and pulled Todd inside.

Mae had said to break the guy's nose and maybe an arm. John had already busted his nose with the first punch, and he was bleeding like crazy, but Wood punched him hard again to make sure the nose was conspicuously crooked. Then he and John flipped him onto his face and pulled his arms back. Wood handcuffed his wrists.

The guy said, "Who the fuck are you? What do you want?"

Wood said, "This is for the girl you fucked up in Vegas."

"What? I haven't been to Vegas in months. That wasn't me."

"Your name is Todd? Or should I say, Rod?" Wood pulled the wallet from his back pocket and checked the driver's license.

"Yes, Todd, but I don't know no Rod. And it wasn't me that fucked up the girl, whoever she is." The guy took gasping breaths, panting like a dog.

Wood felt the guy's arms. They were huge and tense, almost twice the size of his own, and he knew it had to be from steroids. There was just no other way to get that big. No raw eggs, protein powder, amino acids, or working out around the clock would give a guy twenty-inch biceps. Todd was ripped, and Wood wanted what Todd had. It made him think. "I saw you at the beach. Some of those guys are huge. They use steroids? Injectables?"

Todd's breathing slowed, and he paused as if maybe the beating was over. "Yah, injectables, sometimes orally—Dianabol."

"Where do you get it?"

The guy turned his face toward Wood. The nose was twisted and bleeding and a dark spot was growing on the carpet. "Why you want to know?"

"Just tell me, asshole." Wood pressed his knee into the guy's back.

"There used to be a doctor, but he stopped supplying. Now, we get it from Tijuana. A pharmacist there knows how to dose veterinary supplements."

"Veterinary supplements?"

"Steroids for farm animals, like horses."

"What's the name of the place in Tijuana?"

"I don't know. Fucking Mexican, *farmacia*. Right next to a club called, 'Oh.'"

"'Oh,' like zero?"

"No. 'Oh,' like, 'Oh, My God.'"

Besides the nose, Mae had said to break an arm, but his arms were huge and cuffed behind his back. Even if he could find a bat or a tire iron, he didn't see how to break bone through all that muscle. Then he thought of retaliation, vengeance, and what that would feel like. He pulled out his folding Buck knife that he kept in a leather sheath on his belt. He quickly snatched the rim of the guy's ear and slit it from his skull.

The guy's hands were still cuffed behind him, and he just jerked his head to the side, burying the stump of his ear against the carpet. He screamed, "Fuck."

The ear was small, and what was left in Wood's fingers was like a chunk of Play-Doh. It reminded him of Mr. Potato Head—a small pink accessory. There wasn't much bleeding.

John had been quiet but spoke up after the ear was cut. "What'd you do that for?"

"Fucker deserved it for what he did to Claire." And Wood thought hard for the right word, one that would make it seem like some Hollywood movie. He said, "Retribution."

John looked toward Wood with his serious Jesus-loving stare and said, "Deuteronomy thirty-two. I sharpen My flashing sword, And My hand takes hold on justice, And I will render vengeance on My adversaries."

"Fucking-A."

Wood drove back to Las Vegas that night and arrived early before even a hint of sun glowed on the eastern horizon. He dropped John off at his apartment on Koval Lane behind the Imperial Palace casino, then drove down Flamingo and took a right on Maryland Parkway. He pulled his orange pick-up into the strip mall parking lot in front of Reuben's. Inside, Mae sat at the bar, pushing quarters into a video poker machine. Next to her were ten or so quarter rolls standing on end and ready to be lost to the machine. Mae had a gambling problem with video poker.

Just to freak her out, Wood flopped down, right next to her stack of quarters, a sandwich baggie with the severed ear.

Mae hardly moved. "What the fuck is that?"

"An ear."

She looked up at Wood, "Do I have to have it?" She was wearing a white wife-beater T-shirt with no bra. Wood could see the dark spots of her pierced nipples and the outline of those small gold hoops. He'd seen her tits plenty of times and knew that if he just gawked a few seconds longer, Mae would pull up the T-shirt to give him and the bar a real eyeful.

"It's from that guy, Todd. We took care of him. You want it?"

"Fuck do I want with an ear? No, throw it away, or flush it down the toilet or something."

Wood slipped the baggie into his jacket pocket. He sat beside Mae and ordered a Stoli Cranberry and two rolls of quarters. Mae didn't say much; she was too focused on the machine. She was able to feed her ten rolls before Wood could spend his two. Her hands moved dealer-fast, and by the time the sun came up, her fingers were black from the grime on the recycled quarters.

He got home midmorning. His wife was gone to work at Tramps, where she kept books for her dad, Frank. Wood's stepson was at school, some special program for halfwits. He still had the ear in his pocket and thought about how he should store it. In the freezer? The refrigerator? Could he dry it and wear it strung in a necklace like that Special Forces guy in *Apocalypse Now?* He looked in the fridge and had an idea. A small jar had just a few pickles left. He fished out the pickles with a fork and then emptied the contents of the baggie into the pickle juice. He figured that the ear would keep in the salt and vinegar brine. He took the jar to his truck and hid it behind the bench seat. If he opened the driver's door, he could easily slip his hand back underneath and grab it. And it became something he liked to look at—something that gave him goose bumps and a hard-on, just like his orange truck.

CHAPTER THREE

It took a month for the swelling to go down, for Claire's nose to work as it should and move air through the nostrils. The bridge of her nose was no longer the curved crescent moon—it was definitely better—but she was now far from a perfect Cher. The whole thing bent slightly to the right, the direction of the oncoming fist, and the bridge itself was no longer smooth and straight. The break and the follow-up closed reduction procedure had left a red knot like a knuckle in the middle of the bridge, like a huge pimple boiling up. Like Barbara Streisand, but crooked. To Claire, the nose was an optical allusion—she was looking straight-on into the mirror, but her reflection seemed to look elsewhere, somewhere over her shoulder. It was as though her own reflection couldn't look at the deformity of her face.

She stayed at home and watched TV. She rarely went out. Apple brought her food and did her best to get her back on her feet, back in the business. "You can fix it. You got the money. Mae at the service said she'd help out." Claire thought about the service. Escorting was beyond dangerous—a random phone number sent to a beeper, a call to meet a *guy* in an anonymous hotel room *alone*, and then sex. The business was all so ludicrous, a last-resort profession if you were a Vegas girl who wanted quick money and had little or no skills. And it helped if you were cute.

Claire knew she'd been lucky, and it took that one time—that one scare—to let her know just how lucky she was to still be alive. What she remembered before hitting the floor was the jerk of his shoulder, then the punch, the violent move forward that was so unexpected. She didn't think she could look at her beeper again, or step into a casino with her pink purse, or walk up to a hotel room behind some guy, some larger man that smelled like cologne and soft cheese. She couldn't see closing the door and doing her thing. She was scared, and she felt done. And she didn't feel like fixing her nose, and she couldn't escort with a crooked nose—she wasn't cute Cher with the pink purse—and there was no going back. She'd keep her nose, a deterrent, her locked chastity belt. No going back.

———

Claire made her decision, but now the reality of life without quick money sunk in. She traded in her red Porsche for a five-year-old Ford Fairmont station wagon. It was a straight-up trade, and she knew she'd lost out in the deal, but the Ford had only forty-thousand miles on the odometer—more practical in her new life, whatever that would be.

Her pink purse wasn't anything special—leather that felt like vinyl, a subtle step-and-repeat pattern that was supposed to look like Gucci, and a bent bamboo handle that was probably plastic. She gave the purse to Apple along with her beeper. She said, "Tell Mae I quit."

She decided to move from the apartment and live on her own, someplace cheap, because her money needed to last. Someplace alone—she needed to be completely out of *that* life and away from *those* people. It took her a month, but she eventually found what she was looking for.

Near the airport, down Tropicana, she saw an old adobe home on a large commercial lot. A waist-high chain-link fence surrounded the property, with a locked driveway gate. One large tree shadowed the south side, and in the back were two smaller buildings—a shack and what appeared to be an outhouse. The adobe home looked run-down, but all the windows were intact, and only the front steps were busted. She climbed the low fence, then walked around the house and looked through the windows. She saw empty rooms with litter on the floor, mostly fast food wrappers. In one bedroom lay a bare mattress and blanket. Someone had probably squatted there, but now a heavy padlocked hasp was screwed to the door and frame. A sign in the yard listed the property for sale, Greco Commercial Real Estate. Below was a phone number next to the name, Wayne Greco.

She called the number at a gas station pay phone and spoke to the man. A half hour later, she was north on Las Vegas Boulevard close to downtown. The real-estate office was in a strip mall and just big enough for a counter and one desk. Wayne Greco sat at the desk and looked up over his reading glasses as she walked through the door. The first thing Claire noticed was his Elvis-black hair combed into a helmet, covering his ears and framing his face. His mustache was pencil-thin, razor-parted, and stretched past the edges of his mouth. He looked less like Elvis, more Wayne Newton. For a second, it crossed her mind that he could have been a past date, but lately, every man looked like a date. And she would've remembered a guy who'd looked like Wayne Newton.

The man stared at her nose and then tried to look away. "What can I do for you?"

She introduced herself and said, "I'm the one that called about the property off Tropicana."

She noticed a tautness around his eyes—from a facelift or facial cream. A signed photo of the man and the real Wayne Newton was on the wall. A framed poster advertised Wayne Greco as Wayne Newton in the lounge at the Showboat Casino. It seemed impersonators were everywhere in Vegas: Michael Jackson, Liberace, Carol Channing, The Rat Pack guys, Buddy Holly, Barbara Streisand, now this Wayne Newton—and Cher.

Greco put his hands on the counter. "So, you want to buy, rent, what?"

Now he looked her over, past her crooked red nose to her T-shirt and jeans. She was no investor; she looked like a kid. "I was just thinking of living there for the time being."

"Living there?" He paused to consider his next words. "The place is a dump."

"Well, I was hoping to take care of the place while you look for a buyer, clean it up, and make sure no one trashes it." She smiled, a big fake smile. "What I'm saying is, I'll clean the house, make it livable, and keep out the vagrants. It'll be like security. I'll be there along with my watchdog." The dog part was spontaneous, but just then, a dog appealed to her—a friend with few questions.

Wayne Greco stood on the opposite side of the counter. He thought—slowly—and what Claire hoped he thought was, *fuck-it, what do I have to lose?* And maybe *she's cuter than the bum that was living there before.* What he finally said was simply, "Sure, why not."

Claire stretched out her hand. "Okay then."

He shook her hand and then looked from her eyes to her nose. He said, "I know a plastic surgeon. With a straight nose, you'd be a perfect Cher. You know, like Sonny and Cher." She looked down and away.

She knew he was still looking at her nose, lost in the potential vision of a fellow celebrity lookalike. He said, "Can you sing?" And before Claire could answer right away, Wayne sang, "*Danke schoen*, darling *danke schoen*."

Claire finally answered, "Like nails on a chalkboard."

———

She spent a week cleaning up the adobe house before moving in. There were two bedrooms, one with a soiled mattress. The kitchen was gross and disgusting, with animal excrement of some species on the floors and counters, but all the appliances were there and worked. In the front room were two soiled chairs and another mattress. She started by throwing everything away.

She owned some furniture at the apartment she'd shared with Apple. She also had her own bedroom set. She bought whatever else she needed at the Goodwill along with an older color television with a remote control that clicked mechanically.

Claire found her dog at the Animal Foundation near downtown. The label on the cage said he was three years old, part Lab and part Spaniel. His name was "Bud," and the reason he was abandoned was listed as "relocation"—probably another dejected Las Vegas newcomer who'd turned around and headed home. The dog was black and just big enough to be scary. On the drive to the adobe house, Bud curled up in the passenger seat with both eyes open, watching her. After parking the car, she closed the gate and let Bud have the run of the place. First thing he did was sniff out a feral cat and chase it off. She smiled without much thought, maybe the first time she'd smiled sincerely since the assault.

———

She sat in a booth at Reuben's, waiting for Apple and Mae. The two had wanted to have lunch, probably a last plea to get her back to the service. It was early afternoon and she'd been up since nine o'clock but knew Apple and Mae would be just waking up, slipping into jeans, pulling hair back into scrunchies, and, except for lipstick, skipping make-up altogether. She looked around. Ten older people sat at the bar, played the poker machines, and sipped free cocktails—probably gambling with their Social Security cash. A few booths were filled with people having a late lunch with cocktails. She ordered coffee from Reuben's day waitress, an older woman who wore large bug-eyed glasses. The woman fit tight into the black shorts, heavy nude stockings, and white tuxedo shirt that Reuben made all the girls wear. Reuben usually hired knock-outs—young, thin, with big hair—and Claire figured the woman had to be some regular's sister or a cousin, someone with connections. Claire needed a job and wondered if Reuben would hire *her* for the day shift.

Apple showed up first, wearing jeans and her brown hair tied back like Claire had imagined. And even with just lipstick, she looked good. Her eyes were big, like doll's eyes, and her nose was small and perfect. They'd attended the same high school in Henderson, just south of Vegas; they were best friends and both cheerleaders. Alicia was her real name, but she hated it, and even back then, everyone called her Apple. She was the most popular girl in school. And bad—drinking-smoking-fucking-getting-high bad. During her senior year, Apple started doing dates on weekends. Her parents? They both worked the gaming tables at Sam's Town Casino, working and sleeping at all hours. They were just relieved Apple was out of the house and not making noise. She sat down across from Claire and lit a cigarette.

Apple said, "Long fucking night."

"Yeah?"

"Four dates back-to-back. A three-hundred-dollar night. Not bad for a Thursday. Some convention in town, like hardware store owners."

It was November, and a few smaller conventions were in town. But in January, the big season would start: AAIW (big-shot auto dealers), CES (stereo nerds), NAB (hip TV and radio guys), CONEX (construction guys, but with money). Thousands of guys—most without their wives—hitting Vegas with that bottomless expense-account cash. During the big conventions, Claire had made more than a thousand each day, sometimes two—these were non-stop parties without any downtime; she had dates at seven at night and seven in the morning. The auto dealers' convention alone would last almost a week, and she'd be lucky to sleep four hours each day. She'd made enough during the last convention season to pay cash for the Porsche.

Apple was trying to show off with all the money she was making. Claire knew what she was missing and just pushed the conversation along, "How do you suppose a guy ever becomes a hardware store owner? It's not like any of the kids we knew in high school said, 'Boy, I sure wish I could own a hardware store someday.'" Claire had been thinking about professions, how you become something.

Apple smiled, thought about it, and said, "Don't you remember Tommy Noonan? His dad owned the Henderson Hardware Hank. Tommy worked there through high school. He'll probably take over the business. I suppose that's how you become a hardware guy."

Claire said, "I suppose." Then Mae walked in.

Mae was older, in her mid-thirties, and owned the service. The business was called Sincerely Yours, and Mae recruited the girls, hired illegals to pass out fliers, ran the call service, and provided security. Mae once had a boyfriend and a partner, but the guy was caught with two kilos of cocaine and was now serving time at the Nevada State Prison in Carson City. As far as Claire knew, Mae owned and ran the business herself. And Claire could see it. Mae was tough and instructed the girls, security guys, and everyone as though no alternative existed. But she did it like a tough mom, and she could be nice and generous like a mom. She'd often be at Rueben's early in the morning playing video poker, chatting up her girls, and buying rounds of drinks. And when she sat down next to Apple and looked at Claire, the first thing she did was touch her hand and then reach for her nose. Claire sat unflinching.

"It's healed?" Mae had seen her after the beating, after the hospital procedure, and she'd asked her about the guy, what he looked like, and if he said where he lived. Claire told her what she could.

"It's healed as good as it's going to get."

Mae ran her fingers down the bridge of her nose, and Claire could feel her touch the still-red bump and follow the curve. "I know a surgeon. Not a boob guy, but a real nose guy. I could set it up." Everyone, it seemed, knew a plastic surgeon.

She didn't like saying no to Mae, and she didn't. "Let me think about that."

"You okay for money?"

"I'm fine."

Apple said, "She's living in a dump over by the Airport."

Mae looked at Claire but kept silent.

Again, Claire said, "I'm fine."

They ordered coffee and breakfast from the older waitress. Mae led the conversation and kept things light—gossip about the girls, daytime soaps, and the upcoming holidays (slow times before the convention season started). It wasn't until dishes were cleared that Mae came right out and said, "I know it's tough. I've been there. Early on, I made the dumb mistake of trying to sneak up to a room at the Riviera. I got up to the fifth floor through the fire escape, but later, on the way down, security was waiting for me. The two guys had all kinds of fun, held me in handcuffs, beat me, and then took their turns getting off. I was shaken after that, sorry for myself, and didn't want to go back. But then that sorry feeling turned to anger, and I just said, 'Fuck it, I got to work.' And I got back on that horse. And you know something, Claire?"

Claire pushed her coffee cup aside and set her hands on the table. "What?"

"The bruises hurt, but the rest was all just more monotonous cock."

Mae looked at her, raised her eyebrows, and smiled. Apple laughed.

Claire said, "I don't know."

Mae continued, "And don't be worried about that creep, Rod. He wasn't hard to find. Registered with a fake name and credit card, but the idiot valet parked and charged it to his room. It wasn't hard to track down his California plates. His real name is Todd Winkler. I sent your brother-in-law Wood down to LA. Rod, Todd, has been taken care of. You do not need to worry about that asshole."

"Fucking Wood," Apple said.

Claire said, "I wasn't worrying." Wood was an asshole too, and not much evolved from the creep, Rod or Todd. Apple said it all, *Fucking Wood.*

"Good. Don't. Convention season is coming up in two months. That's plenty of time to fix your nose and get back in the saddle. We can work out how to pay for it, but you'll have no money worries after the season." Then Mae added, "You know Cher got her nose done before she did *Silkwood.*"

Claire looked at Mae. She was still beautiful—curly brown hair, a pinched nose, and full, fake boobs with tiny hoop nipple piercings that she loved to show off. And she could still do dates, and she would if she had to, if there was an obligation and no other girls were available.

Claire wanted to please her in some way but couldn't. "Mae, I appreciate everything you've done for me. I know it's a business, but I know you care. And I know you respect that we can walk away at any time. You said it when I first signed up, and you've said it since. And now I want to walk away. I don't know what I'm going to do, and maybe I might have a change of heart, but for now, I just can't do it anymore."

"Why?"

"You're right, it *is* just all monotonous cock. I know that. But now I just don't want to touch anyone. I don't want to be touched. It's personal." That's how she felt. She wanted to be by herself in her own house. Find a job that was regular, inconspicuous. Be normal if there was such a thing.

"You'll get over that."

"And then maybe I'll be back."

———

Claire woke late the next day to her dog, Bud, standing below her bed and wagging his tail beside a small puddle of urine. She looked down at Bud and half-heartedly said, "Bad dog." With the attention, he wagged his tail harder. Claire stood, slipped on her robe, and let the dog into the yard. She cleaned up Bud's mess and, later, switched on TV soaps and watched from her couch. People—all beautiful—talked, kissed, argued, fought, hugged, and smiled. The drama drifted through her brain without once connecting with a nerve or providing a thought—she'd paid more attention to the commercials. One advertised cosmetic surgery, but she was too tired and maybe too depressed to pick up the remote and turn the channel. Another commercial advertised a local school for jobs in the medical profession: lab technician, dental assistant, home-care professional, office assistant, occupational therapist, and nurse's assistant. Ten minutes later, the same commercial, and she took more notice. After a lunch of Campbell's Chunky Chicken Soup, she watched the commercial for a third time. After the fourth time, she stood from the couch, showered, and dressed. She didn't know what a nurse's assistant job entailed but walked down the street to the public phone at the gas station and called the number.

The assistant's course was one of the least expensive and required only a high-school degree, which she had. It was a twelve-week course, and if she passed all the tests, they had jobs waiting. The next day, she walked into the admissions office at the Nevada Technical College and signed up for classes.

She needed a job and wanted something entry-level at a

hospital where she could eventually nurse-assist. She applied for a cafeteria position at Sunrise, the hospital she'd gone to months before with her broken nose. She filled out an application and referenced experience years ago working for her dad in the kitchen at his nightclub, Tramps. She was almost hired on the spot.

CHAPTER FOUR

Tramps was the hub of Wood's existence, where everything had come together since moving to Las Vegas. He'd met his wife, Sally, at Tramps, and Frank, the owner, was his father-in-law. Wood worked security on busy Thursday, Friday, and Saturday nights when the club had a line around the building from eleven until sometimes four or five in the morning. Wood made a decent hourly wage now that he was the Head Doorman, plus he could pull down side money at the front door by palming ten or twenty-dollar bribes from guys who wanted to skip the wait. He wasn't supposed to. Frank catered to the working Joe-Schmoes: the dealers, car valets, servers, desk clerks, bellhops, shop girls, and show workers. They came to the club after work, knowing there wouldn't be a cover charge. And they wouldn't have to watch big shots, who *they* catered to, cut the line. So, Wood had to take his bribes discretely like some drug dealer. Regardless, he loved Tramps and thought that he'd married into a real goldmine.

Wood managed five other doormen. Holt, a Mormon kid

who'd played linebacker for the BYU Cougars up in Provo, worked the line with Carl, a senior and gymnast at UNLV. Holt did the counts once Wood started a line—ten out, ten in— while Carl checked for fake IDs. Three guys worked inside. Nash the Smasher worked the back exit—called "The Smasher" because, during one brawl, a beer mug was smashed into his face. Now, he had a long scar from forehead to lip that circled one eye. Paul, Holt's brother, stood just inside the front door and could signal the guys from outside to work inside or vice versa. Paul was younger than Holt, but the two looked like twins—short blond hair parted in the middle, cut jawlines, thick Cro-Magnon foreheads. John stood in the back next to the cocktail waitress station and just waited for the signal that his sap-gloved fists were needed. He'd stand there all night lifting a fifteen-pound shot put, building up his right wrestling arm. They all carried Mini-Maglite flashlights in their back pockets for signaling and for checking ID's. They all had chrome handcuffs looped over their belts like some punk-rock accessory.

He and John had worked together since Wood came to Vegas. He'd met John at another club, now closed, called The Brewery. By Tramps' standards, The Brewery was out of control. The club had just the two of them inside, and both stood together and handled disturbances as a team, their own buddy system. Back then, they wore their sap gloves openly. They knew how to strike first when a guy tensed up with balled fists. And they weren't above taking a thief out back and breaking a few fingers. They worked together and, for a time, lived together, sharing a shitty apartment on Koval Lane where John still lived. Wood met Mae at the Brewery and picked up side work escorting the escorts and protecting them from creepy dates. The Brewery was closed by the city after a guy was gunned down in the parking lot. Both moved to Tramps.

Even then, John was a Jesus freak, but he never tried to convert Wood or tell him what he should do. His religion was more internal, maybe just trying to ensure a good place in heaven for himself after all the evil shit he'd done on Earth. Wood really didn't know; he didn't talk to John about his religion. But John was Wood's guy, his backup, his partner, and now he was also letting John in on the foolproof scam he'd been working up.

He hit on the scam one night while talking with a guy at the bar. It was early in the morning, and the guy had just gotten off the second shift at the Westward Ho casino where he was employed as a mechanic. He worked on the slots, which got Wood asking, "How do you beat the machines?" People were always trying to beat the casinos, and Security was always looking out for card counters or guys stealing chips at the craps tables. Wood was sure people were trying to scam the machines. After a few drinks, the mechanic started listing the ways. There was the Yo-Yo scam, where you dangled a coin on a string up and down through the slot to trigger plays. There were fake coins and shaved coins. The sensors in the current machines, though, were getting better with the coin tricks. The machines were now more electronic, so the newer scams were about tricking sensors with magnets or fiber-optic lights to get the hoppers to whirl and spit out coins. Wood asked the guy, Mike, what *he* would do.

The mechanic had clearly been thinking this through. "See, working a regular machine inside the casino is peanuts. You trick the hopper and out spits massive quantities of quarters. But if you somehow manage to get out a measly five hundred dollars, that's twenty-five pounds in a huge sack that you now have to lug through the casino—very conspicuous and very risky. You won't get away with that scam for long. They will watch you and check the machines.

"So, the trick is to make one big score at one big machine. The jackpot on the Mega Slot at the Westward Ho is fifty grand. That's a nice score. But for that score, you've got to have a team. Someone's got to rig the machine. Someone's got to keep people from watching. Someone's got to block the cameras. And someone has to win."

All this got Wood's head spinning. Over the next few weeks, he worked up the plan with Mike The Mechanic. Making the machine pay was easy. Mike was the inside guy and had a key to the machine. He could easily open it and then rig the machine's clock with a piano wire to pay out on the next pull. Once the machine paid, Mike obviously couldn't take the payout, so someone who looked like a winner needed to win. Wood had already talked his wife, Sally, into winning. She was nervous and suspicious at first, but he walked her through the risks. She'd just be a lucky passerby, put a coin in the machine, and then scream in surprise as the tray filled with dollar coins— fifty thousand in dollar coins. She'd be that lucky gal. John didn't know it yet, but he would stand there with Sally while Mike did his thing. John would block the one camera mounted on a pole just outside the casino entrance. Wood's genius was coming up with a way to keep people from watching because people loved to watch the Mega Slot. Westward Ho was right on the Strip, and the Mega Slot was out front and almost on the sidewalk. Wood would provide a major distraction by driving his truck with the lift kit and monster extreme-country tires right up onto the sidewalk, honking his horn, and screaming. He would be way more entertaining than the Mega Slot.

So, it was set. They'd do it the next Wednesday when Mike

was working, and Wood and John were off. It was early Saturday morning when Mike came into Tramps, ordered a Jim Beam on the rocks, and they worked out the final details. Mike was older than Wood, thirty or so, and already balding. As Mike talked, he fidgeted nervously with his beverage napkin, twisting the corners like the ends of a rolled joint. They had the scam worked out—the distraction, the wire, the cameras, the payout.

Wood said, "What else?"

He then talked about the split, something they hadn't discussed. Wood had assumed equal shares. Mike said, "I just want to be upfront about this thing. I brought you the idea, and I bring the skills. I just want my half on this, fifty percent. You and your guys can have the other fifty percent. I don't care how you work this out with John and your wife."

Wood went through the numbers in his head. He'd get twenty-five grand to split three ways. Sally would be pissed if she didn't get a full share, but what was hers was his. John would be happy with five grand. "We all got the same risks. We get caught, we're all going to the same jail. I get what you say, but how about sixty-forty? You still get the bigger share, and I split thirty-thousand three ways. We each get ten. You get twice as much." After paying off John, he was getting twenty-five thousand (what was hers was his).

"Fine," Mike said. "Sixty-forty. I just want it to be fair." They looked at each other and nodded. Agreed. Mike picked up his bourbon, "Here's to our payday." They touched glasses.

Even after his shift was over, Wood instinctively kept his eye on the front door, and he was watching when Lamar walked in. Lamar knew where to find him and his two hundred dollars from the dead-pet route. He sat down on the barstool next to Wood, on the other side from Mike. As soon as Lamar started talking, Mike stood up and left.

Lamar said what he always said, "You got my two hundred?"

Wood was already starting to regret the business. He'd cleared over six hundred the previous week, but it took all his Monday and Thursday to do the route, and then he had to work Thursday night at the club. His spot in the desert was an hour and a half away, just north of Pahrump. The last few miles were on rugged trails with washouts and boulders that were tricky to maneuver and tough on the truck. He had to wash it twice a week, ten dollars each time, not including the tip. And Lamar was driving him crazy; he couldn't escape the guy. He was in every Friday night, and if he couldn't collect, he was back on Saturday. So here he was.

"Listen, Lamar, this hasn't worked out the way I planned. The Mortician takes half, and my truck eats gas faster than I can fill it up. I made maybe three hundred last week, so if I give you two hundred, that barely covers gas. Somehow, we got to switch this up, or I got to give it up."

"You said two hundred. That was *your* number. The business is rock solid." Lamar ordered a light beer. He was Mormon and drank, but only light beer. His regular job was waiting tables at Hugo's Cellar in the Four Queens downtown. It was one of the better steak houses in Las Vegas, and Lamar easily did over two hundred in tips five nights a week. Lamar always came to Tramps after his shift. He didn't change clothes and wore his black-and-whites from work that smelled like wet food garbage. Wood was thinking Lamar's appearance was somehow an insult. He wanted people to dress up, or at least clean up, when they came to the club.

Wood said, "I'll be right back. I got to pee." He placed a cocktail napkin over his drink to keep his spot—a Vegas thing—and then walked to the bathroom. He peed and afterward pulled out five twenties and slipped them into his front pocket. He didn't want Lamar to peek inside his wallet when he paid.

Wood sat back down and then pulled out the twenties. "Here's a hundred. You can have the business back if it's so rock solid."

Lamar took the hundred, finished his beer, and stood. "I might just do that."

Wood didn't care. By next week, he figured he wouldn't need to be hauling dead pets around Nevada anyway. He finished his drink, a Stoli Cranberry, and left.

———

The house was his wife's domain and still, legally, in her name. She'd bought it with her first husband, who owned a dive bar off Paradise Road moronically called Bird Off Paradise—or just The Bird. The house was ranch-style with two bedrooms on the one story. The front was sheathed in a random rock siding, while the other three sides were stucco. Out front stood two ornamental Japanese-looking trees surrounded by more rocks. No grass grew on the property, though they planned for a lawn in the back. That was one item on his hubby-do list, to put down rolls of sod and install a sprinkler system, but he wasn't a landscaper, and they didn't have the money to hire one. So, for now, the backyard was mostly fenced-in, hard-packed desert with one bricked-in square for their gas Weber. Inside was a living room and dining room with delicate furniture that hadn't changed since the first husband. Wood stayed out of those two rooms but allowed himself the sunroom, where he had a color TV set, a small couch, and his

La-Z-Boy recliner. He also stayed out of the finished basement. That was the domain of his stepson, Frankie, who Wood thought was probably brain damaged. It was fine that Frankie took the basement—out of sight, out of mind.

The stepson's dad, Sally's first husband, Dominic, was long gone. He was finishing the morning deposit at The Bird when two guys entered the bar with sawed-offs and cut him in two. In her grief, Sally sold the bar. If Wood owned The Bird now, he'd be set for life, and that thought bothered him—a lot. Instead, he was bouncing at her dad's nightclub, dropping dead pets in the desert, and doing security for hookers.

He came home after working out the slot scam with Mike and haggling with Lamar over dead-pet money. The sun was just climbing over the edge of the desert, and Sally was already up and getting dressed. When they'd first met at the club, she'd worn a tight skimpy dress with moccasin boots, her dark hair permed and big. Her eyes and tits were big too, and she was the boss's daughter. He could tell she was flirting with him, standing around the door and gossiping about the bartenders, waitresses, and regulars. So, he asked her out. They went to a Willie Nelson concert outdoors at Caesars Palace, free tickets from a concierge who traded favors. They were a couple after that. He remembered she made him feel good. She seemed to dig his body and liked going out to bars and restaurants with him at her side. She bought him new clothes at the Chess King. Now, Sally was getting ready for work at the club. Her hair was pulled back in a sloppy knot, and she wore her glasses instead of contacts. "Hi, Hon," she said, "how did it go?"

Wood knew what she meant—*Was the club busy? Was it a good night?* "Yeah, packed. Line from midnight until four."

"Okay, babe, see you tonight. Let's go out, maybe to Hugo's downtown."

Lamar worked at Hugo's, and he really did not want to see him. "Yeah, let's go out. But not Hugo's, maybe Friday's or Carlos Murphy's." He liked the chimichanga at Murphy's.

"Sure, fine. Whatever you want."

"Listen, Sally, that thing is on for Wednesday. I need you to be there Wednesday night at around ten. At the Westward Ho."

"What was that again?"

"You know, the Mega Slot. It hasn't paid in months, and the guy I know knows the machine's clock. He says it's going to pay on Wednesday night. Guaranteed."

"Sounds like bullshit to me." She opened her purse and pulled out her car keys.

"No bullshit. This guy is the mechanic, and he knows. And if you win, he wants half. But it's fifty grand, babe. Half of fifty is twenty-five. That's real money. We could finish the backyard or *party like it's nineteen ninety-nine.*" This was a line from a Prince song DJ Dan D had been playing at the club. He smiled and held up his arms like he was ready to dance.

"So do it yourself."

"No, babe, I told you. The Mega Slot is going to be crowded. I'll create a diversion with my truck so you can get in at the right time and take a few pulls. You have to be there at exactly ten-fifteen. You have to be playing the machine at that exact time."

"Fine," she said. "Whatever."

"Great, Sally. See you tonight. I feel like having that chimichanga at Murphy's."

"Keep an eye on Frankie, okay?"

"Sure, I got to get some sleep, but I'll make sure he stays in the basement. I'll get him fed."

Wood was in bed asleep when Frankie woke up. He was

thirteen years old, a teenager, but acted like he was five. He wouldn't ever look Wood in the eyes, even if he told him, "Look me in the eyes." He couldn't talk but would make involuntary noises— chirping like a bird, squealing like a pig, bleating like a goat. Sally had him in a class for kids with special needs at the local public school. He'd do what you'd say, though, which for Wood was mostly, "Stay in the basement."

He heard a high-pitched squeal and knew Frankie would make a mess in the kitchen and make more noise if Wood didn't get up and feed the kid. In the kitchen, the kid stood staring down at the floor. Frankie wore pajamas from his favorite TV show, *Inspector Gadget*—a show for five-year-olds. His favorite toy was his Inspector Gadget bag, a canvas tool bag that opened from the top like a Mary Poppins carpet purse. His blond hair was matted on one side from sleeping, and his arms hung motionless and useless. The kid looked like his father with the same blond hair and blue eyes. And he was skinny. Secretly, Wood liked that this kid was all that remained of his predecessor—something fragile and flawed. It was as though Sally had moved up and found someone better and more worthy. Frankie made the same squeal again. Wood pushed him aside and pulled down a box of Honeycomb cereal. Frankie always ate his cereal dry with his hands, so Wood just filled a bowl and pushed him toward the basement door.

Twenty minutes later, Wood was back in bed. He felt like things were lining up nicely, and he slept like a kid with a spent erection.

CHAPTER FIVE

Sally pushed the button on the garage remote, then pulled her Chrysler LeBaron past Wood's ridiculous truck parked conspicuously in the driveway like some tacky lawn ornament. She opened and closed doors quietly, knowing Wood would still be sleeping at three in the afternoon. Frankie had an after-school program, so he wouldn't be home until five. She had two hours to herself and settled into the living room couch with a stack of magazines—*People*, *Self*, *Mademoiselle*, and *Cosmo* with a quiz she thought she'd take: ARE YOU NEUROTIC?

The house faced west and the sun streaming through the front picture window felt warm and comforting. The living room was her favorite place to be alone, where Wood or Frankie hardly ever bothered her. She could see the oak-framed mirror in the front hallway that had belonged to her grandmother back in New Jersey, which supposedly had come over from England with her grandmother's mother. The living room furniture was bought new with her first husband, Dominic. She and Dominic had also bought their bedroom set new, solid oak from Bassett. Dominic wasn't so different from

Wood in that he couldn't have cared less about the furniture and just wanted the color TV in the sunroom—once Dom's room, now Wood's. The house was still in her name, though she owed plenty to Countrywide Mortgage.

The first question in the quiz was, "If a friend comments on the weight she's lost, do you: 1.) Comment on how well she looks. 2.) Ask her how many pounds. 3.) Go home and look in the mirror. Or 4.) Get in your car and cry." Sally would definitely ask how many pounds. She was a bookkeeper and wanted the numbers.

Before Wood had moved in, she took down all her photos with Dominic and purged his clothes from their closets. She put up new pictures around the house. Across from the couch was a large, framed photo of her and Wood after their wedding at the Chapel of the Bells. Frankie was in the picture wearing a light-brown corduroy three-piece suit that she'd bought him especially for the occasion. Another framed photo of Frankie showed him on his third birthday when the noises he made were still funny and cute.

Every time she looked at Frankie, she thought of Dominic. Both had blond hair and blue eyes. Dom's family was northern Italian. His grandparents lived outside Venice, and a cousin worked the tourist gondolas. They had planned a trip to Venice so that she could meet his family there, but they never stepped on the plane. Dominic was a bartender for her dad, and as a wedding present, he loaned them the money to buy the old Bird Off Paradise bar. They then had a business to run and couldn't be away for a two-week honeymoon. He was killed in a robbery before they could take a trip. Anywhere.

She read the next question, "On meeting a first date at a restaurant, do you: 1.) Show up fifteen minutes late. 2.) Show up on time. 3.) Show up fifteen minutes early. Or 4.) Get to the restaurant thirty minutes early and wait at the bar to see who walks through the door." Show up early? A girl needed to play a little hard to get—you can't look *needy*. Definitely 1.

The bar's name had been stupid, but who could afford to have a new sign made? The bar inside was a dump, but it paid and was a start. They had the gaming license limit of fifteen video poker machines, which brought in a thousand a week in pure profit. And Dominic was a great bartender. He worked the bar at night alone with one cocktail waitress, and they had a group of hardcore regulars, mostly dealers from the nearby casinos—the Desert Inn, Riviera, The Silver City, Vegas World, and Circus Circus. Before Frankie was born, Sally worked days cocktail waitressing and doing the books. They passed each other in the mornings, then had a few hours alone with each other in the afternoons before his shift started. She'd come home, remove her clothes, and crawl into bed. He'd have wake-up sex while she had midday full-sensory sex. Afterward, they'd eat whatever they wanted, sometimes breakfast with pancakes and bacon and sometimes dinner with steaks or delivered pizza. Dom was good to her. It was a fluke that he was shot and not her. She did the books and the deposit in the mornings, even after Frankie was born. That morning, she had a doctor's appointment with Frankie. He'd never grown out of making those noises, and he could barely talk—they were worried. Dom made the deposit for her, and it was Dominic who was cut nearly in half by the sawed-off shotgun blasts of the robbers. They were never caught.

She knew Wood hated Frankie. He could be mean and demeaning to the boy. He tried at first, especially before they got married. He took Frankie to see kids' movies and one time, they went to see *The Secret of NIHM*. Frankie loved the movie and came home with a new sound, a squeak like a mouse.

Wood laughed at that. But Frankie wasn't big. He couldn't play sports, like tossing a football around, so maybe that was why Wood lost interest. But she and Frankie were a package deal; if you loved one, you needed to love the other. That's what Wood didn't understand.

Wood was a dreamer and probably a hustler too. He worked at the club only three nights a week, and Sally wasn't sure what he did the rest of the time. There were freelance security jobs and something about a veterinary disposal service with his stupid truck—like he needed a jacked-up, four-wheel-drive truck in Las Vegas. The thing was so high that she could barely step in without his help. His household commitment to her was just fifteen hundred each month, and she was lucky to get a thousand. And he kept hounding her to have a joint checking account. He tried to explain that married couples had a shared financial responsibility—like she was stupid and hadn't done accounting for The Bird and then Tramps. And it wasn't like he was offering to share the debt and be on the line for the mortgage with Countrywide. She figured Wood just wanted access to more money, her money, and that wasn't going to happen. Now this Mega Slot thing. What was that?

Sally finished the quiz and dutifully put her answers, the numbers, in the spaces provided. She totaled up the numbers to a score of twelve. And for any score in the range of ten to fifteen, she was deemed NOT NEUROTIC. In fact, cool as a cucumber.

Later that night, after they'd had a dinner of hot dogs and macaroni and cheese, and Frankie was in bed, Wood drove with her out to the Westward Ho casino. She vaguely heard what he said, "The machine has been clocked to pay. It's going to be simple. Just play the machine at exactly 10:15 p.m." He gave her a stubby roll of one-dollar coins.

She asked just one question, "Is this legal?"

Wood looked back and forth from the road to her, talking in quick bursts. "It's like counting cards. Think of it like this—the dealer is down to a stack of mostly face cards. You know your chance of winning or pushing is like one hundred percent. It's just like that. The guy I know has been clocking this machine. He's been keeping track of the wins and knows the payout schedule. It's mathematical. It has to pay out tonight, and it will pay out to whoever is pulling the lever at 10:15. He says he might be off a few minutes, but after 10:15, he's sure it will pay. And what do we have to lose? Twenty-five bucks in dollar coins? That's risking almost nothing." He looked at her hard, almost driving into oncoming traffic. "Do it for me."

She saw the oncoming car, "Watch it!" But before she could reach for the wheel, Wood had steered back into his lane.

She went along with it, though in her gut, she knew the whole scheme was far-fetched and unlikely. She thought Wood was full of shit. But the worst case would be losing a roll of coins and a few hours of her time. The best case was that she'd win fifty grand—the unlikely best case.

The Westward Ho was a dump of a casino between the Stardust and Circus Circus. Unlike the other two big casinos set back from the Strip with driveways and valet parking, the Westward Ho was right on the Strip, the front entrance only steps from the sidewalk. The locals called it simply "the Ho," and it attracted tourists who walked between the two bigger casinos. It advertised seventy-five cent Heinekens and St. Pauli Girls, nickel slots, and two-dollar blackjack tables. Out front were strange multicolored, lit-up umbrellas, like a garden of gigantic psychedelic mushrooms or a set for the H.R. Puffin Stuff show. Sally couldn't quite put her finger on what the umbrellas were supposed to look like, and there was possibly no rhyme or reason. Standing under the tallest green umbrella was the Mega Slot that advertised the $50,000 jackpot. The Mega Slot stood fifteen feet tall, and the lights and tumbling fruit could be seen from the sidewalk over the heads of the crowd entranced by the turning tumblers and dancing lights. Sally mixed in with the crowd and watched her time. It was 10:05 p.m. A lady in her fifties with a '60s bubble-flip hairstyle was pumping coins into the machine. She held a plastic quart-sized bucket printed with the likeness of the Mega Slot.

At 10:10 p.m., Wood drove his jacked-up truck up onto the sidewalk. He drove slowly, honking his horn and shouting, "Get the fuck out of the way." He stopped abruptly before hitting one of the lit-up umbrellas. He began shouting obscenities, "This casino sucks! This casino will fucking steal your money. The dealers are fucking cheats. They fucking call it the Ho because it fucks you and takes all your money…" He kept yelling while honking his horn and flashing his emergency lights. Sally looked away, embarrassed.

People close to the truck stepped back or walked clear of it. The crowd at the Mega Slot turned and watched. The lady with the bubble-flip hairstyle paused and looked up toward the strange man in the monster truck. Sally turned sideways and budged in front of the lady, then lifted her hand to drop in a coin. At that same moment, a slot mechanic dressed in khaki coveralls and holding a toolbox said, "Just a moment, lady." He turned a key to quickly open a chrome door beneath a coin tray the size of a dish sink. Sally could see the mechanic quickly twisting a wire through its guts. It took seconds, and then he said, "Go ahead, lady, play." And then she saw big John standing beside her and in front of the mechanic. John smiled and said, "Play." The mechanic was gone.

Then, the lady with the bubble-flip hair complained

loudly, "It's still my turn. I wasn't done yet."

John stepped in front of the lady as Sally finished slotting her coin. He told the lady, "It's okay, ma'am; I understand your concern."

The lady turned on him. "Who the fuck are you?" To Sally, the *F* word coming from the mouth of a woman the age of her mother or grandmother was incongruous and offensive, and she had an instinct to side with John and give the lady a piece of her mind. But now, the coin was clinking its way through the maze of sensors and switches, and the lights of the Mega Slot began flashing brightly.

Sally pulled the huge lever the diameter of the exhaust pipe on Wood's truck, topped by a black knob the size of a bowling ball. The cylinders turned, and the fruit spun. The first tumbler stopped at Mega Slot, the only graphic that wasn't an orange, cherry, lemon, watermelon, or apple. The second tumbler stopped at Mega Slot, and then the third. Now bored with Wood's ranting, people watched the tumblers fall into line. Each time a Mega Slot came up, there was a roar of "Yes." Sally realized she was going to win.

The fifth Mega Slot came up, and the crowd and the machine went crazy. Sally heard the cheers and shouts of "Oh, my God," like a football touchdown or Neil Armstrong stepping out onto the Sea of Tranquility. The machine wailed like a car alarm with squealing sirens and flashing lights. She heard drivers crawling along Las Vegas Boulevard honking horns. She had won the Mega Slot fifty-thousand-dollar jackpot, and the machine was raining silver dollars into the massive coin tray. Along with the crowd, she screamed, "Oh my God."

People were patting her on the back and offering congratulations. The older woman with the bubble flip stood behind John, glaring but silent. Sally jumped up and down with her fists pumping—she was a winner, a champion.

Moments later, a manager and two security guards were at her side. The guards were all badges and patches, leather pouches and holsters, ear-pieces and walkie-talkies. They stood on either side of the machine, holding their arms spread out to keep the spectators at bay. Both had matching Fu Manchu mustaches that dropped to their jawlines. The manager said, "Congratulations, ma'am. Now, you should come with us. Security will collect your coins."

The manager gently touched her upper arm and pointed toward the casino entrance. For a moment, the manager's hand frightened her. She had never been arrested, but this was what it probably felt like, and she was rattled. She moved toward the entrance, the man's hand now touching her upper back, guiding her like a criminal. She sensed the two security guards walking behind the manager, probably carrying the coins from her win. She smiled at the onlookers watching, playing the part of a woman who'd just hit the jackpot. She had slotted her dollar coin and pulled the handle. She had won, and the fifty grand was rightfully hers.

The manager led her through the casino to the cashier's cage with its barred windows. Inside, all the hoopla of the win was over, and the people moving between tables and slot machines paid no attention to Sally or her escorts. At the cage, he asked her to stand at a closed window while he opened a locked door and then looked through the bars from inside. The manager's hair was thinned to long wisps combed over a bald crown, and his thick gray mustache was neatly trimmed to the corners of his mouth. Sally noticed creased half-moons of skin under his eyes. Old, tired, and—she hoped—bored. The man didn't seem happy for her and was probably just going through the routine motions of his job. The exhilaration of winning had subsided, and now she was thinking of getting the cash money and then quickly leaving.

The manager looked up from the cage and forced a smile, "Congratulations, Miss…"

"Mrs. Harding."

"Miss Harding."

"Mrs. You can call me Sally."

"Excuse me, Sally." He paused. "Congratulations, Sally. How would you like your winnings? Obviously, you can't take fifty thousand-dollar coins with you; that's over a thousand pounds. So, we can do cash or a certified check. The check, of course, is safer. Fifty thousand is a lot of cash to carry around, and you could easily deposit the check at your bank tomorrow."

Sally was the bookkeeper for her dad at Tramps. She counted the daily receipts, filled out the daily ledger in pencil, and prepared the deposit for Frank to review and then deliver to the bank. She wasn't naïve; cash could be kept off the books if Frank wanted. "Cash is fine. I'll have my husband pick me up. We'll be okay with cash."

"Fine, Sally. Fine. We just need you to fill out this form, then we can disburse the winnings." He slid the detailed form through the cage window. His forced smile was gone. "There's a pen right on the chain. I'll also need to see your identification."

The form said IRS and W-2G. Fuck, taxes. "Is this necessary?"

"Yes, Sally, any payout from this cage over fifteen hundred dollars must be reported to the IRS. You're lucky; next year, we'll have to also withhold the taxes, like from a paycheck."

Sally stared at the form. The manager had already written in the winning amount, a five with six zeros, a comma, and a period. She picked up the pen and filled out the form. It included her social-security number. She tried to figure out the taxes in her head. Thirty percent of fifty grand was three times five, or roughly fifteen thousand dollars she would have to pay to the IRS in April. So, the fifty grand she'd be walking out with would now only be thirty-five after taxes. She finished the form and pulled her driver's license from the wallet in her purse. She slid them through the window to the manager.

The manager took both and wrote the driver's license information on the form. He spoke to her without looking up. "So, you're a local?"

"Yes, born and bred."

"And where do you work?"

"Tramps on Flamingo. I'm the bookkeeper."

The manager seemed to make a mental note, a connection. "The nightclub?"

"Yes."

"What brings you to the Westward Ho?"

Sally looked up through the bars of the cage window, annoyed and nervous. The simplest answer was always the best. "I like to play the slots."

"Of course, I'll be right back with your winnings."

The manager filled out a slip and went to one of the open cashiers. The cashier looked at Sally, smiled, and then pulled out five thick bundles of hundred-dollar bills from her drawer and passed them to the manager.

The manager then insisted on recounting the bundles. Sally thought it would take forever, and she just wanted out. "That's okay," she said.

"This will only take a moment." And it did. The manager

held each bundle between the second and third fingers of his left hand. Then, with the thumb of his right hand, he flipped through the bills in a blur of speed, licking his thumb between each bundle. He finished in minutes, almost as fast as an electric cash counter, and slid the pile through the cage window toward Sally. He also slid back her driver's license. The manager said, "I'll have Security escort you to your car."

"That's okay." She knew the manager would insist, and he did. She figured Wood was already waiting somewhere in the parking lot, but then she didn't want security to see her step into the obnoxious neon-orange truck, the one that had just pulled up on the curb with a guy yelling obscenities out the window.

As Sally was being escorted outside, it occurred to her that the slot machine had been rigged. She knew something was fishy all along, but just then, she put two-and-two together. She remembered the mechanic just moments before pulling the handle. She remembered John, Wood's sidekick, standing behind her, making sure *she* was playing and not the old lady. And whatever that mechanic wound through the machine had rigged the payout and was probably still wired in the guts. Wood had lied to her or, more likely, fed her half-truths with convenient omissions—Wood-style. With the security guard behind her, Sally walked to the street and raised her hand to hail a cab. She turned toward the guard with a Fu Manchu mustache and wondered if she was supposed to tip him. In Vegas, you tipped everyone, it seemed, but she wasn't going to open her purse and show the bundles. She looked at him, smiled, and said, "Thanks." She climbed into the back of the cab.

By the time Wood got home, Sally was pissed. She now knew for sure it had been a scam, and she was not only pissed at Wood but also pissed at herself for not seeing through his lies earlier. He'd made it seem like it was a luck thing, like the probability of winning would be extremely high because the machines were programmed to pay out, and the mechanic was keeping track. Blah, blah, blah. Really? Ten-fifteen on the dot? She was a sucker. How stupid could she have been? What she'd done was certainly a felony and meant jail time if she were caught. And she had a kid with learning disabilities. Why had Wood done this to her? And she was supposed to split the money fifty-fifty with the mechanic? The guy was crazy if he thought he was getting twenty-five grand. She was stuck with all the taxes, so her twenty-five was only worth—she quickly went through the math in her head—seventeen thousand five hundred. She wasn't risking jail time for seventeen thousand five hundred. And Wood could get nothing, zip.

Wood walked through the door with a big stupid smile on his face. "Incredible," he said.

Sally glared at him. "You fucking asshole."

"What?"

"You didn't tell me the machine was rigged, that a mechanic would open the thing and set it to pay off!"

Wood's smile quickly turned into a tight, downturned mouth. "I told you that the clock was set to pay out. The machine was going to hit a jackpot at that exact time."

"Bullshit. I'm not crazy; I'm not *neurotic*. The guy rigged it just before I pulled the handle. And John was there. You planned out this whole scam, this rip-off." She was near the kitchen, and Wood was just inside the front door. They both staked out their areas and left the space between them a no-man's-land.

"I told you..." Wood tried to finish his sentence and tell a good lie, but the idiot hadn't thought it through and was now tongue-tied. Why had she married him? She'd been a single mom already in her thirties with a thirteen-year-old kid who needed constant help. She was lonely. But that didn't explain why him? There was a time when he was attractive, a strong and good-looking man with confidence who paid attention to her. Blah, blah, blah. Simple—desperate and stupid. But maybe not forever.

Sally jumped in before he could collect himself and tell that one next lie. "Also, did you know I would have to fill out an IRS form to get the money? I have to pay taxes on the whole fifty grand. Do you still think I'm splitting the whole fifty with the mechanic? I'm not."

Wood dropped his hands to his sides. "I didn't know about taxes."

"Of course you didn't."

"I'll talk to the guy. He probably knew there would be taxes. What's right is right. I'll explain it to him. What are the taxes, like ten percent?"

Sally glared at Wood. Ten percent? Wood had probably never made enough reported income in his life to pay taxes. They'd only been married three years, and they did separate returns. He probably never even filed. "Try thirty percent. Since you're not good with math, that's seventeen thousand five hundred."

"Okay, he's just going to have to take that. He'll understand. I need to meet him tonight and pay him off. So, can you give me the seventeen-five?"

Giving him anything from her purse made her uncomfortable, an evolved natural reflex. "Fine," Sally said. She went into the kitchen and pulled out two bundles. She counted twenty-five hundreds from one bundle and returned those bills to her purse. For the first time, she noticed that they were crisp and new. She came back into the living room. She slapped the two bundles, one partial, into his outstretched hand.

Wood stared at the cash, "Wow. Thanks, I'll be home after I give the guy his split." He looked back at her while he was leaving. "Just so you know, that money you have is ours. Yours and mine." Then he was gone.

Sally entered the kitchen and put the remaining bundles and loose bills on the table. For the first time, she used the words to herself, "stolen money." She could go to jail. She thought of how she could get caught. The mechanic had strung a wire through the machine. She hoped that the guy wasn't stupid enough to leave it there. He would probably pull it out later in the night. She hadn't touched the machine, except the handle, and she'd never met the mechanic. Even if they found a wire, nobody could connect her to the guy—unless the guy talked. But she couldn't go there in her mind. There was nothing she could do about it anyway. What was done was done. So she was just passing by and lucky. Now she had some real money to help with the mortgage and car payment and maybe get Frankie professional help. Wood barely contributed to the household bills and thought he was doing her a big favor when picking up a restaurant check. She needed that extra money.

Sally thought about where to hide the remaining thirty-two thousand five hundred. She thought about Frankie's room in the basement, a place Wood avoided like hot, steaming vomit.

CHAPTER SIX

He needed to pay Mike forty percent of the $50,000 minus the thirty percent for taxes, and the math was really hard. He needed a calculator and the exact amount, and he couldn't be flashing one-hundred-dollar bills and making change at the bar. He passed a Payless Drug Store and pulled into the lot. Inside, on a wall next to the checkout stand, he found a ten-dollar Casio calculator that didn't need batteries and could work on solar power, which seemed space age and cool. He tried to pay with a hundred. The girl at the checkout had hair dyed blue-black with mascara painted heavy around the eyes, hollow-looking like Alice Cooper. She said, "This ain't no casino," holding the bill up like a dead rodent. She added, "You got anything smaller?" He flashed her a smile that wasn't returned, then pinched a twenty from his wallet and gave her that. In the truck, he unwrapped the calculator and found the ON button. He did the math: three five zero zero zero times four zero and then the percent symbol. He owed Mike $14,000 after taxes. Then he figured out John's cut of $5,000 after taxes, and that came to $3,500. So he had the $17,500 to cover both Mike and John. He took John's cut from the loose bundle of hundreds and then put the remainder, Mike's cut, back in his front pocket. The $3,500 went into his now thick wallet.

Just past midnight, Wood walked into Tramps. The crowd was small, and the dance floor was mostly empty, with just a few regulars moving in their jerky rhythm—people who danced non-stop like it was exercise. He went to the bar and ordered a Stoli Cranberry from Big Tony. The bar was a wide wraparound horseshoe job with two bartenders on each side, both named Tony—Big Tony and Little Tony. Both had Sicilian black hair jelled and combed back from their foreheads. Both seemed to know every line from every De Niro-Scorsese movie: *Mean Streets, Taxi Driver, and Raging Bull.* After Wood ordered his drink, Big Tony looked over his shoulder and pointed to his chest, "You talkin' to me?" He'd say that line a few times every night and somehow always get a laugh. Big Tony had him sign the cash register receipt for the comped drink. Wood held his wallet under the bar and pulled tip money—two singles from the wad of hundreds—that he fanned on the bar. He sat and waited for Mike The Mechanic's shift to end, which wouldn't be until two, so maybe he'd be at the club by two thirty. John was off on Wednesdays, and he'd pay him on Thursday. Wood sipped his drink and looked around.

Across the horseshoe bar was a regular, Chris, whom he knew from Tramps and Eiferman's gym. Chris was muscled, built, and had short blond hair gelled into a cowlick. He wore a tight gloss-white T-shirt that showed off his arms and pecs. Chris was into cool stuff and had shown Wood his motorcycle the previous summer, a Honda Interceptor 1000 with a full race fairing painted red, white, and blue. It could do wheelies in fourth gear going seventy, the top speed something like one hundred fifty. He also drove a white Datsun 280ZX—a real chick magnet. The car looked fast just sitting still. Chris made his money dealing drugs, and Wood thought a hit of cocaine would be nice.

Their eyes met, and Wood nodded, lifting his glass in a toast. Minutes later, he picked up his drink and took the empty stool beside Chris. "What's up?"

"Not much," Chris said, "slow tonight."

"Wednesdays are slow. Frank needs to do something. Like a dance contest or ladies' night. Nothing's happening on Wednesdays."

"Something," Chris said.

Wood felt the thick wallet in his back pocket and the bulge of hundreds in his front pocket. What the fuck, he thought, time to party. "You got some coke?"

"Sure, in the car."

The 280ZX was backed into a parking spot away from the front entrance. Wood saw the newer white fiberglass skirt that extended the body close to the ground and made the car look race-ready. They got in, and Chris started the engine. It came to life with a low throaty sound—custom exhaust. Across the lot, they could see Wood's orange truck, and Chris said, "I love your truck. Sometimes, I think about trading this thing in on a 4x4, something I could have fun with out in the desert."

"Yeah, but chicks dig this ZX. In fact, this car feels like," and Wood worked hard to find the right word, something that said it all. And there it was, "A wet pussy."

Chris laughed, "I like that…wet pussy. Step into my wet pussy and do a line. So how much you looking to score?"

A gram was a hundred, Wood knew. He could snort up a gram by the time Mike got there. An eight ball was almost four grams and was three hundred. An eight-ball would last all night and then some. "You got an eight ball?"

"Sure." Chris pulled out the plastic ashtray from the dash. Behind the ashtray was his stash of brown glass vials in a large plastic baggie. Most of the vials were smaller and contained grams. There were two larger eight-ball vials, and Chris handed one to Wood. Wood pulled out his wallet and flashed the hundreds. He pulled out three. Chris said, "Nice, business has been good."

"Yeah, good."

Chris replaced his stash behind the ashtray. He then reached into his pocket and pulled out another vial. This one had a cap with a turning nob that measured out easy hits. He flipped the vial upside down and turned the knob to load the coke. He offered the vial to Wood. "This is on me."

Wood was familiar with the device, a carburetor or carb. He turned the knob another quarter turn and then did the hit through his right nostril while holding a finger to his left. The coke slammed through his sinuses and hit the back of his throat. First, a metallic taste like chewing raw aspirin, then the numbing. It felt good and clean.

Wood had always liked the idea of selling coke. He worked at the hottest nightclub in Vegas, and he knew everyone. But his father-in-law, Frank, owned the place; if he were caught, there'd be trouble. Then he thought about the guy, Todd, in LA. He wondered if there was a market for steroids, and he figured Chris would know. He asked, "You ever mess around with steroids?"

Chris did another hit and passed the vial back to Wood. "I don't use the stuff and don't sell it, but there's a guy that works out at Eiferman's who's actually a doctor. He's that guy with the thick glasses. I think the steroids fucked up his eyes.

Anyway, he used to sell steroids, but he stopped. Steroids are a touchy subject now. Eiferman doesn't allow them in the gym, and he's cracking down. There's talk that steroids are going to be illegal. Like coke." He looked at Wood and smiled.

So, there *was* a market for steroids. Wood had all these good ideas, had them almost every week. Hell, every day, and wondered if maybe he should get one of those little blank books that smart people carried in their breast pockets so he could write down ideas as they came to him.

Before leaving the car, Wood realized he didn't have a carburetor, spoon, or mirror to do his coke. He asked Chris, "You got a spare carb?"

"No, but I got a spoon. One's in the glove compartment. Help yourself."

Wood opened the compartment. The inside was littered with lighters, a miniature scale, pens, fast-food napkins, ketchup packets, and swizzle sticks from Reuben's on Maryland. The swizzle sticks had a tiny cup on one end that could be used to snort coke. He'd been to Rueben's countless times and never noticed. Wood took two and laughed. "Fucking clever," he said.

The coke was good, and he felt so good back in the club that he walked to the bathroom and into a stall to scoop more with his swizzle-stick coke spoon. When Mike arrived, Wood was peaking, and everyone was his friend. Mike was like a childhood friend, though he'd known him less than a month. Wood smiled hard, the edges of his mouth stretched and sore. "What's up, brother?" He wanted to hug Mike, but that would have been uncomfortable, gay. Instead, he held up his arm to do a high handshake. Wood held Mike's hand in the arm-wrestling grip a second too long.

Mike replied, "What's up?" He gave Wood that look, like

why are you being so weird? He still wore his khaki mechanic's uniform and black leather shoes with wedge soles, like mailman shoes. Mike sat on the stool beside Wood and ordered a Jim Beam and Bud longneck. Wood ordered another Stoli Cranberry. The cocktails came fast, and they toasted each other. "Fuckin' A," Wood said.

"Fuckin' A," Mike replied.

They sat in silence for a minute. Wood wanted to talk and celebrate and again thought of hugging Mike. But he needed to be cool; he needed to settle down. "We all good?"

"Yeah, fine. Perfect." Mike lifted his Beam glass, emptied it in one swallow, then drank half the Bud. "Drink up; let's get out of here."

Wood drained his cocktail and put a ten down on the bar. "Okay, let's go." The drink seemed extra strong, and the vodka added to his clean, coke high. He felt aware of everything in the club—Big Tony wrapping his fist on the bar, a drunk stumbling on the dance floor and stepping on a girl's toe, DJ Dan D smiling, saying, "What's up, Wood," Holt—or was it his brother Paul—saying, "Later dudes."

They walked across the parking lot to Wood's truck. There was a glow from lights on the Strip calling to him. It was Vegas, that whore, telling him to party until the sun rises, then party until it sets. Once inside the truck, Wood offered the coke to Mike who took the vial and scooped a hit in each nostril. He leaned back in the bench seat, waiting for the rush. "Nice," Mike said.

Wood asked again, "You sure we're good? The bosses don't think anything's up? Nothing to trace this back to you?"

"Yeah, nothing. I pulled my wire. The machine hadn't hit for a while, so the bosses expected it. We're clean." He paused. "You got my money?"

Wood did another hit. The fourteen thousand was bulging in his front pocket. He'd thought this through. Show Mike the cash, let him see the green, and then explain. He pulled out the wad and placed it on Mike's outstretched hand. Wood looked at the two bundles now in Mike's open palm. The hand stayed open between them, Mike holding the cash away from him like it was something offensive—a dog turd. Wood should have known the mechanic would see it instantly. "One bundle's light. What the fuck?"

Wood was ready, "You see, it's like this. Sally collected the jackpot but had to fill out a tax form. Did you know she'd have to fill out a fucking IRS form?" Turn it around, Wood thought, don't apologize, and always put it on the other guy. It was Mike's fault, like it was Lamar's fault he had to do his dead-pet route the next day, or was it today?

"I didn't fucking know," Mike said.

Wood could feel Mike looking at him. He did another hit with the swizzle-stick spoon. "So it's like this. Sally got the fifty thousand. She figured she'd have to pay taxes on the whole fifty. Like, *you're* not claiming it, right?"

Mike's hand closed around the two bundles, which disappeared into a pocket. "You're right, I don't fucking claim stolen money. We agreed on my forty percent cut of fifty thousand. That's two full bundles. You give me a short bundle, and I figure I've been screwed. Are you trying to screw me?"

"Listen, have some more coke." Wood handed him the vial and spoon. Mike unscrewed the cap and took four hits, two in each nostril. Wood thought one hit was customary, two hits were taking advantage, and four was like Mike recouping his full twenty thousand. "Sally figured thirty percent for taxes, so your forty percent was actually fourteen thousand." The solar-powered calculator was on the dash. He grabbed it and handed it over toward Mike. "Check it out." Mike's left hand held the vial, and his right, the spoon. He looked at the calculator and then at Wood. He did a fifth hit. Wood felt his blood pressure rise, felt the blood jump in his veins—he was getting pissed. "We did the math," Wood said and looked him in the eyes, daring him to take the issue one step further.

Wood put the calculator back on the dashboard where, in the morning, it could recharge.

Mike took a sixth hit and handed the open vial and spoon back to Wood. "Fuck it," he said. "Let's party."

"Fuckin' A," Wood said. He took two hits himself and then started the truck's eight-cylinder engine.

CHAPTER SEVEN

It was almost nine o'clock in the morning on Thursday, way past sunrise, when Wood pulled into the driveway of his—Sally's—house. The night, then early morning, had not gone well. After Tramps, he and Mike went to the Crazy Horse Saloon, a strip joint on Flamingo. Wood knew the doorman and didn't have to pay the cover charge, and he knew some of the girls—a few worked for Mae on the side. He felt like a big shot, a Vegas guy, with the girls saying, "Hey, Wood," and "What's going on, Wood." And Mike turned out to be like a fiend with both the coke and the girls. The first thing he did was change out a hundred-dollar bill for singles. Then they sat on the runway and Mike threw out singles like confetti. Then to the bathroom for more coke. The vial was now half empty. Then Mike wanted a blow job, so Wood fixed him up with one of the girls who took him to a back room for maybe a half-hour. Then Mike had to buy champagne for the girls, and Wood had more Stoli Cranberrys. The night's bill came to over five hundred bucks, which they split. So, out of the thirty-five hundred that was supposed to be John's cut, he was closer to twenty-five hundred and now needed to replenish. But Sally had gone to work, Frankie to school.

Wood sat down at the kitchen table and spilled a small pile of the coke he had left onto the linoleum tabletop. He pulled his bank card from his wallet and moved the coke around, forming, then reforming rows. There was enough for two lines or just one fat line. He chose the fat line. He rolled one of the crisp hundreds into a straw, bent over, and took the line in one nostril. The familiar metallic taste, then the weird drip where his sinuses met his throat, a drip that turned his throat numb. He wiped up the last crumbs of coke with his finger and pressed the crystals against his upper gum. The coke was nearly gone, and he wanted his money.

He also had dead pets to pick up.

The bundles of hundreds he'd handed Sally were stashed somewhere. Wood looked in the places he thought she would've hidden the dough, mostly in their bedroom: her jewelry box, her undies drawer, shoe boxes in the closet, under the mattress, in her nightstand, and under the bathroom sink. He looked in the refrigerator and freezer, opening Tupperware containers with leftover spaghetti, mac and cheese, and something that looked and smelled like dog food and made him nauseous. Fuck it, he thought, go out and make some money.

He climbed back into his truck and started his route. He liked to do a loop starting south in Henderson and then moving north. He stopped at the vets Lamar had established, but many others wouldn't work with him. The larger pet hospitals contracted with a regular medical supply company to drop off orders and pick up dead pets. Those trucks were fitted with a freezer, and the pets were taken to a plant in LA. After that, the burnt remains were sent back to the vets. The medical supply company charged five dollars a pound—more than twice what Wood charged—and they had to order the pickup days in advance. So vets could save three dollars a pound if they paid cash to Wood. The vets thought Wood worked for the Mortician in Barstow, so part of the deal was that Wood would write out a receipt with the crematorium's name and logo on it. Wood had taken a stack of these receipts when he first learned the route, and he'd since made copies. From Henderson, he did Paradise Valley, then downtown and into North Las Vegas, and finally to a veterinarian on the far north end of town near Corn Creek who dealt more in horses and farm animals. He would've liked a payday of two dollars a pound for a two-thousand-pound horse, but as far as he knew, they buried the horses on the owner's ranch. That or they sold horse hamburger and steak to unsuspecting or indifferent restaurants. From there, he drove northwest on Highway 95 through Indian Springs and then south on Highway 160.

By the time he finished with the vet pickups, the sun was straight overhead and pounding down on the black asphalt road, and his coke high was leaving him with jitters and confusion. It would take him another few hours to complete the route, and then he'd have a few hours of downtime before his shift started at Tramps. It was nearly ninety degrees in the desert. The sun reflected off the hood of his truck, and even with sunglasses, Wood squinted. He felt tired and his eyes blinked, but he knew sleep was out of the question. He just needed more coke. While steering with his knees, he did two small hits with a swizzle-stick coke spoon. He held the vial to the light—the coke was nearly gone.

His secret spot was off-road, just before he got to Pahrump, near a little town—more a ghost town—called Johnnie. From there, a four-wheel dirt road went east into the desert. Five miles in, he took his truck off-road and went north. A cloud of dust rose behind him, and all around, he saw nothing but loose rock and plants that looked like dead coral. He thought of this place as the moon, and in his head, that's what he said, "Takin' the pets to the moon." On the moon, he didn't have just one spot, but many. At first, he regularly returned to the same place, but the smell and the flies were overwhelming—bloated dog and cat bodies with flesh-eating maggots like electrified white rice. Turkey vultures, coyotes, and crows fought over the flesh. So his strategy now was to move around. Driving north, he looked for the vultures swarming over the last haul and the one before that, and Wood just went a couple hundred yards further. He found that after a month or so, the carcasses had turned to dried bones and tufts of fur—no more flies, maggots, or birds—and he could use the same dumping spots over again. He figured he had about eight or ten piles total.

Wood took the bags of carcasses from the cooler mounted on his truck bed and dropped them off the back. He'd collected eighteen bags that day, maybe two hundred pounds, which added another $400 to his wallet, good for another eight ball. He jumped to the desert floor and cut the plastic zip ties on the bags with his folding Buck. He dragged the bags one at a time a few feet away and emptied the carcasses over old bones. He stopped and noticed a bright blue and yellow parrot in one bag, and he reached down to touch its feathers. He was spaced out and just stood there stroking the feathers that felt like soft panties. Then he thought he felt the body twitch, like a carpet spark, and he jumped back and dropped the bird in the dirt. He stuck his foot out and flicked the bird with his toe and saw the head and neck flop like a limp dick. Fucking focus, he thought. In the truck, before he left,

Wood scraped the bottom of the vial for one more hit. He wiped the insides with his pinky finger, the only finger that would fit down into the hole. He pressed the last crystals to his upper gum.

His circular route took him south. He stopped, filled up with gas, and bought a liter bottle of Mountain Dew. Further south, entering Pahrump, a sign for the Chicken Ranch Brothel read, BENDING OVER BACKWARDS TO SERVE YOU! Sally once told him that her mother had moved up to Pahrump and worked there as a whore when it first opened. Her parents had long since split up, with she and Claire raised by their dad. Sally never liked to talk about her mom and rarely spoke to her sister, who was now a whore, too. The fact was, he saw Claire more than Sally did. Claire was always dressed up in some hot outfit and looked great in her Porsche—she did look like Cher. Sometimes he wished Sally could be more like Claire, though not a whore.

From Pahrump, it was another hour to get home. He wanted his money, and he needed more coke.

CHAPTER EIGHT

Wood pulled into his driveway late in the afternoon. Sally's LeBaron was gone. Inside, he heard something in the basement and, in his sleep-deprived, drug-induced confusion, was startled—maybe someone looking for his money. But then he realized it was just Frankie moving around, playing Inspector Gadget or some shit. The kid was like a rodent—a mouse or a squirrel—and it bugged him that he needed to take care of some other dude's offspring. Then his mind raced back to the same old nagging thoughts. Sally's dad, Frank, had bought her and Dominic the bar, which was now gone. He could have taken over that bar. The slot money alone could have kept him in cash, and he wouldn't need to do three or four jobs just to keep up. He wouldn't need to be scamming slot machines and carting dead dogs and cats into the desert. And when he married Sally, Frank didn't do squat for them. Where was *his* bar? He just had his three nights a week at Tramps, making fifteen bucks an hour and what he could pull in from the line. Nothing. He felt sweat dripping from his temples. He pulled a

Coors from the refrigerator and sat in his La-Z-Boy recliner, watching TV. He wanted to close his eyes and sleep before his shift at Tramps, but he was twitchy and couldn't. He turned on a sports channel and watched some basketball game. He tried to figure out who was winning and who he wanted to win. The players moved fast, in a blur, so he closed his eyes and just listened. The beer tasted sweet.

Wood thought maybe he'd dozed off for a second. Then he heard the front door open and close. Probably Sally with his money. He expected her to come into his room, but minutes passed, and he couldn't hear footsteps or keys on the counter or a voice. He stood up and walked through the house. No one. He looked out the front window. He saw his truck door open and Frankie's Inspector Gadget tool bag tipped over on the driveway. *Fucking idiot*, he thought, *I fucking told him to never touch my truck*. Wood opened the front door. He walked slowly, his anger blasting off, and he could feel the tension in his jaw and gnashing teeth.

Frankie had climbed up into the driver's seat. In his lap was the pickle jar. He had fished out the severed ear and now held it to his nose, sniffing.

Wood looked at the kid, the jar, the ear. Fuck, Fuck, Fuck. "Give me that," he yelled. He grabbed the ear and the jar and then dropped the ear back into the brine and closed the top. With his free hand, he pulled the kid from the truck and yanked him to the driveway. He put the jar back under the seat, closed the door, and locked it with his key. The kid was lying on the ground and making a sound like a bleating goat. "I told you to never fucking go near my truck. You fucking moron. I told you never." Then he kicked Frankie in the stomach. Later, he would think that the kick wasn't full-on like he'd done in past fights. The kick was more like a quick punt from the knee, something you'd do against an outside step to get mud off your boots. Not that bad. But there he was, doubled over.

"Just get up," Wood said. "Get back in the basement." His voice was calmer now.

Frankie kept making his noises, groans now. Slowly he rolled to his knees and stood. He was bent over, holding his stomach. The front door had been left open. He reached for his tool bag and then walked into the house. Wood followed and heard the kid's footsteps on the basement stairs.

By seven, Sally was still not home. Wood tried to sleep again in the La-Z-Boy, but his thoughts kept swirling. The basketball game ended, and a panel of ex-players and talking heads debated the merits of play. He tried to follow the conversation, but his mind drifted elsewhere—the slot money, more coke, Frankie. He thought about the ear and figured the kid probably mistook it for a pickle and would have eaten it if he hadn't gotten there in time. And he thought again about the money—always the money—and wondered where Sally was. Why wasn't she home watching Frankie? Then he couldn't sleep because he was thinking about having to eventually get up from the La-Z-Boy and work that night. Maybe he could call in sick, but he wasn't sure Sally would cover for him. She would say it was his job and responsibility or some shit. He'd have to go to work, but what he needed was more coke. The swizzle-stick coke spoon was still in his pocket, and he knew that he could always find coke at Reuben's. The bartenders there sold it like Long Islands or lemon drop shooters.

He stepped into his truck and drove to the bar. On Maryland Parkway, he remembered he hadn't eaten in over twenty-four hours and was suddenly hungry. He pulled into the drive-through of the Naugles Tacos and ordered two combo burritos with a large Mountain Dew. His truck window was two feet higher than the pickup window, and normally, the exchange for food and money worked fine, but the kid behind the counter was short, like almost a Munchkin, and Wood had to crumble and toss him the ten-dollar bill. When the kid came back with his food and change, he thankfully brought along a stool. Wood started eating before he left the parking lot and finished the second burrito in front of Reuben's just a few blocks farther down on Maryland.

The sunlight was fading, but inside Reuben's, it was already nighttime. Reuben, the owner, sat in a booth by himself with the *Daily Racing Form* and looked up as Wood walked inside. Reuben was an older guy with curly gray hair and a big nose. Wood knew the place had been mobbed-up in the seventies, a hangout for guys like Tony Spilotro and "Fat Herbie" Blitzstein, and maybe still was. He nodded a greeting at Reuben and walked to the bar.

The bartender looked familiar, but Wood couldn't remember his name. The bartender, though, knew *his* name and said, "Hey, Wood, what can I get you?" He threw down a beverage napkin. The logo on the napkin was a caricature of Reuben with his Jewish nose exaggerated wildly. Underneath the logo was the catchphrase, THE NOSE KNOWS. Wood ordered a Coors; he couldn't get too fucked up on booze before his shift.

When the bartender came back with the long-neck, Wood motioned him closer. The music was loud and playing some Frank Sinatra shit. He cupped his mouth and whispered, "How can I score a gram or maybe an eight ball?"

"Let me check." The bartender moved to the end of the bar and spoke to another guy sitting by himself and smoking. The guy wore aviator-framed glasses with a faggy pinkish tint. Wood saw nods and then saw the guy look up to Wood and give another nod. The guy stood up and walked to the bathroom. Wood followed. It was all business, and they did a quick exchange, two hundred-dollar bills for two vials of coke, one gram each. Wood stayed behind and locked himself into a stall. It had been hours since his last hit, and his hand shook as he dipped the swizzle-stick spoon into the white crystals. He kept the vial close to his nose and did four quick hits, two in each nostril. He sat back on the toilet seat and felt a rush of energy that was almost calming.

When he returned to the bar, he instantly recognized a girl who had just sat down—Apple. Wood picked up his beer and sat next to her. "Apple, what's up?"

"Hey, Wood." She lit a Marlboro Light and blew the smoke toward the ceiling. Wood had done security for Apple, accompanying her up a casino elevator to a date who'd refused to come down. Apple looked hot in her tight neon-orange mini dress that matched the color of his truck. Her permed brown hair was past her shoulders and teased big like Kelly Le Brock in *Weird Science*. "Heard about you in LA. That was sick." She smiled.

"Asshole had it coming," he said. "How's Claire?"

"Her nose is still fucked up, and she won't fix it. I tell her it can be fixed, but she won't listen."

Wood thought of Claire and Cher, and then he tried to imagine the nose permanently broken—a shame. "So what's she doing?"

"Going back to school to learn some medical thing. She got a shit job at Sunrise Hospital. She doesn't want to escort anymore, even though convention season is coming up."

"Time to make some money." And Wood thought about the side money he could make doing security. "So you two still living together?"

"She moved out to some dump near the airport, an old house that looks like the first settlers died there. She bought a dog." The bartender returned with a Long Island iced tea, and Apple took a sip through the straw. She'd only taken two drinks when her beeper, on silent, buzzed. "Gotta go," she said. She stood up from the bar. The bartender came over and poured the drink into a plastic to-go cup. "Thanks, Vin," she said and left.

Now he remembered—Vin, Vinny. Wood finished his Coors, paid, tipped, and left. On his way out, he stopped at the end of the bar, at the cocktail waitress station. Standing in a lowball glass were the swizzle-stick coke spoons.

He looked up to the bartender and asked, "Vin, you mind?"

Vin winked. "Knock yourself out."

CHAPTER NINE

Wood pulled up behind Tramps. He walked past the Dumpsters through the back door and punched in fifteen minutes before his shift started at ten o'clock. Inside, the club was quiet, with maybe fifty people playing video poker or eating bar food in the booths. The lights were dimmed, and the music was still low and canned—DJ Dan D wouldn't start until eleven. At that time of night, the place didn't seem like a dance club, more like a theme restaurant with the wrong theme. When he'd first heard about Tramps, he figured it meant tramps, like loose women, sluts. But the theme was tramps like hobos who rode the rails. Circling the back bar was a model train that went around and around and puffed little clouds of smoke. The walls were covered in rough-cut wood to resemble boxcars, and in the ceiling were thick rafters as though the building was a barn for trains. Other train memorabilia surrounded the room, like train-crossing signs, signal lights, and old outdoor advertising signs like Nehi soda, Prince Albert tobacco, and Lucky Strike cigarettes. In the margins of the food menu was a dancing hobo character like the clown Emmett Kelly. He asked Frank once how he came up with all this shit, and he told him that his one hobby growing up had been model trains. Frank loved trains.

John clocked in at eleven when the DJ music started. He stayed in the back corner near the cocktail waitress station and exercised his arm-wrestling arm by lifting the fifteen-pound shot put. John was good with his fists but not good with people. Wood had tried to use him out front checking IDs when Carl wasn't working, but John was a sucker for any story. Wood saw him let through a pimply teenage kid that used an old, dog-eared draft card from the seventies. The ID said he was twenty-eight. Wood pulled him from the door, and he'd been stationed in the back corner ever since. When Wood saw him, John didn't ask about his cut on the slot scam.

The club was packed by midnight, and Wood could barely move through the crowd. He started a line outside, with Carl checking for fake IDs. Wood stayed inside the front door to collect the side money from regulars and high-rollers. He tried to pace his coke. He'd snorted most of one gram before coming to work and would need the other to get him through the night. He planned to do a couple of hits every hour.

Time dragged, and then he just wanted to be done, have a few cocktails, drive home, and sleep. But sleep was far off, and he was spaced out and confused. He could barely remember the names of the regulars, and when someone tried to casually slip him a twenty, he somehow forgot the motions—the simple sliding of the palms in a handshake, the simple movement of fingertips around the folded bill—and the twenty fluttered to the floor. Fucking embarrassing. He still needed to explain to John that his five thousand was now thirty-five hundred because of taxes. And he only had two thousand on him.

At two in the morning, a girl he knew—a regular—stomped up to him at the door. She acted crazy mad and gestured wildly with her hands as she talked. She complained about a guy that had propositioned her—had asked how much she wanted for a blowjob. She told him to fuck off. Then the guy called her a fucking cunt. Wood listened to the tirade, nodding his head and touching her shoulder. He really didn't care but knew he needed to do something about it. Frank had pounded the words into his skull—*No Girls, No Club*. Wood used his Mini Mag flashlight to signal John in the back corner of the club. It took a few minutes for him to make it through the crowd to the front door. He'd already slipped on his sap gloves. The two followed the girl to the back bar near the DJ booth. "Him," she said, pointing to a guy in a red silk jacket with a tiger head embroidered on the back.

With John behind him, he approached the guy and tapped him on the shoulder. He turned around and Wood said, "Hey, buddy, I need to speak to you outside."

The guy looked at Wood and then at John behind him. "What did that bitch say I did?"

"I just need to speak with you outside, not here. We can straighten this out outside."

"I'm not fucking going anywhere." The guy's arms hung down, his hands balled into fists. John started to move around to the guy's back.

"This can go one of two ways," Wood said. "One way's not going to hurt."

John was behind the guy now and ready to move with just a quick head signal from Wood. Behind John, though, Wood saw another guy stand up from a table and step toward them. He looked huge. When he was close, he asked, "What's going on?" He wasn't talking to Wood but spoke directly to his friend in the red jacket.

The guy in the red jacket said, "They're throwing me out because of some shit this chick said I said."

"No, they're not." He said it loud enough for Wood and John to hear. He then turned and stared directly at Wood.

Wood looked closely at the guy standing next to John, towering over him. He was probably six foot five and weighed two-fifty or more. He wore a green Incredible Hulk T-shirt that outlined his bulging muscles, the sleeves bunched in his armpits, unable to cover his biceps. And for a moment, Wood spaced out again, thinking about the steroids. He'd never seen this guy at the gym and figured he was probably up from LA— probably worked out with Todd at Venice Beach. Wood wanted to be bigger like these guys, and he needed steroids to do it. In the meantime, he knew he was outgunned. He said, "No, I guess we're not." Wood stepped away, and John followed him back to the front door. They were going to need reinforcements.

Wood figured it would take six guys, two for Red Jacket and four for the Hulk. He pulled Carl and Holt from outside and shut the doors. Holt's brother Paul was already inside and stood with the others. Then, he used his Mini Mag to catch the eye of Nash the Smasher with his Zorro scar. The six of them huddled, and Wood explained the situation. Holt and Paul needed to take out Red Jacket. John, Carl, Nash, and Wood would go for the Hulk. They'd have to take him down and carry him out.

The big guy, the Hulk, saw them coming and stood up. His arms hung down against his side with fists clenched. Wood, John, Nash, and Carl had done this countless times. Maybe with no one this size, but the motions were the same. Most fights started as shouting-and-pushing matches that escalated to more violence. Unless the guy was a real street fighter, he wouldn't expect it when Wood and his guys moved fast with fists and a takedown. The Hulk was no different, and just by his stance with his fists down, Wood figured they'd have the draw on him. Wood had full clarity with his adrenalin up and his coke high, and he felt strong. John was the first to move and went for the one punch. It landed, and the Hulk stumbled. Nash went for his chest with a high kick and knocked him to the ground. The Hulk struggled to get up, but Wood held one arm, John the other, with Carl and Nash on each leg. Wood said, "Let's go," and they started dragging him through the parting crowd. The Mormon brothers, Holt and Paul, were behind with Red Jacket, who surprisingly didn't attempt to fight or resist. Fucking pussy.

They dragged the Hulk to the front and used his head like a battering ram to open the heavy wooden door. Outside on the sidewalk, they pinned him to the ground. John took out his handcuffs looped over his belt and cuffed the left wrist. He could barely stretch it around the thick wrist and could only tighten it to one click. John lifted the cuffed arm to the guy's back, and Wood tried to bend the huge right arm to get the other wrist cuffed. The Hulk's arm bulged around the bicep and tapered into a thick wrist. Wood used both hands to push, but the Hulk's arm was twice as big as his.

The guy was superhumanly strong, and the arm wouldn't budge far enough to get to the cuffs. Wood felt his adrenaline and his rage and knew that the only way they were going to get the Hulk in cuffs was to really hurt him. Wood pushed the arm back to the sidewalk and pinned it with his knee. He grabbed the guy's head by the hair and started banging and smashing his face over and over into the cement. Wood could see the blood now flowing from the guy's nose. He kept banging the

Hulk's head until he felt the arm go limp. Wood finally stopped, and he and John were able to pull the arms around and cuff the other wrist. Wood looked up to see the line of customers staring. He smiled and felt like he'd given them a good show. Red Jacket was already in cuffs, and they took both around back by the dumpsters and had them lay on their stomachs. The Hulk's chin, nose, and forehead were bloody and pulpy. There wasn't a scratch on Red Jacket, and Wood had the impulse to change that, to beat the guy who'd started all this. Carl, Holt, and Paul returned to the line, John watched over the two, and Wood called the police.

Before he left for home after his shift, while he was winding down and finishing a second Stoli Cranberry, John asked for his five grand. Wood tried explaining the whole tax thing—the IRS form and the government's thirty percent cut. John just stared at him like he was talking gibberish. John was his best friend in Las Vegas, maybe his only real friend. He didn't say much, but he had his back. Wood could count on John when breaking up a bar fight or when things got nasty on a security job. And somehow, he felt that he owed John the full amount—only another fifteen hundred—so Wood said that he'd come across with the whole five grand but that he had only two on him. Wood finished his drink, and they walked to his truck. Once he laid out the twenty hundred-dollar bills for John, only two were left in his wallet. Now, he felt he had nothing to show for the Mega Slot score. Mike and John had theirs, and Sally had his. Wood climbed into his truck and scraped out the last coke crystals with a swizzle-stick spoon, the final two small hits. He drove home.

CHAPTER TEN

Who was this woman screaming at him? It was a weird out-of-body experience, like he was in a thick glass bottle and there was someone on the outside trying to say something, but he couldn't hear, and he was trying to read the person's lips, but they were moving too fast, and he couldn't. Then Wood felt a shove, just one hand pushing against his chest, and he snapped out of it—all instinct, like if anyone shoved him that way at the club or anywhere, that hand would be crushed. Then he said out loud, "Why are you screaming at me?"

Sally's hair was tied back again, and she didn't have her contacts in, just big glasses like a scuba mask. Her face contorted into rage, and she was crying and screaming. "Did you even check to see if Frankie was okay? Did you even look or think about taking him to the hospital?"

"What'd I do?" Then he remembered what he'd done. "It was nothing. He was messing around inside my truck, and I told him never to mess with my truck."

She shoved him again. "He's got a cracked rib. He can

barely breathe without pain. I found him lying on the floor in the basement. His chest is one big bruise." She shoved him again. "You fucking asshole. Why don't you get the fuck out of my house?"

"Your house?"

"Yeah, my house. You're fucking worthless and contribute nothing. My house, my son, my life. Why don't you go back to one of those whores you're always hanging out with? Anyplace, but not here. I'm done with you."

Wood heard the words clearly now, his adrenaline pumping once more. "Divorce? You want a divorce?"

"Yes, divorce. Like in, get the fuck out of my house and my life. I don't want to see you again."

That was fine, Wood thought. If she wanted a divorce, that was fine. However, it wouldn't end there, and it wouldn't be easy. He didn't care if his name wasn't on the mortgage or title; he would have half. And she owed him the money for the Mega Slot score, and he wanted that money now. He yelled, "Fine, I'll fucking go. And fuck you. I'll go as soon as you pay me the slot machine money. That was my idea and my score."

"You used me, you fucker."

"Yeah, so?"

Sally stood in front of Wood, her hands on her hips. "Yeah, so that money's mine now. I took the risk, and it's my name on the IRS form. If something goes wrong, if your mechanic friend fucks up and they suspect something, they know who I am. And you contribute next to nothing around here, and I've always paid the bills. I'm keeping the money."

And then it didn't seem to matter anymore. Everything was so fucked up. Wood had made a fifty-thousand-dollar score, and now he had nothing and still owed John three grand. He'd leave, but not without the money. "Sally, you need to tell me where that money is." He spoke calmly now; she was just someone who owed him money.

"No." Sally turned away and walked toward the kitchen. And in that split second, so quick that it was like missing frames from a film, Wood tackled her from behind and dropped with all his weight onto the kitchen floor. Her body and head slammed against the linoleum. He pushed himself up and put his forearm against her back.

"Tell me where the money is?" He put more weight on her back, pushing her body down, but there was no pushback, no tension. He turned her over, her body limp to his touch. He looked into her eyes and said, "Sally?" There was no blood, but her forehead was different, misshapen like a deflated ball. He put his ear near her mouth. Her breathing was faint, and then it slowed. And he knew he'd killed her.

The next moment, he heard a door open and footsteps coming from Frankie's bedroom. He yelled, "Frankie, go back to bed. Now." Frankie stepped into the kitchen dressed in his Inspector Gadget pajamas, his hair bent against the grain from resting on the pillow. He looked down at his mother and made a sound. The sound was a single tone, like when Wood left the keys in the ignition with the door open—a buzzer sound like that, but mournful.

"Frankie, your mom is just sick, but she'll be okay. Now, go back to bed or down to the basement. Go. I'll take care of your mother. Now *go!*" Frankie walked to the basement door, opened it, closed it, and then walked down the steps.

———

Sally was dead, and on one level, she was just another dead pet that needed disposal. He walked out through the open garage door and climbed into his truck. He wanted to back his truck into the garage and then put Sally's body into the cooler on the truck bed, but halfway in, the cab hit the top of the garage door. Wood checked for damage and was pissed when he found a small dent—just one more thing to deal with. In the kitchen, Sally didn't weigh much over a hundred pounds, so he easily lifted her up and over his shoulder. He dropped her onto the truck bed and pushed her into the cooler.

Before he left, he went through Sally's bedroom, looking for the money. He checked the obvious places: her closet, shoe boxes, under the mattress, and in dresser drawers. Her clothes made him think. And he thought he needed a story, which would be that Sally left him and left town. He packed some of her clothes into a suitcase. He spent more time looking—the bathroom, Frankie's room, the living room, and again through the kitchen. He couldn't find the money. By then, he'd already decided that the body was going to the moon; no one would find her on the moon.

He was tired and out of coke—coked-out. The drive through Pahrump to the turn-off at Johnnie was an hour and a half, and he caught himself dozing at the wheel and almost dreaming. And in that dreamy state, thinking about Sally and about kicking Frankie, he thought that what he did to Frankie was nothing compared to what his own dad had done to him. The memory of that pain started with the time he saw his first dead body, that of his best friend, Sam, lying across the tracks. Wood was fifteen at the time. It was one of the first warm days of spring, and the two of them had skipped class to hang out in the freight yards and drink beer. Sam looked older and had his brother's ID, so he bought a twelve-pack of Old Style from the liquor store. They hung out, drank, and felt the warm sun on their faces. Then, a freight train came through.

Sam said they should hop the train and maybe go as far as Albany, which sounded fun. They ran alongside the train with what was left of the twelve-pack. There was an open boxcar. Wood jumped in first, and Sam handed up the beer. Then, he placed his palms on the boxcar floor to push himself up. He didn't make it in all the way, went teetering down, and disappeared beneath. Wood jumped off and ran back. The train was still moving, and its wheels ran over Sam's torso— over and over. The train seemed endless, and for a split second, he thought he could see Sam looking at him and pleading. By the time the train was gone, Sam's eyes were vacant, and he wasn't moving. Wood was scared—scared that he'd killed his friend, scared that he would be blamed, and scared that his dad would find out and also find out that he'd skipped school. Wood ran.

The body was discovered that day. The following morning, the news was on the front page of the *Republican*. His dad asked him if he'd been there, and he lied. His friend's death was a big deal at school, and everyone remembered how much they liked Sam. A funeral service was held at the Blessed Sacrament Church. He was Sam's best friend, and Sam's parents hugged him and cried.

The day after the funeral, his father asked him again if he'd been there. This time, his father said that a friend who worked in the freight yard had seen Wood there. Wood broke down and cried. He told his dad the whole story. That same night, his dad beat him with a belt. He beat him so hard that there were cuts that bled through his T-shirt the next day. He had welts for weeks. His dad never told Sam's parents the truth or anyone else. Wood finished high school that year, and the first day after graduation, Wood left Springfield and never looked back. He had an older brother somewhere, and maybe his parents were still alive. But he didn't care—so long, good riddance. He'd lost his wife now, and it was time to move on again. Good riddance.

Out past Johnnie, out on the moon, Wood dumped Sally's body and found soft sand to bury the suitcase that couldn't be eaten by scavengers. He was tired and angry—angry at everything and everyone, especially Sally. *What a cunt*, he thought. Then, without thinking, he reached for the folded Buck he kept in the worn leather sheath on his belt. He pulled open the blade and reached for Sally's hair. He thought maybe he'd take a lock of her hair, a memento, but as he lifted the hair, he saw the ear, and without much thought, Wood slit it off with the Buck's sharp blade. He let the ear drop to the desert floor, where the dust and dirt absorbed what little blood oozed. Afterward, he put the severed ear in the pickle jar.

He felt nothing, vacant—just another dead pet—and now he wanted more coke.

CHAPTER ELEVEN

Claire's shift at Sunrise Hospital started at seven in the evening when she clocked in, wrapped herself in a white plastic apron, and covered her hair with a thin disposable net. Her job was technically Kitchen Assistant but should have been Dishwasher Assistant since what she did was assist the dishwasher. By seven, the patient dinner trays were back from the hospital rooms and stacked in tall, slotted carts. On the trays were the detritus of the cafeteria meal: half-eaten chicken breasts, hardly eaten vegetables, bread wrappers or intact wrapped bread, and usually empty dessert bowls. Her job was to scrape the leftover food into a fifty-gallon garbage bin, stack the trays, bowls, and plates at the end of the dish stand, and then toss the used silverware into bus tubs filled with soapy water. After the trays, bowls, plates, and silverware were washed, the process was reversed, with Claire stacking the trays in the carts with clean silverware, ready to be filled again several hours later with breakfast. The smell was ever present and didn't change regardless of the meal, something like rancid bacon grease. The smell hung on Claire well after her shift ended at three in the morning, right up until she could light a cigarette and cloud it, like washing a skunked dog with tomato juice.

The work reminded her of high school and taking a few evening shifts weekly for her father at Tramps. She was the actual dishwasher then, a step up from her current position as assistant. The work had been mindless and oddly relaxing, and the hours would drift by while thinking of school, friends, and probably boys. The work was mindless now.

At nine, she took a smoke break outside near the loading dock, then at eleven, her thirty-minute dinner break. She walked down the hospital halls toward the cafeteria, where she had a fifty-percent employee discount on everything. She was still new and self-conscious and still worried that someone might recognize her from before, from when she was an escort, and call her Cher. She walked the edges of the hallway with her head down, watching the shoes of others, sometimes flattening against the wall to avoid collisions. Then a man's voice, "Hey, I know you." The exact words she dreaded. Her head stayed down, and she saw shoes blocking her lane—black trainers with three white stripes. She stopped and looked up, her dread turning to relief. She recognized the man as the emergency room doctor who'd tried to straighten her nose with a butter knife. "You're the girl I treated in the ER."

"Yes, that was me." With the mention of her nose, she instinctively reached up to cover it with a hand. Then she realized how stupid that was, covering the nose he'd worked on. Instead, she fumbled to push hair around an ear. But her awful hairnet was still holding all the loose strands in place. She was flustered like a teenager and just stood there motionless— like a dope.

The doctor leaned forward and looked closer at her nose. She looked up past him to let the doctor examine her further.

"Not such a great job, I'm afraid. I'm not a plastic surgeon." Then he added, "Sorry, I'm Dr. Meiser, Harold Meiser, or just Harry." He was maybe five years older than her, thin and, in fact, hairy with a hedge of black hair sticking up from the V-neck of his light blue scrubs. His hair was full and curly, and a stubble of beard poked through his skin. He was, in a way, tall, dark, and handsome.

The thought of Harry as hairy made her smile. "Hi, Claire."

"You work here?"

"Yes," she said, then added, "in the cafeteria." She didn't want him to think she was part of the real hospital, a healer of some kind. Though to anyone who worked here, that was obvious: Doctors wore blue scrubs. Nurses, technicians, and medical assistants wore green scrubs. Kitchen workers wore maroon.

"I got to go, but come by the ER sometime. I can refer you to a surgeon who can fix that nose. Since it's related to an injury, you should still be able to get it covered by insurance."

The emergency room visit had cost over three grand and consumed a chunk of her savings. "I don't have insurance." She thought of the next sentence and the term to use—accident. She had told him that she was in a car accident but couldn't bring herself to say the lie again.

"If you're working here, you should have insurance now." Dr. Meiser—Harry—turned and walked down the brightly lit hallway.

At three in the morning, after her shift and after lighting up a cigarette in the Ford station wagon, Claire stopped at a 7-Eleven near her house and bought a four-pack of Bartles & Jaymes wine coolers. At home, she let Bud out in the yard and then settled back to watch TV and unwind. Only two stations were still broadcasting, and over the past week, she'd settled on *The PTL Club* with Jim and Tammy Faye Bakker. She'd watched the show before, back when she was escorting. They sang, preached, and pleaded. *The PTL Club* singers were soulful and uplifting, and she got caught up in their message of hope. Toward Christmas, Tammy would sing her holiday songs, her voice crystal clear in contrast to her regular, squeaky, ear-piercing pleas for money. That night, Jim and Tammy talked more about the story of little Stevie, who after prayer and multiple operations, was now sitting up in a wheelchair and able to feed himself. Stevie needed more prayers and more operations, and the Bakkers, through their Heritage Foundation, were paying for it all, and they pleaded for more money. Claire opened a second Bartles & Jaymes as they brought Stevie out in his wheelchair. He held his own microphone while he spoke in a high-pitched voice like he'd sucked helium from a balloon. Part of her wanted to believe, wanted purpose, but her cynicism was never far away, and she saw through the carny routine and knew it was all nonsense, a con. And all the Tammy Faye crying and streaked mascara broke the spell for Claire. It was just too much. She was no sucker.

———

The next week, Claire started her coursework at Nevada Technical College, and she was able to schedule her work around classes. She slept when she could and cobbled it together somehow. Bud was the one that suffered, and one afternoon, she came home and opened the front door to a terrible stench. Bud had done his business near the back—again. He crept up to her, looking sheepish with his tail down, nose down, and eyes cast upward. He was nervous and stood inside the living room, waiting for Claire's reaction. Claire walked past Bud, through the kitchen to the backdoor. She shouted, "Bad dog." Bud stayed in the living room. Claire came back through the kitchen and said, "Bad dog," again. Bud couldn't meet her eyes and slunk to the floor. His tail now wagged nervously. She grabbed him by the collar and pulled him to the back door. She was tired and angry. She worked forty hours a week, attended classes, and lived in this dump of a house. She drove a station wagon and cleaned up sick people's dishes. And now she was supposed to clean up the dog's shit too? She wanted to stick his nose into the mess and make him smell it. She held his collar tight but then stopped. She opened the back door and let Bud out into the yard. She wanted to sit at the kitchen table, feel sorry for herself, and just cry. Instead, she cleaned up the mess and then sat outside on the steps. Bud eventually came back.

She stroked his head and whispered, "Sorry, Bud."

CHAPTER TWELVE

Wood drove his truck with Frankie in the passenger seat. Frankie made no sound. It was Sunday morning, two days since he'd dumped Sally's body.

The previous Friday, he'd returned from the desert to find Frankie in the basement, still in his Inspector Gadget pajamas, and not at school. The phone rang. It was Frank at Tramps wondering why Sally wasn't at work. Wood had thought this through. He said he didn't know and thought she *was* at work. He called Frank back an hour later, part of his plan. He told Frank he was worried, that Sally's car was still in the garage, but she'd packed suitcases and was gone. Frank had questions. Did they have a fight? Was she going somewhere, and had Wood just forgotten? Was Frankie all right? Wood's answers: No big fight. Maybe he did forget but didn't think so. Yes, Frankie was fine. Wood said he would stay with Frankie and would probably need to take Friday night off. He'd wait to see if Sally showed up. Then he went to sleep and finally slept hard after being awake and wired for forty-eight hours. That evening, he woke up briefly to feed Frankie and put him to bed. Saturday morning, Frank called again, and Wood again said that Sally hadn't returned or called. He'd watch Frankie and take Saturday night off, too.

Wood stayed in the house all day Saturday and Saturday night. Bored, he watched TV and drank beer. Off and on, he looked for the Mega Slot money. He thought about what he had to do the following week. He needed the cash from the dead-pet runs and needed to get back to his job at Tramps. He was still trying to work out an angle for making money selling steroids. He couldn't do any of that and still take care of Frankie, and on Monday, Frankie would need to go back to school. Wood had never taken him there and didn't know where the school was. Or was there a school bus stop? Then he thought of Sally's sister, Claire, and remembered that she'd left the escort business and was living in a run-down house somewhere near the airport. Sunday morning, he packed Frankie's clothes into trash bags and loaded them into the bed of his truck. He lifted Frankie into the passenger seat and then roamed the streets just north of the airport.

On Palo Verde Road, he pulled up to a stoplight that had just turned red. Next to him was a cyclist on a ten-speed bike with downturned handlebars. Wood had recently seen more of these guys around town—guys in helmets with tight black shorts and fingerless gloves. He thought they were funny and maybe gay. The light turned green, and Wood accelerated hard, sending a plume of dark oily exhaust into the path of the bike—*eat that, faggot.* Wood laughed and then looked over at Frankie to share the fun. But it was just like Frankie to not get it, the kid looking down at the truck's floor mat and not even paying attention. Then, the exhaust spewing wasn't fun anymore, and Wood felt relieved when he finally spotted the old house. It was the only home in a commercial neighborhood of hotels, warehouses, a strip mall, the post office, and a gas station. He pulled his truck in front of the low chain-link fence surrounding the property.

What did Wood see? The FOR SALE sign was still in the yard, and Wood figured the adobe house for a teardown once the post office next door brought the property, or some entrepreneur made plans for an auto body shop, lumber yard, or something else. The house was like a bunker: square, small, almost windowless, with thick concrete-looking walls. The roof was flat, with a swamp cooler in the center like a chimney. A closed gate led to a dirt driveway and a parking spot beneath a big tree. The car parked there was a shitty Ford station wagon without accessories, tinted windows, or even fake wood paneling. Another small building or shed was in the back; otherwise, the property was all dry desert dirt and weeds. Then he noticed another shed, much smaller than a phone booth, and realized it was an outhouse. Didn't the place have plumbing? Was Claire using an outhouse? What he remembered about Claire was Cher with her long black hair and red Porsche 924. He always thought Claire was the hotter of the two sisters. He couldn't imagine her in this dump. But that's what Apple had said, a dump like something the original settlers had died in. This had to be the place.

He left Frankie in the truck and opened the driveway gate. On the front porch, he looked for the doorbell, then gave up. He knocked. A dog barked, and Wood remembered Apple had said something about a dog. He heard footsteps. Claire cracked the door, "What do you want, Wood? I'm trying to get some sleep."

Wood first saw her nose. He knew she had been beaten up, and he knew his trip to LA a couple of months ago had been for retribution, but he figured the nose would be healed by now or fixed. The bridge veered slightly to the left with a red lump in the middle the size of a marble. The tip itself looked larger and tougher, like leather. After the nose, he barely noticed her black hair braided into a thick rope or that she wore no makeup. He kept looking at her nose. "Can you breathe through that thing?"

Claire repeated, "Wood, what do you want?"

Wood looked away from her nose and let his eyes fall and settle on the cleavage of her breasts covered by a thin, silky robe. He stared a second too long, now self-conscious. He then just looked across the yard at the Ford station wagon. "Sally left me," he said.

"It's about time."

He now looked her in the eyes, "Yeah, she left me all right, but she also left Frankie."

"She wouldn't leave Frankie."

"Well, she did. She packed up on Friday and left while I was at work. Her clothes are gone. I haven't heard from her since. Neither has Frank. I've got Frankie in the car." He paused. "You need to watch him for me until she gets back."

"You watch him. He's your son."

"He's Dominic's son. Anyway, I'm not equipped. I got no idea how to take care of this kid—his special needs."

"Wood, do you see diapers on the clothesline? Is there a sandbox in my front yard? Do you see a child's seat in my car?" She looked toward the Ford, and Wood followed her gaze. There was no child's seat in the car. "You got more experience than I do. It's me and the dog here. I can't take Frankie, and you need to just step up. Now get out of my yard." Claire shut the door, and Wood heard a deadbolt slide through the doorjamb.

Wood felt his anger physically. Tension in his jaw caused a twitching motion, and his shoulders squared up and locked. The anger swelled in his muscles, like the tension after a solid workout. He subconsciously touched his leather knife sheath. Anger was familiar—a good friend.

He walked back to his truck and opened the passenger door. Frankie sat upright, still staring at the floor mat. Wood lifted him with two hands and set him down on the ground. Wood then reached into the truck bed and pulled out both garbage bags of clothes. He grabbed Frankie's upper arm and led him back toward the door that had just been shut in his face. He dropped the two bags on the stoop and knocked. He didn't wait.

He was almost to his truck when he heard the door open, and Claire yell out, "Wood!" He stepped into the truck's cab, closed the door, and fired the engine. The extreme-country tires dug into the soft driveway dirt and sent a cloud of dust into his rearview mirror. He saw the cloud and smiled.

————

A half-hour later, he knocked on John's apartment door. Wood thought he'd stay away from his house for a while, make sure the kid didn't boomerang. John lived in a one-bedroom apartment on Koval Lane just behind the Imperial Palace casino. Inside, John was watching football. Wood asked if he could stay and watch, maybe buy some beer.

"Okay," John said. He added, "You got the rest of my money?"

Wood looked at John and realized the money issue wasn't going away. "Bro, Sally left me, and she took all the money. The bitch is gone, and I have nothing."

John switched positions in his elbow-worn easy chair and continued watching the football game. "Timothy 6: verse 10. For the love of money is the root of all kinds of evil."

Wood was used to the Bible quotes and liked their fortune cookie sound. "Fuckin' A," he said.

CHAPTER THIRTEEN

The boy in front of her stood motionless and stared ahead. Claire watched the orange monster truck explode in a cloud of dust and then take off down Palo Verde. *Fuck*, she thought. She went outside dressed only in her silk robe. She crouched and tried to look the boy in the eyes. He looked down and away. Frankie was her nephew, but years had passed since their last meeting, and Claire wasn't sure he knew who she was. She said, "Hi, Frankie, I'm your Aunt Claire."

She reached to hold his hand, to guide him inside the house, but Frankie pulled his hand away and kept it stiff beside his body. She then touched his back to guide him, but she could feel the tension in his muscles—he did not like to be touched. Finally, she just said, "Come on in," and held the door open. Frankie walked through the door and stood in the living room. Bud ran over to sniff his pant leg and then jumped up playfully. "Down, Bud," Claire said. Bud ignored Claire, and Frankie ignored Bud.

The last time she had seen the boy was at Dominic's

funeral four or five years earlier. He must have been eight then but seemed younger, like a five-year-old. Sally was seven years older than Claire and more of a mother to her than her own mom, Deedee. Sally would make her cereal in the morning, get her off to school, and then have dinner ready in the evening. And what Claire remembered about her mom was that she always dressed in a glamorous, sequined dress to go out. She wore high heels, her hair sculpted in some carefully woven style, a cigarette holder, and pearls. Claire would get a kiss on the forehead before she went to bed and before Deedee went out for the night. During the days, Deedee slept or didn't come home at all.

Deedee might have loved her, but she didn't know for sure. To Claire, kids seemed overrated and not worth the trouble—possibly her mother thought the same. Deedee abandoned the family when Claire was only ten. When Claire was twelve, Sally became pregnant, moved out of the house, and married Dominic. They had Frankie five months later. Claire stayed with her dad after that, and she pretty much raised herself without Sally. She looked at Frankie. He was about the same age as she had been when Sally left.

She hadn't seen Deedee in fifteen years. Sally had told her once that their mother had turned prostitute and was working at one of the brothels out in the desert. Sally told her that when she found out Claire was escorting. She said, "Like mother, like daughter."

Had Sally really left Wood? Wood was a tool, a meathead, all muscle below the neck and none above. She never knew why Sally married him and figured it was just out of panic or desperation—a willing replacement husband. She could see Sally leaving Wood, but Frankie? Maybe, maybe not. Deedee had abandoned her kids, and Claire thought, *Like mother, like daughter.* She looked at Frankie and knew Wood could never help this kid on his own. She knew, for the time being, she was stuck. She carried the two garbage bags of clothes from the stoop into the second bedroom.

That day, she figured out a few things. He wouldn't talk or look at her, and he didn't like to be touched. But he wasn't stupid. He followed instructions. When she told him to sit on the couch, he did. She said to go ahead and watch TV if he wanted, and Frankie picked up the remote control for the Zenith and, within minutes, was switching through stations. He found the cartoons. While watching, he made his first sound, a high-pitched noise with no equivalent in nature that she could think of. She tried to get him to answer simple questions like, "Frankie, do you want something to eat?" or "Frankie, do you like the TV show?" But it was as though he couldn't hear or she wasn't even in the room.

In the afternoon at Safeway, she told him to follow her through the store, and he did. She bought what she thought a thirteen-year-old boy would want: macaroni and cheese, Oscar Meyer bologna, white bread, mayonnaise, yellow mustard, hot dogs and buns, milk, eggs, frozen pizza, and Marie Callender's frozen meals. He showed interest only in the cereal aisle. Claire told him to pick one, and he did, grabbing a box of Honeycomb from the shelf and then holding it to his chest like a blanket. At the checkout stand, Claire asked him to put the box on the moving belt, and he did. After shopping at Safeway, she drove to the Goodwill and bought a small chest of drawers and a blue-striped bed ticking that she could roll up and load into the station wagon. She made one last stop at Woolworths, where she bought bedsheets and a pillow.

She called in sick that Sunday night and unpacked Frankie's clothes. In one of the garbage bags was a wide-mouthed canvas bag, like a purse. Inside were tools: screwdrivers, an adjustable wrench, pliers, a small hammer, a tape measure, and a dull toy saw. She made up the bed, which lay flat on the floor. She told Frankie to change his clothes and put on pajamas. Frankie went through the drawers and found the ones with the Inspector Gadget print. Claire asked him if he liked Inspector Gadget. Frankie didn't immediately acknowledge her, but moments later, he made another sound, different from the first, almost birdlike. Frankie then took off his shirt to change. Claire saw the bruising around his chest and the bandage. She touched it and Frankie winced. She said, "What did Wood do?" She didn't expect an answer.

He watched more TV that night. No cartoons were on, so he switched to a new show that had just started on Sundays, *MacGyver*. They watched together silently. Bud jumped up on the couch next to Frankie and lay down. Frankie didn't move or acknowledge Bud in any way, but partway through the show, his hand reached over and touched Bud's fur. For the rest of the show, the hand stayed there, not petting, just feeling, like Bud was a soft pillow or a fur coat.

———

Monday morning, Claire took Frankie to her sister's house. No one answered when she rang the doorbell and then pounded on the door. Afterward, she simply followed the neighborhood kids to the school. Rowe Elementary was in a sprawling one-level cinderblock building. The school mascot was painted on a wall near the entrance with the sign beneath, THE ROWE RUNNERS. The cartoon mascot, roadrunner, wore a black leather jacket and held its thumb up. Claire figured it was supposed to be like Fonzie in *Happy Days*. But what she recalled about Fonzie was that he was a high-school dropout, a rebel, and a garage mechanic. And somehow, the cartoon figure summed up her whole education experience—aspire to be a dropout, be cool, have sex, have sex for money, get beat up, and wash dishes for the rest of your life. Out of the car, Frankie knew right where to go, and Claire walked behind him and stopped just outside his classroom.

The heavy institutional door had a large glass window, and Claire watched for a few minutes. Frankie took a desk in the back and simply stared at the laminate desktop. About fifteen other kids were in the room, but Frankie didn't interact or seem to acknowledge any friends. The other kids were a mixed bag of ages and afflictions. Some were obviously mentally disabled with mongoloid features. A skinny kid with a crew cut couldn't keep his hands to himself and reached forward to tap another kid on the back. The kid turned with a blank stare, and the skinny kid laughed. He then drummed on the desktop, began mouthing words to himself, and shook his head back and forth. He used the desk next to him to extend his drum set. The girl at that desk glared at him behind thick glasses and then crossed her arms over the desktop to block the drumming. Behind Frankie was another kid in a wheelchair contraption with a battery and joystick. The kid's head listed unnaturally to the side, his mouth open, and Claire could see his pink tongue. Her view was limited, and she couldn't see the front of the classroom or the teacher.

Later, Claire sat alone in the waiting room outside of the principal's office. She'd been sitting and waiting for almost an hour and needed to pee, but the thought of walking into an elementary school bathroom and getting stared at by seven or eight-year-olds kept her holding it. The principal finally came past the reception desk and through the waiting room.

"Are you waiting for me?" The principal was small, old, and completely bald. He wore wire-rimmed glasses that were once fashionable in the seventies with John Lennon, but Claire figured his glasses went back to the fifties and were probably out of fashion even then. He wore a thin, short-sleeved white shirt and a patterned tie that bled in shades of blue like a desert scene at dusk. The sleeves of his undershirt were too long and stuck out around his thin arms. She could see the low-cut neckline of the undershirt and realized that the principal was Mormon. Las Vegas had a huge population of Mormons, and Claire knew the particular look of temple garments. Claire wore Gloria Vanderbilt jeans and a blue T-shirt with an ocean-wave-and-sunset graphic. She instinctively crossed her arms over her chest.

"Yes, I'm Claire Welch. I'm Frank Harding's aunt."

"Frank Harding? I'm unfamiliar with a Frank Harding, and I pride myself on knowing every student."

Claire thought about the name and remembered Dominic. His last name was Barleto. Wood had never adopted Frankie. "Oh, I mean Frank Barleto. That's his deceased father's last name. We call him Frankie."

"Yes, Frank Barleto. In Mrs. Sander's special needs class. Please come into my office."

The office was stark, with a large wood desk facing two chairs. Behind the desk, on the wall, were three framed diplomas. The principal motioned for Claire to sit. A name plaque on his desk facing outward said, PRINCIPAL AMMON K. SMOOT.

She started to address him. "Thank you, Principal Smoot, for seeing me." She wondered if that was how she should address him—Principal Smoot. He didn't correct her, and she continued, "My sister, Sally Harding, formerly Sally Barleto, apparently left town or is missing. Her current husband, Wood Harding, refuses to care for Frankie and essentially abandoned him on my doorstep. I'm doing the best I can." She stopped; she was getting ahead of herself.

Principal Smoot leaned back in his chair and folded his hands. "I'm sorry for your situation. What is it I can help you with?"

Now she wondered that herself. "Well, I just thought the school should be aware of the situation." She paused and added, "Do you know Frankie's condition?"

"Condition?"

"Like, what's the matter with him? Has there ever been a diagnosis?"

"We're not doctors here; we're merely educators."

"Well, what kind of class is he in? I saw mongoloids."

He corrected her, "Kids with Down syndrome. Yes. He's in the class for all kids with special needs. Frank, unfortunately, has special needs."

"Well, I don't think he's completely…what's the word? Mentally disabled? I've seen him figure things out."

"He does have special needs. I'm unfamiliar with Frank Barleto's condition, but I understand that he doesn't speak or interact. In fact, Mrs. Sanders has said that he may, in fact, be *seriously* mentally disabled. But we're not doctors. We're educators. And like you, we do the best we can with all our students whether they should be here or not." Principal Smoot looked around the room, seemingly now bored with the conversation. He removed his glasses and cleaned them with the end of his dusk-blue tie.

"So you don't think he should be here?" Claire sat forward and put her hands down to her side, uncovering the surf-and-sun print on her shirt.

"That's not what I said, though currently, he is the oldest student at Rowe. He'll have to move on eventually, but I believe he started here late. Regardless, the Disabilities Education Act prohibits us from discriminating against any student with disabilities or special needs." Now, he looked at her. "Mrs.…I'm sorry, I missed the name?"

"Miss Welch."

"Miss Welch, what legal rights have you established with Frank Barleto?

"Legal rights?"

He leaned forward. "Have you contacted the police or social services? Do you have custody?"

"The police?"

"Child abandonment is a felony in the state of Nevada. If Frank Barleto has been abandoned, the crime should be reported." Then he added, "In fact, if you cannot show that you have legal rights, I shouldn't even be talking to you."

This was all happening too fast. She hadn't thought through the situation, and now it had spiraled out of control. She was doing the best she could, and she was trying. She knew if she called the police, they'd either make Wood take Frankie back or take the kid to Social Services. She knew nothing about what the state did with abandoned children but imagined it was like a jail with steel doors instead of bars, school lunches for every meal, and maybe a common room where they all watched the same TV show, where bullies controlled the remote control and stole desserts from kids like Frankie. She wanted to yell "Fuck you" to the Mormon creep. But that would just cause more trouble and push the principal to call the police himself. She needed to get out of the office without causing any more damage. All she could think to say was, "Thanks."

Claire stood and left the office without saying another

word.

Principal Smoot instinctively stood when Claire did and said, "Thank you, Miss Welch."

———

That night, Frankie watched *TV Bloopers and Practical Jokes*. Claire sat with him on the couch, with Bud between the two. Again, Frankie rested his hand on Bud's fur. The practical joke that night was on Jerry Lewis in Las Vegas, and Claire recognized City Hall from the few times she'd gone there— once to get a Sheriff's Card that would allow her to take the escort job at Sincerely Yours. Anyone who wanted work in Las Vegas had to go through the same application and background check—the idea was to keep felons and gangsters out of the casinos. The joke on the show was that Jerry Lewis was attending a mock ceremony proclaiming him as Las Vegas's number-one citizen. Part of the honor was the unveiling of a sculpture in his likeness. The joke was that the statue was made of ice and was melting in the hot desert sun. Claire didn't think it was all that funny and was looking toward Frankie to see if he got it. Frankie watched. When Jerry Lewis finally saw the ice sculpture and did his laugh, Frankie made a sound like a high-pitched buzzer that seemed to mimic the laugh. Then, Frankie mimicked Jerry Lewis's funny schtick, where he tried to clap, but his hands kept missing each other. Did he get it? Claire wasn't sure.

Claire went to the grocery store the following Saturday, leaving Franking alone for the first time. She didn't think much of it; the kid hardly left the couch and had never shown interest in going outside. She left Frankie in front of the TV set, watching a football game that she was sure he didn't understand. The game had come on after the *Inspector Gadget* show that morning. She told Frankie she'd be back shortly, told him to stay put, and thought he understood. When she came home two hours later, another game was playing, but Frankie was gone. Bud was also gone. She searched each of the other three rooms. They were empty. She panicked and ran outside, looking across the back yard and then around to the front. She kept yelling, "Frankie," and then, "Bud, come!" She noticed that the front gate was closed. She ran to the back of the house again, again yelling, "Frankie! Bud, come!" She was scared.

Finally, Bud did come, running with his tail high and wagging. He came from the larger of the two outbuildings, the one filled with old garden tools she thought of as the shack. She ran into the shack and found Frankie sitting on the floor with his legs straight and spread. His face was smudged with oil or grease, and metal bolts and engine parts lay between his legs. His tool bag was open, and he held an adjustable wrench in one hand. Next to him was the lawn mower that was now missing an engine. In his other hand, Frankie held a part that Claire remembered was the piston. She remembered the name of the part because it was featured in the last episode of *MacGyver* that she and Frankie had watched together. The show was set in the Amazon jungle, and MacGyver impressed the plantation owner by fixing a broken water pump piston by welding it together with a generator, jumper cables, and two half-dollar coins. Frankie had taken apart the lawnmower engine and found its piston.

She remembered that later in the episode, the plantation was overrun by flesh-eating ants. MacGyver fought the ants by flooding the canals between the fields, but the ants crossed the canals on floating leaves. Then he improvised a flamethrower fed by a huge tank of gas. That's when she realized there was a smell in the garage and saw that Frankie was sitting in a puddle of gasoline.

CHAPTER FOURTEEN

Saturday afternoon, Wood tore apart the house looking for the Mega Slot money. He went through her drawers and closet again, this time checking the insides of boots and the pockets of coats. He threw over every mattress in the house and checked under every piece of furniture and behind every photo. He went through the basement and dumped out every box of Christmas ornaments and family mementos in storage. Then he started again in the bedrooms, going through every square inch. With his Buck knife, he slashed the sides of mattresses, and with a screwdriver from the kitchen, he removed vent covers. He slit the couch and seat cushions in both the living room and the basement, not bothering to simply unzip the covers. When he got to the kitchen, he was panicky and enraged. He pulled the food, dishes—everything—out of the drawers and cupboards and onto the floor. He kicked apart any box large enough to hold a bundle of bills. Most of the glassware hit the floor and smashed. By the end of three hours, the house looked like a family of wild bears had gone rummaging for food, and only piles of excrement were needed to complete the scene.

Then he started looking outside, and to the neighbors, it would have seemed as though Wood was finally landscaping. He turned over every large rock in front and pulled out the ornamental Japanese trees to check inside the pots. The rock garden was laid on a membrane of thick, dark plastic sheeting, and he pulled at a few of the edges before it occurred to him that Sally would have never gone that far. He then searched the backyard, which was still just bare desert, looking for any fresh marks that suggested digging. The yard was flat and hard, like kiln-dried clay. He yelled, "Fuck," to himself and then smashed with his boot heel the only breakable object he could find—a rusted yellow Tonka Toys dump truck. Then he wondered about Frankie; he wondered how stupid he really was.

He decided to work his shift at Tramps that night. He went in early to talk to his father-in-law. Frank was going to ask questions, and Wood just needed to have some answers. He found Frank in the office on the phone. Wood stood in the doorway and waited. Frank was an odd man to figure out, odd because he was always smiling. He could be pissed off and yelling at Wood for something stupid, like for letting a bum in off the street, and he'd still be smiling. He may have been burning mad, but it was as though underneath it was all a joke, like the world was just a surprising and funny place. At least, that's what Wood thought. He could never read his father-in-law—just didn't know *what* he was thinking. And he wasn't to be underestimated. Frank was a battle-hardened veteran who had done tours in Korea and Vietnam.

Frank knew about guns, collected guns, loved guns, and kept loaded guns all around. He had a loaded shotgun next to the safe and a loaded Remington .45 handgun on the floor of his two-door Mercedes. Those were the two Wood knew about. Frank had said he looked forward to when he could blow away anyone who tried to rob the club. Payback for Dominic. He kept the office door unlocked when he was inside and the safe open. Practically begging for a robbery. And he delivered his own bank deposits, usually late at night, just hoping for a chance to use the handgun. Frank was one man who actually put a scare into Wood.

Frank took his time finishing the phone call—Wood guessed to make him sweat. Frank asked, "Sally back?"

"No."

"She hasn't called?"

"No." Wood knew it was best not to elaborate too much with Frank. Frank wanted simple answers—just the facts.

"Where's Frankie?"

"At her sister's house. Thought it best that a woman take care of the kid. Family."

"Claire's a whore. You dropped my grandson off with a whore?" There it was. Frank was getting mad at him but still smiling like it was all a joke.

"Thought you'd heard. She got her nose broken by some date. Her nose looks like…" He tried to think of what it looked like but couldn't. "Well, it looks like it's busted. She quit escorting. She's now living alone in a house with a dog." He didn't think it was a good idea to mention that the house was a dump.

Frank looked at him closely, smiling, and for a solid minute, didn't say a word. Then, "So you didn't get in a fight with Sally? Didn't hit her or anything?"

"I wouldn't hit a woman." Another kind of smile burst on Frank's face, and Wood realized that Frank had seen him manhandle and drag plenty of women out of the club. He'd seen Wood hit women. It was part of the job.

"So what do you think happened?"

"I think she's just run off. Sally's been gone from the house more than usual lately, and I don't know what she does late nights on weekends while I'm at work."

"I suspect she takes care of Frankie late nights on weekends."

"Frankie takes care of himself mostly. Sally goes out plenty by herself. Frankie just plays in the basement. Sometimes he sleeps on the couch down there."

"So she ran off with another guy and left you to take care of Frankie?"

"That's what I think. But Claire is taking care of Frankie."

"A whore."

"Used to be."

They were going in circles, and Wood wanted off the merry-go-round. "I'll find the guy. Then I'll find Sally."

Frank made his widest grin. "I think that's a good idea."

So now Wood needed to find a guy. The Sally story needed to play out—that she'd left Wood (no surprise to anyone who knew Sally), that she'd been seeing another guy (again believable), and she'd taken off, abandoning her halfwit kid (not so believable, but then again Frank's wife had abandoned him and her kids). He needed the guy to make it stick and give the story believability. The image of Lamar popped into his head.

Wood asked Carl to cover for him later that night. He asked the other guys if it was okay if he left early after the line dwindled.

Just after three in the morning, he sat in his truck waiting for Lamar. Lamar would be at Tramps after his shift downtown at Hugo's like clockwork. He'd be looking for his weekly payment. Lamar drove a small silver Volkswagen Jetta, and Wood saw it pull in and park. He called to Lamar as he walked toward the club and asked him to jump into the truck. Lamar nodded, then stepped up into the passenger seat. Wood had bought a gram that night off Chris and asked Lamar if he wanted a hit. Wood knew he was Mormon and would refuse. He did. Lamar asked for his $200. Lamar was smaller than Wood with permed blond hair that was maybe fashionable ten years earlier. As usual, he hadn't changed out of his work clothes, his black-and-whites. Wood thought Lamar was pathetic and was fed up with being asked each week for the lousy two hundred bucks.

He'd thought the story through—Sally had run off with this guy named Lamar, who worked at Hugo's Cellar. Frank didn't know Lamar, didn't know what he looked like, didn't know he was a weird Mormon dude, so the story was very possibly believable.

Wood did a quick hit of coke in front of Lamar and then screwed down the vial cap. He moved slowly and effortlessly, first reaching over and wrapping his thick arm around Lamar's neck. He hardly struggled. The trick to a good choke hold was to get his arm completely around the neck so that his elbow lined up with the chin. Then, using his other hand for leverage, pinch the neck and arteries. Wood had done it countless times and always with the same result. With no oxygen flowing to the brain, the guy would pass out in ten or twenty seconds. He'd be unconscious for a minute before the blood flowed back into the brain. Wood knew that if you held the choke hold for a few minutes, five tops, the guy would be dead. Lamar hardly struggled. In seconds, Lamar was lifeless. Wood continued to pinch his neck. He could see the face of his wristwatch and the sweeping second hand, and he watched it pass the twelve mark five times. It wasn't that hard, and no bloody mess. It wasn't that hard to kill someone.

Wood drove his truck west down Flamingo until the strip malls and apartment complexes abated and the lots became empty desert. He turned into one lot and shut off his lights. He waited until there were no cars on Flamingo. He reached across Lamar's limp body and opened the passenger door. He gave the body a push and it tumbled out, falling four feet from the passenger-seat cushion. He heard the body hit the desert floor, a soft, muffled sound. Wood opened his door and walked around the front of the truck to the body. He dragged the carcass to the back of the truck and lifted it onto the open bed. Wood stood on the desert floor and went through Lamar's pockets. Like a Vegas high roller, Lamar carried his cash and cards in a folded bundle bound with a thick, blue rubber band used in grocery stores to wrap broccoli stalks. Wood opened the bundle and counted over three hundred in tip money. In the center of the bundle was Lamar's driver's license, bank card, and credit card. Lamar's keys were in his other pocket. Wood climbed into the truck bed and dragged the body into the pet cooler. Would Sally ever run off with a guy like Lamar? Fuck no, but who'd be the wiser? And he was killing two birds with one stone. He had a story for Frank and was rid of the nagging, continual, two-hundred-dollar kickback.

Next, Wood needed to get rid of Lamar's Jetta. Sally's car was still in her garage, so the story needed Lamar's car gone. His plan was simple. Take the car to the slums on the north side and abandon it to the ghetto rats who'd strip it down to its bones within hours. Wood drove back to the club and parked his truck. When he was sure no one was around, he walked over to the Jetta, opened the door, started the car, and drove east to Interstate 15. He followed 15 north past downtown and the waterfall lights of the Union Plaza casino. He got off on the Owens Avenue exit.

For Wood, the only reasons to ever enter the north side were to pick up pet carcasses or visit The Palomino strip club. The club was an oasis on the north side, a Vegas bastion of bright lights in an otherwise poor, fucked-up neighborhood. His idea was to stay close to the strip club so that he could catch a cab just outside once he abandoned the Jetta. A few blocks away, he found the Shady Acres Mobile Home Park, a real shit-hole of rented trailer homes, crappy cars, plastic kid's toys, old tires, cast-off appliances, random chairs, cinder blocks, and weeds. He stopped the Jetta on a dirt road just inside the mobile-home park, turned off the lights, and rolled down the driver and passenger windows. He needed to pull the plates but didn't have a screwdriver. Instead, he used his folding Buck knife, careful not to break the tip. He dropped the plates into the nearest storm drain and then returned to The Palomino.

Huge letters spelled out PALAMINO in neon beneath a spinning horseshoe mounted heels-up to catch luck. In the middle of the horseshoe was a rearing Palomino horse. The marquee said BURLESQUE, and underneath, SILKI ST. JAMES. There were cabs lined up along the curb, but Wood took his time, walking into the club and sitting at the bar toward the rear of the theater. The older bartender wore a gold vest and a white silk tie. Wood ordered a Stoli Cranberry and watched the show. At five in the morning, the Burlesque show with headliner Silki St. James was long over. Now, the regular strippers took turns on stage, slowly shedding their few clothes—no headliner gimmicks, no fans, fire, whips, or feathers.

Wood had been to the Palomino before with John and

other guys. It was the only place in town where you could get a drink and watch completely nude dancers. Back then, they'd gotten up close to the stage to see real anatomy. Now, he sat back in the high bar chair, sipped his drink through a small straw, and watched. There wasn't much to it—more tits and ass—and he didn't recognize anyone in the club. One of the girls approached him. She was petite, cute with blond hair, and tits too big for her body. She wore a tight blue mini-dress with a large oval cut-out in her midsection. The oval revealed her pierced bellybutton and the undersides of her gigantic breasts. She asked if he wanted to buy her a drink. Wood knew the routine—a drink meant paying for a hundred-dollar bottle of cheap champagne. He declined, then pulled out the wad of bills he'd taken from Lamar's front pocket. He pulled off a ten, folded it in half lengthwise, and pushed it toward the girl. She smiled, thanked him, and then moved on. Wood finished his drink and left.

Riding in the cab on his way back to his truck, Wood couldn't think of a single detail he'd screwed up on—not one thing that would come back to haunt him.

CHAPTER FIFTEEN

Red drove by an adobe house near the airport and saw the FOR SALE sign. Two-plus acres of commercial property for $79,000. The two-plus acres were mostly desert dirt and scrub grass. There was a big shade tree out front, leafless this time of the year, with a station wagon parked beneath, a Ford Fairmont. The house looked like an Old West outpost of some kind—a place where cowboys could get a drink of whiskey, exchange hides for coffee and beans, and maybe bed down for the night with a local sporting gal. He wondered if, in fact, the building had historical significance. When he looked closer, though, he could see that the window casings were rusted metal and that the flat roof was held up by internal joists rather than timbers that would've been exposed along the roof line. He drove by the house several times, circling the block to see the area. The airport property started on the next block south. The two-plus acres abutted a large post office that probably distributed airmail. From the corner of Palo Verde and Tropicana at the end of the block, he could see the Thomas

Mack Center, where Tark the Shark's Running Rebels played basketball. Any way you looked at it, the property would be gobbled up someday by a player with deep pockets—The University of Nevada or the Postal Service or the Metropolitan Airport Commission or some entity like that. And he could live in the adobe while waiting for a payday.

Red was looking for a place to invest his garbage windfall. He had sold his garbage business for $80,000 and now needed to reinvest before the new year kicked in, and he lost a large chunk to taxes. He didn't want to own another business. He was sick of talking to customers and done with managing employees. He remembered when his first employee, a kid, had a problem. He'd knocked up some girl. He wanted the baby, but the girl wanted an abortion, and she needed seventy-five dollars for the procedure. The kid came crying to him in his office. The baby, the money. Red suddenly felt like a real boss, someone who provided not only financial stability but also emotional support and guidance. He felt honored that the kid had come to him. He said the right things: "It's a woman's choice, if she's not ready…" "This too shall pass." He loaned him the seventy-five bucks. He felt good about helping. But the next time an employee came to him, the feeling wasn't the same. By the fourth or fifth time, the feeling was dead gone. Didn't these people have families that could help? Didn't they save a few bucks each month? He was frankly burned out on dealing with other people's problems, and the best investment he could think of in Las Vegas was property. And he needed commercial property, which would leave him exempt from taxes.

It was lunchtime, and he drove to the Tropicana Casino close by. He'd seen a billboard about their $3.99 lunch buffet and wanted to try it. The lady at the hostess stand was older and wore glasses too large for her face that hinged at the bottom. They looked upside down. She took his name and said the wait was thirty minutes. Red looked around the restaurant and saw half the tables empty. "Thirty minutes?" he asked.

She had her answer ready. "We'll seat you as soon as we can."

Sometimes, he was a little slow on the uptake, especially with puns, like the knock-knock joke about bananas—*Orange* you glad I didn't say banana again? The first two times he heard the joke as a kid, his response was, "I guess." Then, late at night, while trying to sleep, he figured it out—*aren't* you, *orange* you. Stupid. But he picked up business stuff pretty quick and noticed the old folks playing nickel slots just outside the hostess stand. He supposed it was hard to make a buck selling all-you-can-eat food for $3.99, so make them wait, and maybe they'll lose a few coins in the machines. But he wouldn't be nudged into playing slots—he just wanted to eat.

What made a good buffet? They all had salad bars, but the good ones had real bacon, not fake Bac-O's. He also liked julienne sliced ham, canned beets, and blue-cheese dressing with chunks of real blue cheese. He'd yet to see shrimp. For the main course, he liked a chef-guy who sliced roast beef fresh under heat lamps, but that was hard to find at lunchtime. He liked a poached fish filet in some sauce, not just fried mystery lumps. The latest thing was a pasta bar where you loaded up with linguini or rotini and then ladled on marinara, alfredo, or clam sauce. He liked the soft white rolls but figured rolls were the cheapest way for a casino to suppress an appetite—Red had a huge appetite. Finally, there was the dessert station. The pies sucked at every buffet he'd been to. There was probably one huge bakery somewhere in Las Vegas that supplied the stuff—short on fruit, heavy on the doughy crust and gelatinous sugary goo. What he really liked was a soft-serve ice-cream machine with toppings like fudge, whipped cream, caramel, flavored syrups, and broken bits of Heath bars. The Tropicana had real bacon, a stewed fish, soft white rolls, and crushed Heath bars. He was mildly impressed and walked back to his car, satisfied. He'd resisted the slot machines, so was only out the $3.99.

The real-estate office was coincidentally just down the Strip from where he stayed. The agent was weird looking—jet-black hair all swoopy and coiffed, Elvis sideburns, a pencil-thin mustache, rings on each hand, and a gold bracelet. Red figured the guy was supposed to look like someone, but it wasn't Elvis—Elvis never wore a mustache. It was the aren't-you-orange-you thing all over again. And where did these Las Vegas cats come from? Not many were born here, and they didn't look like that back in New York or Cleveland or Dallas. Back there, they'd have been ridiculed or worse. And they certainly wouldn't be selling commercial real estate. But this was Vegas. Start over, reinvent yourself, buy two acres of desert near the airport, and dress up like Liberace. But this guy wasn't trying to be Liberace—Liberace never wore a mustache, either. Red would get it that night or maybe in a month while sitting around and thinking of nothing in particular.

Turned out he liked the agent, a guy just slightly older than himself with a relaxed, easygoing way. Red talked a little about the garbage business in Connecticut, where he grew up. The real-estate guy was originally from New Jersey but had lived in Las Vegas for almost thirty years. He'd been a dealer at the Flamingo during the Rat Pack sixties and had some good stories about seeing Sinatra and Sammy Davis. He told a story about how Dean Martin, drunk one night, drove a golf cart along with two show girls into the pool. The agent had started buying real estate when he was still dealing cards. Then real estate started to boom, and he went at it full-time. He owned the property on Palo Verde and needed the cash from selling it to do another deal, an upscale apartment complex west of the Strip. Red said that he could pay cash and offered seventy grand even. They agreed on seventy-two, and both signed a contract right then and there. Red would have seven days for due diligence, but he figured there wasn't much to inspect, just an old building and open desert. Whoever bought the property from him would tear the building down and start over. When the transaction was finished, and after Red had said, "Thanks, Wayne," the guy replied, "*Danke schoen*," and that's when it hit him: Wayne Newton. How stupid could he be? Red just smiled and walked out of the office.

He returned to his hotel to watch TV and wait around until dinner. He was staying at the Holiday Motel on the Strip. The place was not to be confused with either the Holiday Inn chain or the Holiday House Motel next door, where you could get a bridal gown at the Bridal De Paris and a quickie marriage at the Hollywood Chapel. The Holiday Motel had none of that, just a pool that was empty during the winter months. Red had a first-floor room that opened to the parking lot, and he could drive his Monte Carlo right up to the door. Inside was a small refrigerator, microwave, and color TV. His by-the-week rate was only eighty dollars with once-a-week cleaning and laundry. He figured he could almost stay forever at that price. A bonus to his living situation was a casino—Bob Stupak's Vegas World—just across the street that had one-dollar blackjack tables, seventy-five cent Heinekens, and a decent $9.99 dinner buffet.

Red was sure he'd stayed at the same motel his first time in Las Vegas. It was almost ten years earlier, right after he'd dropped out of college his senior year at UCONN. At the time, he was studying English literature—a good liberal-arts curriculum which was supposed to culminate in a wider appreciation of the world and maybe provide good communication skills. But he had no idea what he wanted to do. His dad worked in sales and made good money, and his mother stayed at home, a homemaker. He couldn't see himself doing sales, didn't want to be an English professor, and overall, he was questioning everything. And graduation was looming.

That spring of 1977, he took a midcentury American poetry class from a well-known tenured professor, Graham Atwood. Professor Atwood was shy and introverted, but inside the classroom, he was dogmatic and protective of his interpretations and analysis. As a student, you could try to disagree with him, but over the years, Atwood knew all the arguments and was quick with his stock rebuttals, moving on before you could rebut. This was his arena and he guarded it jealously. Midway through the class, they studied Robert Lowell's *Skunk Hour*. Lowell had a line about a millionaire who auctions off his nine-knot yawl to a lobster fisherman. Atwood discussed the obvious: the millionaire was no longer a millionaire and couldn't afford the boat. Then he went further and talked about the millionaire's penis—that the lobster fisherman would have no use for a sail-powered boat, and that he would surely cut down the mast. So, the mast was a phallus—the millionaire's penis—and the lobster fisherman would metaphorically emasculate the guy. Well, whatever. Then Red raised his hand. He had grown up in Connecticut around boats of all kinds. He knew that a yawl had two masts and said so. Maybe Atwood's interpretation of the metaphor was incorrect? Maybe Lowell's yawl was just that, a fast sailboat now too expensive to maintain? Atwood glared at him. There was no stock rebuttal, and uncomfortable seconds passed before Atwood chose to ignore Red and move on to the next stanza. It was then that Red felt truly lost, almost four years of lost, and he simply packed up his few clothes the next day and hitchhiked west. He was done with school.

Red had never been to the Pacific coast, so he headed to Seattle. He'd hitchhiked and camped during past summer breaks, and he traveled like before with just a backpack, a small nylon tent, and a down sleeping bag. He looked like a college kid on the road and found rides easily. Going northwest of Minneapolis, he saw freight trains that paralleled the highway. On the North Dakota border, he found a freight yard and, after half a day waiting, hopped an empty boxcar. The train followed the Missouri River through Montana to Whitefish, where he switched trains. Two days later, he was in Seattle and stuck his toe in a saltwater bay that he knew was connected to the Pacific Ocean. From there, he hitchhiked south to San Francisco, where he found a cheap hotel room near streets of porn theaters called the Tenderloin District. A random guy sold him a hit of windowpane acid that turned out to be nothing but a clear cellophane chip—bogus. Then, finally, to Los Angeles before turning back east and hitchhiking through the desert, through Barstow, to Las Vegas.

Red read. He enjoyed Tom Wolfe's book, *The Kandy-Kolored Tangerine-Flake Streamline Baby*. Wolfe had written an essay about Las Vegas—how it was new and uniquely American, where history and tradition were either forgotten or never learned, how the city's style came more from the influence of custom-car designers than classically trained architects. He stayed in Las Vegas at the Holiday Motel and just walked around. He was fascinated by the lighted and bejeweled Stardust sign. Circus Circus was a weird adult carnival with trapeze acts flying above the gambling tables. He had a drink on the rotating bar where Hunter Thompson had dropped acid, real LSD. He saw the fountain at Caesars that Evil Knievel had jumped with his Harley Sportster just months before. He ate at cheap buffets. It was all weird and so uncool that it was cool. And he liked the idea of doing the opposite, doing whatever was uncool and unexpected. That thought led him to the garbage business.

Late that summer, he was back in Connecticut near Stamford, where he'd grown up. His parents made it clear that he was on his own now and without a college degree—wasted money as far as they were concerned. With the little money he had saved from his college job, he bought a used Ford F10 pickup. Then he started driving through the back roads around Stamford, New Canaan, and Pound Ridge, looking for construction sites. He offered to haul away their construction debris from demolished kitchens, bathrooms, and other remodeling projects. He was cheaper than a roll-off container. He started following regular customers from project to project.

A year later, he bought another truck and had his first employee, the kid who had knocked up his girlfriend. Then, he invented the Red Bag. He'd been called Red since middle school because of his red hair (his real name was Robert Thomas). The Red Bag was his idea to make hauling construction debris easer for the contractor and easier for him. He had four-by-eight, heavy, red canvas bags sewn by a sailmaker near Bridgeport. The bags had low two-foot walls and strong, looped handles. The construction guys could load up the bags daily to be hauled away by him and his employees. Red mounted a simple boom with a cable winch on each pickup. With the winch and boom, anyone could easily lift the bag and debris into the truck bed. Simple. He tried to add two more pickups to his fleet each year after that.

Just after Ronald Regan was elected, Red got married. The woman was his employee who answered the phones and did the scheduling. The marriage lasted two years, and they never had children. In the end, the woman found another guy who was maybe more exciting and less fat. In retrospect, he thought he was a boring husband, not very passionate, and drank too much beer. Most of the time, when he wasn't working, he just liked to watch dumb TV or read a book. He gave her a settlement, and she quit answering the phones.

By the time Ronald Regan won a second term, Red made good money, had over thirty employees, and grew his routes to cover a big chunk of southwestern Connecticut and New York along the Hudson. He was getting noticed by the other garbage haulers, traditionally a Mafia business. It wasn't good to be noticed.

Ultimately, they offered him eighty thousand for his business, probably worth five times that amount. "They" were the Tri-State Waste Haulers Association. Red's company was not a part of the association that decided routes, and he was poaching their business. He was familiar with the association and the Italian names on the membership roll. He'd gotten a call one afternoon. His presence was requested at their next quarterly meeting. He knew better than to refuse. He sat at a round table in the private room of a roadside Howard Johnson's, surrounded by larger and older men with dark hair. They congratulated him on his entrepreneurial abilities and clever invention, the Red Bag. They threatened him and said he could easily be run out of business. They intimated worse. But it would be easier for all parties if Red agreed to a simple buyout. If he wanted, he could stay on as a manager for one of the association's companies; they welcomed his abilities. Instead, he took the eighty grand and left town.

Ten years after first seeing the city, he still thought of Las Vegas as the place that was new, the place to start over—a second-chance city. He packed up his one car that wasn't company-owned, a brown Chevy Monte Carlo, and headed west again. He drove three days straight, stopping only to sleep at wayside rest areas. In Las Vegas, he found the same Holiday Motel where he'd stayed ten years earlier.

———

Red closed on the property three weeks after signing the purchase agreement. He never did inspect the property—there was nothing to inspect—but he'd driven around the two acres many times and knew a younger single mother was living there with her boy and a small black Labrador retriever—a detail Wayne had told him about, referring to her as the caretaker. He parked outside the gate the afternoon after the papers were signed and the keys handed over. It was January, and the west winds coming down from the mountains were cold, almost Connecticut cold. In March the weather would start to get warmer. April and May would be the best months before the summer hit with blast-furnace highs in the nineties and hundreds. He opened the gate and walked toward the adobe house. He heard the dog bark from within, and before he could ring the buzzer or knock, a woman inside cracked the door open and asked, "What do you want?" The dog had stopped barking and was just inside the door. Her hand was holding the dog's collar.

He just came out with it. "I'm the new owner. I own this

place now. My name is Red." He could see she had a broken nose, but overall, not unattractive.

The woman kept the door open just a crack. "I had an agreement. I've been fixing the place up and watching over the property. Are you aware of the agreement?"

"Wayne told me someone was watching the place, like a caretaker, but there was no lease or formal agreement." Red had every intention of getting her off the place. He would sit on the property until another buyer came along. He'd live there and not have to rent an apartment or pay the weekly motel rates. He added, "I suppose Wayne didn't tell you the property was sold."

"No, he didn't. I suppose you want me out. I'll need to see some papers, some proof. I'll need to see an eviction notice."

With the words "paper" and "notice," Red thought of lawyers. He didn't have the time, money, or appetite to find a lawyer. "I'm sorry, Wayne didn't give me your name."

"Claire. Claire Welch."

"Can I come in, Claire? See what I bought?"

"Suit yourself."

Claire opened the door slightly wider and moved back into the living room. She released the dog, who stood in the doorway and sniffed at Red's pants.

Red walked in and stood just inside the door. He reached down and let the dog sniff his hand, then petted the dog on the head. He hadn't thought this through. He knew someone was living there but just assumed it was like buying a truck— one day, it was someone else's, then the next day, you had a set of keys, and it was yours. If you were lucky, the glove compartment would be cleaned out with only the owner's manual still there. Red had checked out of his motel room that morning, and all his clothes were in the car. He looked around the living room and saw the couch, an easy chair, a TV, old magazines, and what looked like textbooks. This was going to be a little more complicated than buying a truck. "I've got the title documents in my car if you want to see them. I wasn't planning on evicting anyone."

"What *were* you planning on?"

"I frankly don't know. I've checked out of my room and was planning on living here."

"Well, I'm taking care of my sister's kid. I've got a house full of furniture and food in the refrigerator. I thought I had an agreement with the previous owner, and it's not like I can just pack up and go."

"I can see that." Red tried to think through the situation quickly. The motel was $80 a week or around $360 a month. "Can you pay rent?"

"What kind of rent?" Claire had her arms folded over a flannel shirt. Her hair was tied back, and she wasn't wearing makeup. Despite that, despite the broken nose, Red could see she was very attractive.

"Three hundred and fifty dollars a month?"

"Like I said, I'm caring for my sister's kid. He has special needs, and I think my sister ran off with some guy or something. I'm trying to go to school and haven't been able to work. That and this place isn't worth three hundred and fifty dollars. It's a dump, and I've been living here for free, fixing it up, keeping out vagrants."

Red had negotiated garbage hauling for the past ten years. Negotiating was as natural to him as crapping on the toilet and reading a book at the same time. "Okay, two fifty, and I get a room. We'd be roommates."

"Like I said, I have my sister's kid, and he's got the other room. He has special needs, and I want him to have his own room." She paused and thought. "Two hundred a month, and you get the shack out back with inside bathroom privileges."

Red was not particular. "Let me look at the shack."

He followed Claire through the house and out the back door. The shack was sided with vertical hand-hewn boards and looked older than the adobe house. Inside, the electric wires were tacked up on the outside of the walls—at one point in Las Vegas history, maybe in the twenties or thirties, someone had lived here without electricity. A twisting Bakelite switch still worked and powered an overhead bulb. A bolt-on vise was attached to a workbench that had once been a kitchen table with an old washbasin. A tin plate with scalloped edges covered a hole where Red figured a stovepipe once vented a wood cookstove. The shack had two small windows with dried-out and peeling wood frames and wavy glass distorted like a funhouse mirror. The floor was planked and still solid. Years ago, someone had replaced the roof with two-by-six joists, plywood, and rolls of tar paper. Garden tools were hung on the walls with nails, and on the floor was a dismantled lawnmower engine with parts scattered here and there. A noxious smell of tomcat urine was partially overpowered by the more intoxicating smell of gas. Red loved the smell of gas and burning diesel. It reminded him of trains and trucks.

Not too far from the shack was an outhouse with four plank walls, a door with a moon cutout, and a corrugated steel roof. He didn't bother to look inside.

The shack was definitely uncool and unexpected. So it seemed right after all he'd been through—pursue the Las Vegas promise of infinite wealth and possibilities and then move into a run-down desert shack. That, plus he was still rent-free and now up $200 a month. He'd find a bed, clean the place up, and move in.

CHAPTER SIXTEEN

Wood finished his dead-pet run into the desert and drove back to the home he and Sally had once shared. The place was still trashed, and he'd done little to clean it up after his futile search for the money. Once inside the door, he instinctively checked the mail but knew there'd be only more notices for delinquent payment: Citywide had sent statements stamped PAST DUE, Nevada Power threatened to shut off service, and her credit card was incurring late fees. He'd opened Sally's bank statements for the last two months and opened the latest one. The balance was about $2,000, and there was another $5,000 and change in a savings account—no large deposit, so Wood knew that the Mega Slot money was still in the house or somewhere else. He'd searched the house almost every time he came home, sometimes just taking apart a dresser or randomly pulling up carpet, but often searching the whole house again in a thorough, room-by-room, inch-by-inch grid pattern like a TV show detective. He wasn't sure if Sally had hidden the money somewhere outside the house, but after that thought, he ripped apart her car. Then, the only things removed from the house since Sally left were Frankie's clothes and Frankie himself. Wood had packed the kid's clothes and hadn't seen any cash but thought he might visit Claire's house just to make sure.

In his head, he used the word "left." Sally had left. Sally had run off with Lamar. Now, Wood almost believed it himself. He'd told Frank that he was sure it was this guy, Lamar. He used to frequent Tramps two or three times a week, and now he was nowhere to be seen. Wood told Frank he had checked around. Lamar hadn't shown up at Hugo's for work, and his car was gone. The guy had definitely left town. Wood smiled at the thought of Lamar leaving town. He *had* definitely left town, out of this world, and to the moon. His bones were now being picked clean by crows, turkey vultures, eagles, coyotes, and bugs. Everything except Lamar's ear. That Wood had taken, and he now had three in the pickle jar.

The jar was still behind his truck seat. The first ear, Todd's, was starting to pucker and turn a shade of brownish green. He thought he maybe should get rid of the pickle juice and find genuine formaldehyde to keep the flesh fresh. That, or just toss the whole thing out with the dead pets in the desert. But he couldn't bring himself to part with the ears, and it crossed his mind that he wasn't right, some kind of sicko. But that thought drifted away after a line or two of coke. He was the guy who created opportunity, the guy who had the strength and willpower to turn an opportunity into real cash money. What he was doing was, in a way, badass—*Rambo* cool.

He had an idea that night and wondered why he hadn't thought of it before. He searched through a plastic file cabinet where Sally kept tax returns and personal stuff. He found their marriage certificate. The next day, Wood drove to the Wells Fargo on Maryland Parkway across from the Boulevard Mall.

He held the certificate and Sally's bank statement and stood in line to speak with a teller. When it was his turn, he tried to explain the situation to a Mexican girl in her twenties. It seemed to take him forever to get through the whole story, "My wife is gone, it's been months, she abandoned her child that he now had to take care of, the kid was seriously brain damaged. Here's her bank statement; this shows we're legally married. Can I get access to both her checking and savings, or just her checking?" The Mexican girl let him go through the whole song and dance without once saying, "Hold on" or "*No hablo ingles.*" Just let him ramble on. Then, in perfectly good English, after an exasperated sigh and with a valley-girl accent, she said, "Like, you're going to need to speak with a personal banker." Then, "Next, please." It pissed him off.

He waited for a personal banker. He didn't have a good feeling and thought maybe he should have worn slacks and a collared dress shirt instead of stone-washed Girbaud jeans and a Hawaiian flowered shirt. He felt large, conspicuous—out of place. For Wood, bankers were squares like Mr. Drysdale in *The Beverly Hillbillies.* They represented an opposing universe populated by people who worked days, had weekends off, knew how to type, wore ties, and went to church. Squares mostly intimidated Wood and made him feel somehow inferior and subterranean, like a mole or a rat. But sometimes the two universes collided, like when someone with a suit and tie drank too much at Tramps and became belligerent. It happened all the time. Then, he was the master of the universe, and his world was the one that counted. Now, his universe was colliding with theirs, on their turf, and he was sure he wasn't the master.

He was somewhat relieved when a woman asked if he could be helped. She was older and wore a dark-blue suitcoat and a matching skirt that covered her knees. Her hair was pinned up and tied back. She introduced herself as Ms. Jorson, emphasizing the Ms. part like buz-z-z or whiz-z-z—like Miz-z-z was the sound she made when she locked her knees together and counted money.

Wood sat across from Ms. Jorson at a small steel desk in the bank's open lobby. There were no personal items like family photos or knickknacks, and Wood wondered if the bankers shared desks like bartenders shared bar rails. "What can I help you with?" she asked.

Wood thought to preface his situation before he went through the whole spiel. "I'm wondering if you could help with a family situation?"

Ms. Jorson smiled. "I'll try."

Wood placed the bank statement and marriage certificate on the desk facing Ms. Jorson. He went through the story again, slowly: wife left, abandoned him, brain-damaged child, statement, married, checking or savings, or both?

He let the story sink in. Finally, she broke the silence. "I'm very sorry." She locked eyes with Wood and placed her hands palm up on the desk. It felt like real sympathy to Wood, and he held out real hope that he'd get the money. She stood and said, "It will be just a moment while I check that account."

Wood sat back in the chair, optimistic. Ten minutes later, he was still waiting, and his optimism turned into exasperation and nervousness. After fifteen minutes, Ms. Jorson finally came back and sat down. She got right to the point. "Mr. Harding, it seems you are not a cosigner on the account."

Wood gave his most surprised look. "There must be some mistake. We're legally married."

"That may be, but with most married couples, the accounts are joint and can be accessed by either party. It appears that you and your wife do not have a joint account. It's in her name only."

"But she's gone. She abandoned us."

"Have you contacted the authorities about your wife? If she's missing, you should call the police."

He panicked. "There's no reason to get the police involved. She just ran off with another guy."

"Unfortunately, there is nothing I can do. There's no way to access the account unless she shows up to access it herself or if she's deceased."

"Deceased?" He was surprised that she said it. Then he quickly added, "God forbid, what if she is?"

With the mention of God, Ms. Jorson closed her eyes momentarily. "God forbid. If she *is* deceased, you will need a death certificate and then a judge to settle the estate. It is possible to have the judge write us a letter authorizing access while the estate is still in probate. It's happened before. Of course we urge all of our banking customers to either have joint accounts or carry ROS authorization." She paused and then added, "Right of Survivorship."

Wood thought for a moment and tried to figure out an angle. The words "judge," "probate," and "ROS" were throwing him off. He tried to figure out how Sally could be dead for the bank but still alive for Frank, the police, and everyone else. Then he was stuck on "death certificate." With a death certificate, what was hers would legally be his. But then he figured there needed to be an actual body for that—and police and judges involved. The best way out was to buy some time. "Thanks, Ms. Jorson, for your help. I think the best course of action would be to wait." He thought that sounded good, "Best course of action." Like something Perry Mason would say.

Wood drove home. On his way, he stopped at Taco Bell and picked up three double-stuffed tacos and a handful of hot-sauce packets. At home, he ate the tacos with cans of Coors and watched part of a soap opera. Afterward, he took a nap and slept for two hours. He was groggy when he woke up, half in and half out of a dream where he stood at the door of Tramps, and a crowd of people was trying to get in, and some were slipping past him—children, bums, and street whores with needle marks. He tried to shake off the dream, but it stayed with him like a dull headache. The dream left him anxious and moody. He thought of the seven grand in the Wells Fargo account that he couldn't get his hands on. Shit.

Later, on his way to work, he had a thought, an inspiration, and he said the words out loud, "I'll just fucking forge her checks!" Then, he planned out the forgery. Simple. He remembered tracing over pictures in grammar-school. He just needed a bright light and a pane of glass, and right away, his mind went to the living room coffee table. Sometimes, he surprised himself with his mental quickness, making the connections—a gift, really. He smiled to himself and then realized that his anxiety and moodiness were gone—just like that.

CHAPTER SEVENTEEN

Red wasn't fastidious, but he also wouldn't sleep in the filthy, run-down shack. For the next two days, he took a room down the street at the Best Western. He swept and cleaned up and then found furniture at a secondhand store. He scrubbed the floors with diluted Lysol and mostly eliminated the smells. He uncovered the basin and wiped down the counter. The basin still worked and drained somewhere, but there was no running water. He bought a gallon jug of spring water at the 7-Eleven and planned to refill it from an outside spigot. He left the vise where it was bolted to the counter but leaned the garden tools against the wall just outside his door. He put the disassembled lawn mower outside with the random parts stacked in a wood box that was once a drawer from a missing cabinet. It was the beginning of February. The nights in the desert were cold, but he'd get by with a small electric oil-filled radiator from the nearby Hardware Hank. Lastly, he cleaned the outhouse. He lifted the seat and looked down the hole, and as far as he could see, there was nothing fresh and no foul odors. He'd used an outhouse plenty of times and made a mental note to pick up garden lime to drop down the hole and keep future smells to a minimum. It cost him just over $200 to outfit the shack, but he'd get that back with Claire's first month's rent.

That second afternoon, Claire came by the shack while he cleaned to introduce the boy, Frankie. The boy didn't make eye contact and wouldn't reach out when Red offered his hand to shake. He also didn't talk. Red noticed that he mostly looked toward the box of lawn-mower parts. Claire just said, "He's different."

A few days later, one afternoon, Red found the boy outside looking through the box of parts and lining them up on the dusty ground. Red said, "What you got there?" The boy didn't say anything and didn't look up. Instead, he knelt down, lifted the piston, and then made an "ommm" noise like a meditation chant. Red thought that was funny—meditating with engine parts. For him, fixing engines *was* meditation, a mind focus that sped up time and blocked out the world. Red made the "om" chant too. He looked at what Frankie was doing and saw the parts arranged in an order that made sense. The piston was set next to the cylinder head, which was next to the cylinder. Down the line was the crankcase, a flywheel, the flywheel cover, the intact carburetor, the air filter, and the gas tank, all lined up in the order they were taken apart. Red pointed toward the piston and said, "Piston. That's the piston."

The boy's noise then changed slightly. Instead of "Ommm," he said, "onnn."

Red understood and tried to help him, "Pist-on, pist-on, pist-on."

The boy ignored him and kept chanting, "Onnn, onnn." Close enough, Red thought.

Red heard the back door open and saw Claire almost

running toward them. He noticed that her hair was long and spread out over her shoulders. He liked long hair, a step up from when her dark hair was tied back in a tight knot. She reached down, grabbed Frankie's hand, and stood him up. "Sorry, I'll make sure he doesn't bother you again."

"No bother. I think we have the same interest in engines."

"He took that lawn mower apart."

"I can see that."

"It probably won't run now."

Red looked at the scattered parts, now partially covered by sand and dust. He smiled and agreed. "It will certainly not run now." He looked around the yard. It was flat with desert scrub brush, and he wondered if there was ever anything to mow other than a few weeds. Maybe years ago, someone had tried to grow grass in the front yard. But except for the golf courses, he hadn't seen much grass anywhere in Las Vegas. Most residential homes had yards of scattered decorative pebbles like lazy Japanese rock gardens. Then he asked, "Why don't I help him put it back together?"

Claire held the boy at arm's length and, in a loud whisper, said, "At his school, they think he may be severely mentally disabled."

If the boy understood English, which Red was fairly certain he did, then the boy would have heard Claire use the words "mentally disabled." Red figured Frankie grew up hearing those words and others—derogatory, bullying words. Maybe it meant something to the boy, and maybe it didn't. Red had taken Behavioral Psychology at UCONN and remembered some of his studies. Mentally disabled symptoms included difficulty with abstract thinking, memory problems, and a short attention span. Taking apart a small engine and then lining up the parts weeks later in order of reassembly didn't fit. Red said,

"I don't think he's that."

The next day, Claire brought the boy over after school, and he and Red started putting the engine back together. Frankie clutched a cream-colored canvas bag with darker leather handles that Red knew was designed for masonry tools. Red had his own steel tool chest that he normally kept locked in the trunk of his Monte Carlo. The tools and the engine parts were already laid out inside the shack. That afternoon, Red showed Frankie how to clean the parts. He had a cleaning solution in a galvanized bucket and an old toothbrush. He showed Frankie how to brush a part and then lay it on newspaper to dry. He started with the flywheel.

Frankie didn't look up as Red spoke but watched closely at the brushing of parts in the bucket. Red handed over the toothbrush. He stood over Frankie as he carefully cleaned the parts. He started with the piston and made the "onnn" noise. He was strangely meticulous, and maybe he understood that any grain of sand would seize up and kill the engine. He cleaned the parts in the same order of assembly and laid them out on the newspaper. Frankie was definitely not mentally disabled.

The next day, Red showed him how to attach the piston and piston rod to the crankcase. Red found the first nut and washer for the piston rod and attached one side. He asked Frankie to do the other side. Frankie took his time looking at the scattered parts and then picked out the correct one. He attached the other side. Red tightened the first nut and showed Frankie what he thought was the right level of torque. Typically, Red would have used a torque wrench to get it perfect, but it wasn't like he was sending a rocket to the moon. Frankie tightened the other side himself. Red tried again. "Pist-on, pist-on."

Frankie tried. He made the sound of "Pisss" and then

"onnn." He still did the sounds like a meditation chant, but he completed both syllables. Red wondered if he should tell Claire that Frankie's first words were "piss" and "on." He decided to wait until he could teach Frankie another, better word.

A week later, the engine was assembled and attached to the lawn-mower chassis and blade. Red took another day and showed him the ignition points that opened and closed with the turning of the engine flywheel. He showed him how the turning corresponded to a spark in the spark plug's gap. He showed him the path the gasoline took through the petcock, fuel line, and carburetor and showed Frankie how the lever on the lawn-mower handle controlled the flow of gas to the engine. Then Red put some gas in the tank and choked the carburetor. It started after three pulls. Red laughed, surprised. Frankie showed no emotion at all.

That night, after Red had eaten dinner at the Tropicana buffet, he lay in bed and thought about Frankie. He remembered the psychology class at UCONN. The professor spoke about a condition that was at one time linked to schizophrenia but was now treated as a separate disorder, and he remembered it had to do with being disconnected socially. He remembered—autism. Therapy for it once included hallucinogenics and shock treatment. He wanted to know more and planned to look it up at the library. And he wondered if a place like Las Vegas even had a public library.

———

The next week, Red had Frankie disassemble the engine again. Frankie did most of the work while Red showed him the proper tools to use and named each tool and part. Red's Phillips-head screwdriver was worn at the tip, and he looked inside Frankie's canvas tool for a newer one. He found just a regular bladed screwdriver along with a hammer, an adjustable wrench, random open-end wrenches, and a child's dull saw, and he wondered how the kid had taken apart the engine the first time with such shitty tools. Frankie placed each disassembled part on newspaper and, even though the parts were clean, he cleaned them again, which Red thought was a good habit. Frankie then reassembled the engine. When he finished, Frankie choked the carburetor and pulled the cord to start the engine. At first pull, the engine popped to life. Red told Frankie that he'd done a great job—that he was proud of him. Again, he showed no emotion, but Red was getting used to that and sort-of supplied the emotion for him. It was like watching an old silent movie where you just needed a little imagination to fill in the blanks.

While Frankie was at school, Red drove three blocks to the UNLV campus. He quickly found the college library by asking a student for directions. He felt both at home and out of place with kids ten or more years younger than him. He had always liked the feeling of a campus. It was closed off physically from the rest of the world with all these kids who had lofty goals and big ideas. Red had that feeling his first two years at UCONN—focused, confident, smart. That those feelings crumbled over time was just the tectonic plates of the world grinding away.

In the library, he felt sure people were staring at him, like, why is this janitor-looking guy walking through here on his day off. He found the psychology section. He asked a woman at the help counter how to find a book on autism. The world had changed in those ten years, and now the librarian had a computer to type in a search. She printed out the results on accordion-folded paper with perforated edges.

He found a promising book, *The Siege, A Family's Journey into the World of an Autistic Child.* He spent a few hours reading it, then returned the next day to read more. It was written by a woman who raised a child with autism, first getting a diagnosis when the condition was new to psychology and then working through the communication problems and the everyday issues of clothes, food, play, poop, pee, prayer, and sleep. The book was way too detailed and dense, almost a complete journal, so Red scanned the pages for symptoms and hope. Frankie definitely fit the symptoms. In the book, the author's daughter, Elly, *did* make progress.

It seemed Frankie could have taken apart the lawn-mower engine and reassembled it over and over without ever getting bored. Red, though, *was* getting bored. He thought it would be fun to try a minibike or a small motorcycle. As a kid, he'd had both. He first learned engines by fixing his minibike, which always seemed to need new points or a new centrifugal clutch. When he turned sixteen, his dad bought him a small motorcycle that could be ridden both on and off-road. The motorcycle broke down constantly, and he learned how to tear apart the whole bike, replace pistons and worn gears, upgrade the ignition system, and bolt on high-performance exhaust.

Red searched the yellow pages in the phone booth across the street and found a motorcycle-salvage yard just outside town. On a Saturday, he drove Frankie southeast on Boulder Highway toward Henderson. The business was called Sycle Salvage, and the logo on the sign below the name incorporated two *S*'s spelled out in Nazi Storm Trooper lightning bolts. Nice, he thought, fucking Nazis. He pulled into the dirt road that led to the yard and watched for other ominous symbols like swastikas, death heads, or Third Reich eagles. He parked beside a rusting pole shed with an attached office. The big doors to the shed were open, and inside, Red could see old choppers with long-raked forks, high ape-hanger handlebars, fish-tail exhaust, and sissy bars. Most were Harleys, but there were Honda 750s and old English Triumphs, BSAs, and Nortons—biker gang stuff. Red held Frankie's hand and walked. Frankie wanted to stop and stare at each bike, but Red kept them moving.

Behind the shed were old decaying bikes among piles of random handlebars, complete engines, wheels, forks, frames, and seats. Someone had tried to impose some order, but the stuff was rusting and rotting under the hot desert sun.

Red found a rusting early-seventies Honda Mini Trail 70, a bike that he'd always wanted as a kid. The seat was torn, the front fender was gone, and one of the handlebars was slightly bent. Otherwise, everything was intact. The brakes worked, the throttle twisted and moved the barrel in the carburetor, the exhaust was mostly solid, the engine kicked over, and the tires were inflated. Frankie followed behind as he wheeled it toward the office.

Red opened the office door. Inside, the Nazi stuff he had expected was everywhere. Covering the walls were red Nazi banners, some with swastikas, some with Third Reich eagles, and others with swastikas and eagles. A bronze bust of a soldier with a German World War II helmet sat on a table. Next to it was the real thing, a helmet with the Storm Trooper double-*S* logo. On the desk lay a dagger with a swastika stamped on its hilt. Next to that was a red coffee mug with another swastika. The large bald man behind the desk looked up at Wood and sipped coffee. Red said, "Nice collection."

The man just nodded and smiled. And Red figured he'd said the right thing.

Red pointed to the Honda Trail 70 that leaned on its

kickstand outside the door. He asked, "What do you want for that old minibike?"

The guy leaned back in his chair and smiled. "You look a little big to be riding that itty-bitty thing."

"Yeah, funny." Red smiled. He was as big as the guy behind the desk, and maybe it was just a joke between two big guys. "It's for the kid out there. A project."

"Well, since it's like a school project for you and your boy, I'll let it go for three fifty."

"Three fifty is a good price if it's running. Is it running?"

"I'm sure you'll get it running."

"I figure it's worth more like one fifty."

"The parts alone are worth that."

"That's if you got a buyer and the time to part it out." The budget Red had in mind was $220, which was exactly what he had in his pocket. This was the "all I got" negotiation tactic, and it'd been used countless times on him. Red pulled out his wad of cash and said, "This is all I got, two hundred and," Red counted out the bills for show, "twenty dollars."

The man said, "Okay, fine," and reached over and took the bills from Red's hand. "You need a receipt?"

"No." Then Red smiled—his biggest, dumbest smile. All the Nazi stuff made him uncomfortable, maybe pissed off. "You know my old man killed Nazis. Some of his buddies died in the war."

The man smiled back, "So did mine. Daddy took some of this stuff off the rotting corpses of dead Germans—mementos for his little boy. What's your point?"

"No point, I guess. All this stuff just gets you thinking, that's all." What he was thinking was that he never wanted to set foot in this creepy place again.

Afterward, while Frankie watched, Red muscled the

Honda into the Monte Carlo's trunk. It weighed over a hundred pounds, and he barely got it up over the bumper and in. The front fork and tire stuck out the back, so Red used a bungee cord to keep the trunk lid down. As he drove home, it suddenly occurred to Red that once they got the Honda running—and he was certain they would—the kid might want to ride it.

CHAPTER EIGHTEEN

Monday through Friday, Claire took Frankie to school and then picked him up. Between those times, she attended classes at Nevada Technical College and studied for tests. When she arrived home with Frankie in the early afternoons, he always went to his bedroom, fetched the canvas tool bag, and then crossed over to Red's. She was nervous about leaving Frankie with a grown man, a stranger, and she was nervous that something would happen, like gas exploding. She was also anxious about her college tests and finishing the program and wondered how she would take care of this strange kid and work to bring in money. And where was Sally?

Claire had never been this anxious and nervous in her life. It wasn't like her to feel overwhelmed. She thought of herself as steely with all the things she'd been through. And it occurred to her that the anxiety might be biological—like hormones. She'd stopped taking her birth control more than a month ago. While she was escorting, she took only the blue pills and threw out the white placebos, the ones that didn't count, and she hadn't had a period for eight years. Since she'd stopped taking the pill, it seemed she hadn't stopped bleeding. Sometimes, it was only spotty, but other times, it was like the Hoover Dam had collapsed. Her body was fucked up and confused. And she constantly worried about Frankie, even though he wasn't her kid.

Red was a funny guy, and a funny-looking guy. He never cooked in the shack but always went out. When she asked him where, he started rattling off the best and cheapest buffets on the strip. She'd never met anyone who ate at those gross casino buffets. He wasn't tall, but he was certainly wide. It looked like a beach ball was hidden under his T-shirt, and sometimes the T-shirt was untucked, and a roll of reddish-white fat would be showing. She didn't have to ask why people called him "Red." He had short red hair and a trimmed red beard. Red freckles dotted his face, and even his lips were slightly reddish. She saw him walk to the outhouse for his business, but she knew he came into the house to shower and shave while she and Frankie were out. He never left a drop of water on the floor and took his bathroom stuff back with him. She only knew he came into the house because of the fresh droplets on the plastic shower curtain.

Most of the time, Red and Frankie worked inside the shack, but when the minibike (or was it a little motorcycle?) showed up, the two worked on it outside on a large piece of cardboard Red had found somewhere. When they worked outside, she watched through her open kitchen window. Red mostly told Frankie what to do and handed him tools. She saw Frankie unbolt parts and lay them carefully on the cardboard. Red seemed to know when Frankie needed the extra muscle and just reached in and pushed or pulled. Red helped him lift the engine from the frame. There were also sounds. Red talked to Frankie, and Frankie seemed to respond with his noises. If you weren't listening closely and didn't know who Frankie was, you'd think it was just a normal kid working on engines with his dad. She almost wept thinking about it.

One afternoon, she walked Frankie back to Red's place and asked if it was okay if she stepped out to run some errands. "Would you watch Frankie?"

He looked confused. "I've been watching Frankie every afternoon for weeks."

She looked up at the sun and dropped her arms to her side. "I've been meaning to say something. I appreciate what you've been doing. Frankie doesn't seem so…lost."

"Did you know he has a condition called autism? I looked it up at the library. I read a book about it."

"Is that a kind of brain damage?" She didn't know what Frankie was and was starting to doubt her instincts and believe what Principal Smoot had said.

"It's its own thing. Used to be a kind of schizophrenia, but it's just autism. It's kids that have trouble talking and communicating. They don't know how to interact with others. Have you noticed that he doesn't like to be touched and won't look you in the eyes?"

"I've noticed."

"That's autism."

"So what are we supposed to do?"

"I don't know. See if he can fix engines, I guess. The girl in the book I read got better."

"Normal?"

"I don't think so—just better."

The anxiety Claire had been feeling lately made her mind jumpy. She was thinking of Frankie fixing engines, then thinking Red should lose some weight, and then thinking the first of the month was coming up, and she would again owe him the $200 rent. And she had no money coming in. "Would you mind if I go back to work in the evenings a few nights a week? Because I'm paying rent now."

"I guess not."

Claire noticed that he reached back and scratched his ass. She figured it wasn't something he intentionally thought of. "You'll need to put him in front of the TV after you're done working on engines. Then, later, get him to bed. Are you sure?" Red's hand seemed stuck on his backside.

"I guess so," he said.

CHAPTER NINETEEN

Frank could name the things he liked—things that made him feel good. The first was his club. In the mornings, it smelled like stale beer and cigarettes, and that was okay; that's what a bar should smell like, and god bless the people who were still sitting on stools, smoking, drinking, and hopefully playing video poker. Behind the bar was a different kind of smell. The guys knew he liked everything clean, with the stations wiped down with the Stainless Steel Magic he bought by the caseload. The fruit needed to be covered, and the back bar and bottles wiped down with bleachy water. Fruit flies were the sign of a dirty bar, and if he saw one, he'd have his Head Bartender, Ed, call in everyone for an afternoon bleach party—bleach, not beach—off the clock.

He liked the stacks of cash and the simple pleasure of counting bundles for the bank deposit. It wasn't so much that he wanted to buy stuff; it was just the feeling of success—that he had made the club successful. It was funny about the name Tramps. He liked trains and thought the railroad theme would attract both families for dining and guys for the rustic ambiance. The music and DJ were an afterthought, more Deedee's idea than his. He was both stupid and lucky there. He never did attract families, and with the lights low and the dance lights spinning, no one could see the model train that circled the bar or the railroad signs and antiques that he had collected. To anyone in Vegas, Tramps just meant one thing—sluts. And that's where he was lucky.

He liked guns. He had never been a hunter unless you counted Vietnam, where he hunted men. He mostly liked handguns and owned a small collection of Remington's. Colt seemed to be the manufacturer that everyone knew about. Colt had the Peacemaker with its patented revolving chambers. Buffalo Bill, Wyatt Earp, and Billy the Kid used a Peacemaker. But Remington was the oldest gun manufacturer in the United States. They'd supplied most of the Union pistols in the Civil War. Those old guns used percussion caps, black powder, and lead balls that took time to load. Frank had two original pre–Civil War .44 caliber Remington's. He had a Navy New Model .36 caliber and some original percussion handguns converted to cartridge loading. He was even more proud of his five Remington Rand 1911A1 .45 service handguns from the early and mid-twentieth century. He had a rare Type 1 with its Syracuse markings that had been carried and fired in World War II. Overall, he had eighteen Remington handguns, two of which he kept loaded for self-defense. He had one Winchester pump action shotgun, an M870 Mark 1 from 1968, that he kept loaded in his office next to the safe. The 870 had been his weapon of choice when on patrol in Vietnam.

And he liked guys. He always knew he liked guys, but it wasn't until he was in the army that he acted on it. In Vietnam, he was part of the 16th Military Police group and was stationed mostly in Da Nang. As part of his training, he learned to speak Vietnamese, so he was often out in the countryside on patrol with Marine platoons. Part of his assignment was to escort prisoners who might have information. He was expected to deliver, but he kept his interrogations by the book—no torture or threats of torture. Most of the time, he used the simple direct approach because they were scared shitless already. You started by asking administrative questions like their hometown and then moved up slowly to ask about their outfit and where they ate their last meal. He was usually with an ARVN officer with fewer scruples or no scruples at all. Some prisoners wouldn't talk. He was present when an ARVN officer threw one guy out of a helicopter at a thousand feet so that the other prisoner would tell what he knew. It worked. But when he wasn't on patrol, his duty allowed him plenty of free time to do what he wanted, where he wanted. And in Da Nang, he could get anything, and what he wanted was sex with a man. In Da Nang, he had paid for it. Now, in Vegas, getting laid was as easy as ordering a few drinks at the Buffalo Bar on Paradise Road. The Gypsy nightclub was also nearby, but it was a dance club like Tramps, and he would certainly be recognized and outed. Right then, he was seeing someone steady, his radio station sales rep, Craig, from KLUC (pronounced K-Luck), who was unfortunately still married to his wife.

Friday morning meant driving the deposit from the previous two days to the bank and bringing back enough singles and quarters to last the weekend. The deposit was just over fifteen grand in bundles of mostly twenties. The bank was three miles down Flamingo, clear on the other side of the Strip, and any jackass who cased the place could do the math and figure out his routine. His .45 was in easy reach on the floor of his Mercedes, and he constantly watched his rear-view mirror.

At the bank, he bought ten boxes of quarters, $500 per box—each weighing about twelve pounds. He could carry three boxes per trip to his car, which gave any creep four chances to rip him off.

His son-in-law, Dominic, had been dead now for four years. When first hired, Dominic had no experience and worked as a barback. He learned fast and could cover the main bar on Friday and Saturday nights by himself, keeping up with ice, cleaning glassware, and restocking liquor and beer. He kept the bar clean. Frank moved him to the bartender position. He started out working at the high-volume cocktail waitress station, and they loved him. Sally, back then, was a cocktail waitress and the two started dating. Eventually, Dominic ran the whole bar. What he regretted most was helping Dominic and Sally buy their own place. He was happy for them and couldn't think of a better son-in-law, practically a son. He understood that Dominic wanted to make it on his own, so Frank helped them. The Bird Off Paradise was a wedding present. He gave Dominic one of his handguns to protect himself, but he never carried it. He was unarmed when they robbed the bar, and the bastards killed him anyway. If Dom had stayed at Tramps, they could have been partners. He could still be working with his daughter and son-in-law. Frank could be taking vacations.

Now Sally was gone too. Supposedly, she'd run off with a guy named Lamar—at least that's what Wood said. Frank had told Sally not to marry Wood. Frank had known guys like Wood all his life, guys who were always looking for an angle and a way to beat the system, guys who avoided real work. They were everywhere in Vegas. They came looking for a second chance in life only to make the same fucked-up decisions all over again. He tolerated Wood at the door, knowing he lined his pockets with bribes and maybe more. And if Wood was dealing coke and caught, Frank could lose his liquor license. One night, he had a friend try to buy coke from Wood. It didn't work, and Wood told the guy to fuck off and leave the club. So, at least he wasn't selling drugs. But for sure, he did drugs, and Frank just didn't trust him. Frank didn't think that Sally would leave town with a guy and not talk to him first. He didn't think she would leave little Frankie. Sally was no Deedee.

————

He had knocked up Deedee just after he joined the army and before he first shipped out in 1954. At the time, they were both working at the Sands. It was a boomtown then, with a new casino opening every few months. He worked the casino bar, and Deedee did cocktails for the gaming tables. Everyone said she was one of the hottest broads in town and could have been a showgirl if she was four inches taller. All the players and even some of the performers who flew in to work the Copa Room flirted with her. She had a date once with Bud Abbott, the tall one from Abbott and Costello. He took her gambling, and for the night, she stood by his side while he threw dice.

Frank knew Deedee had a crush on him. She'd asked him out a few times after work. The cocktail uniform then was a genie costume with puffy see-through sleeves and pants. Her hair was sculpted up into an exaggerated curl like a crashing wave. She wore eyelash extensions and thick, dark mascara. She was intimidating, and he was too scared and nervous to go out with her. After work one night, just after three in the morning, she was out back in the parking lot by his car smoking a cigarette. He was making good money and drove a lemon-colored Ford Custom convertible. She looked at him and said, "Why are you always smiling?" Then, without waiting for an answer said, "What, am I poison or limburger? I'm not going to ask you out twice." Deedee always got what she wanted back then. They dated, and soon afterward, she got knocked up. By then, he'd already enlisted. His dad had been career army and served in both world wars. Frank had never thought through what he really wanted to do and assumed he'd be a soldier, like a farmer's son was expected to be a farmer. He saw his baby daughter, Sally, just a few times before he shipped out.

The army sent him to Seoul even though the war was over. They didn't need combat troops, but they needed cops, so the army put him in the Military Police Corp, and it was his duty to patrol the bars and brothels around the base in Itaewon and bust GIs for fighting, stabbing, or being AWOL. Then there was a breakout of VD, and they had the MPs round up prostitutes, called *wianbu*, and truck them to an unused barracks where the windows were covered with chain-link fencing. The place was called "the monkey house," and supposedly, there were other monkey houses around Seoul. Frank knew even then that he was attracted to guys, and he knew other soldiers were having sex, but he wasn't going to risk getting caught and court-martialed. Frank knew the brothels had guys dressed up like the *wianbu*, and on one raid, he found himself alone with a younger boy. He was tall, had wavy brown hair, and wore a silk dress that barely hid the fact that "she" was a "he." The *wianbu* looked at him and said, "Nice blow job?" Frank pulled him into a room and dropped his pants. It was just like he had imagined. Then he let the guy go.

By the end of the 50s, he was back in Las Vegas. For those four years, he had sent Deedee money to help care for Sally, and when he returned, he moved in. By then, Deedee had a house just off Desert Inn Road, near the Strip. He married her because that's what you did when you knocked up a girl and had a baby. Deedee's mother, who had helped care for the baby, moved back to Henderson.

Four years was a long time to be apart and then reconnect, especially for a young woman in Las Vegas—a young woman like Deedee. She still cocktailed at the Sands, but she was rarely home when she wasn't working. Then, her clothes were expensive and had nothing to do with her cocktail job or motherhood. One was an aqua-and-royal-blue sequined Gene Shelly cocktail dress that cost several hundred dollars. There were more like it, and there was no way she could afford the clothes from tips at the casino. Frank took care of Sally while he looked for work. He didn't ask Deedee what she did, and she didn't offer. When he finally started bartending again, she paid for a girl to watch Sally.

Deedee and Frank had an understanding. Frank slept in his mother-in-law's old room and played father to Sally, and Deedee didn't talk about her dates. But they stayed good friends, and Frank loved to hear Deedee talk about Vegas and what was happening on the Strip. He loved to hear about who she saw and met. She had gossip about Frank Sinatra and his crowd. She knew Meyer Lansky, the Jewish gangster at the Flamingo, and said there was a rumor that he liked to "watch." She knew Wayne Newton when he was just a kid. Then she got pregnant with Claire. She wasn't Frank's child.

He re-enlisted when he turned twenty-nine. Vietnam was ramping up, and he was itching to get back overseas. He'd felt free in Korea, and living in Seoul—he did what he wanted. Another reason was that after Deedee had Claire, she went back to doing what *she* wanted, which was to party. He signed the papers, and Deedee was out-of-her-mind mad. She sent the kids to live in Henderson with Deedee's mother. His reenlistment came with a bonus of $8,000. He took the money, and instead of giving it to Deedee or his mother-in-law, he bought desert real estate west of the Strip, sixteen acres at $500 an acre. In retrospect, leaving his family and shipping out to Vietnam wasn't a shining moment in his personal history. He'd known it was selfish, and he'd done it anyway. But he wasn't a man haunted by regrets.

The price of land in Vegas skyrocketed while he was away. In the mid-70s, when he finally sold the land, Frank built Tramps with the profits.

———

Deedee made Tramps the hot nightclub. Despite its retro choo-choo train motif, she talked him into hiring a DJ and playing disco-dance music late at night. She was approaching forty, still stunningly attractive, and knew everyone in Las Vegas. She also kept a black book of out-of-town high rollers she dated when they came to town. By then, she had called herself a casino host and was paid by the big casinos to entertain the high rollers and keep them at the tables. Of course, Frank wasn't stupid and knew she was a high-class call girl. But he wasn't about changing people, and he could never change Deedee. She called in every favor on opening night and had half the town at Tramps. The lot was filled with Ferraris, Porsches, Mercedes, BMWs, and Bentleys. The casino executives were there, along with entertainers like Red Foxx, Charo, Lola Falana, Buddy Hackett, Tom Jones, and Wayne Newton. Deedee and Frank danced together that first night— that first song, "Disco Inferno" by the Trammps. The excitement faded a year later, and the fast crowd moved on.

Still, he stayed busy catering to the everyday Vegas crowd of dealers, waiters, cocktailers, parking valets, and bellhops who every night had pockets full of dollar tips and just wanted to party. The lot filled up with Chevys, Fords, Datsuns, VWs, and Yugos.

He'd been quietly and secretly making hundreds of thousands each year since he opened. Part of the reason he kept a low profile was to stay off the radar of the local wise guys. His place was only seven thousand square feet and on the wrong side of Las Vegas Boulevard. The wiseguys were all going to Paul Anka's Jubilation with its table-side waiters serving chateaubriand and champagne while he was quietly selling chicken wings, Budweiser, and Whisky 7s. He wanted to keep it that way. His one extravagance was the three-year-old Mercedes 380SL coupe. He lived in a two-bedroom townhouse in an ungated community.

Frank was fifty years old but had been told he looked younger. His hair was still jet black. He'd had a mustache trimmed to the corners of his mouth for most of his life but shaved it off when it started turning gray. He kept his fingernails groomed with clear matte polish and wore a plain gold pinky ring, just one gold bracelet that Deedee had given him, and a simple gold chain around his neck that he kept buried beneath his shirt. He liked to keep a balance between looking good but not looking too splashy or too showy—too Vegas.

———

Friday night was the big-money shift at Tramps. After picking up change for the weekend and doing the books, he took a few hours for himself and went back to his townhome for a nap and shower. He was back by happy hour when the place filled up with nine-to-fivers. That crowd spilled over into a dinner-and-cocktail crowd that, in turn, stayed around for dancing at eleven. For the servers, cocktail waitresses, and bartenders, it was show time, and everyone was sharp. At eleven, when the music started, there was already a line down the sidewalk with Wood taking side money behind Frank's back from customers trying to avoid the queue.

He didn't like what Wood was doing and thought he made the club look bad. The people he catered to, the service employees and dealers, would stand in line like anyone else, but they didn't like to see high-rollers, big-shots, and tourists get ahead. This was *their* place. So Frank stood next to Wood and made it clear again for the millionth time that there is only one line. "I know, Frank." Always, "I know, Frank."

Frank went outside. Regulars he knew stood waiting patiently, and he greeted each with a handshake and made a mental note to comp them a drink later. Carl was halfway up the line checking IDs. He patted Carl on the shoulder. Carl looked at him and smiled, "Hey, Frank." He walked back into the club and circled the dance floor. The regulars wanted to feel special, big-shots in their local place, so Frank shook hands and comped drinks—he played the club owner. Later, he circled back and saw Wood hold the door open for two guys his age. He hadn't seen the two in line and was pissed again at his so-called son-in-law. Then Wood pointed in Frank's direction, and he knew they were looking for him.

Frank didn't recognize the two and didn't hold out his hand for an introduction. "What can I do for you?"

"We've got a few questions." He could tell they were security for some guy or casino. One had a mustache, short brush-cut hair, and black Wellingtons like bus driver boots.

The other was skinnier and wore military-issue black-rimmed glasses like he'd just been discharged. The skinnier guy had long, out-of-fashion sideburns to go with his never-in-fashion glasses.

"It's Friday night. I've got a club to run. How about you call me next week and make an appointment? Whatever you're selling, I'm not buying it now."

The guy with the mustache said, "It's about your employee, Sally Harding."

Frank was stunned. "Okay, come back to the office."

The small office was across from the bathrooms. On one side were two desks with chairs where the bartenders could count their tills. On the other side was his desk next to a safe the size of a small refrigerator. Next to the safe leaned his loaded shotgun. Frank sat on the edge of his desk with a hand on the safe while the others stood. Frank said, "So what's this about?"

The mustache guy continued; he seemed to be the boss. "We're trying to find the whereabouts of Mrs. Welch. She listed Tramps as her employer. We're Security from the Westward Ho Motel and Casino." They did not introduce themselves.

Frank asked again, "So, what's this about?"

"She won the Mega Slot four weeks ago. We have reason to believe she was part of a criminal enterprise that rigged the machine."

Frank didn't know what to say. He just sat and waited for the mustache guy to fill in the blanks. Then, nothing but silence. Frank asked, "Do you know where she is?"

"We do not. We are hoping you could help us."

Frank was quick and made connections fast. They would have done their research and gone to her house first. They might have already spoken to Wood, who was certainly withholding something. They probably knew he was her father. "I don't know where she is."

"We think it's in your best interest to tell us what you do know."

Frank had been dealing with tough guys and security guys most of his life, and they didn't scare him. In fact, sometimes they made things interesting. "How about you go fuck yourselves?"

The guy with the black-framed glasses now spoke. His tone was soft, like a whisper, but there was tension behind the words, like he was talking to a bad child and holding his temper. "She's been gone for as long as the slot money's been gone. She's left town. We know you're her father. We know she does your books. We'll go easy on her if you can help us get the money back. Her partners won't be so lucky. Frankly, we don't care where the money comes from. In fact, if you'd like to open that safe, we can finish our business right now."

The assholes thought that they could intimidate, extort, and interrogate him. "Like I said, go fuck yourselves."

Frank stared at the man with the glasses. The shotgun was in arm's reach, and he wondered how long it would take for them to pull their holstered pieces clipped into the back of their pants. He figured he could club them both with the shotgun before they could un-holster.

Frank smiled.

It was a simple bayonet drill. He grabbed the shotgun stock with his right hand on top of the weapon and placed his other hand underneath the pump. He came at the guy on his left first, the guy with the mustache and bus driver boots. He made a slashing motion to the side of his head, the muzzle of the rifle catching him in the ear. He reversed the slash and caught the other guy's eyeglasses with a glancing blow. The hinge broke, and the chunky black temple piece flew up and landed on a desktop. The glancing blow also took out a piece of nose. The first guy had slumped to the ground, while the second guy instinctively held his face while blood began to drain from the missing flesh. Frank hit him with the butt of the shotgun. Both were now down on the floor. He opened the office door and motioned to the nearest doorman, Nash the Smasher, who covered the emergency exit. "Two guys just tried to rob me."

Nash and Frank soon had the two handcuffed and lying face down on the office floor. Over the ten years he'd had the club, Frank had seen fights just about every night and multiple fights on weekends. He'd had to deal with guns in the club, and he'd had a knife pulled on him at least once a year. He was fifty years old but could still hang with the doormen and help out. Sometimes, it felt like exercise, and sometimes, mixing it up with the younger guys was just good fun. And over the years, he'd put together a system. Anyone fighting, caught selling drugs in the club, or hustling would be handcuffed, photographed, and eighty-sixed. Eighty-sixed was an old restaurant term that meant something was off the menu, like if you were out of the steak special, you'd say, "The steak special is eighty-sixed." What it meant in Las Vegas was that you were banned from ever setting foot in the place again. The Westward Ho private security guards in front of him certainly knew the routine. He had Nash turn them over. Frank took their headshot photos with a Polaroid and then went through the legalese that the State of Nevada required, "This is to inform you that you are banned from these premises…" Frank had it memorized. Next, he went through their pants pockets and found wallets. He made copies of their driver's licenses and Westward Ho IDs. Frank then called the police and specifically asked for Sergeant Pete Askoff.

Frank had an eighty-six book where he kept the photos. The book had sleeves that fit Polaroids, and he tucked the ID copies behind each photo. The one with the bus driver boots was Clarence Farmer and the other with the broken glasses was Arnold Ramirez. He compared the Polaroids with the IDs. Clarence's left ear was bloody and smashed; it would need a few stitches. Arnold no longer wore glasses, and his nose was still pulsing blood. It would also need stitches and possibly a skin graft. Both lay on the floor, silent.

Frank had deep relationships with the local police. The first year he opened, he or one of his doormen would call the police almost nightly to help break up fights. Pete was just a beat cop then and about the same age as Frank. Pete and the other officers got tired of cleaning up Frank's problems, so they cautioned him, "Either you control the club, or we will." He took it seriously as a threat to close him down. Frank soon found out that Vegas police expected the casinos and nightclubs to do their own security and solve their own problems, even if that meant looking the other way. He beefed up his door staff and made everyone carry handcuffs. The police were not to be called until the brawlers, drug dealers, or hustlers were in cuffs and eighty-sixed. Then he paid the cops for special duty, which was really a gratuity of sorts for taking the cuffed guys down to the county jail. Each month, the local eight or so cops would get an envelope. When Pete was promoted to sergeant, Frank just paid one lump sum.

Sergeant Pete Askoff showed up by himself. He was a big man with stiff gray hair combed back from his forehead and held in place with some old-fashioned hair tonic, like Brylcreem. He came into the office, and Frank had Nash leave.

Pete said, "Hi, Frank."

"Thanks, Pete, for coming down. You know these guys?"

The two had been turned over with their faces to the floor, but hearing Pete's voice, they turned their necks and looked up at the sergeant. Pete said, "Clarence, Arnie. How you two doing?"

Arnie stayed silent, still stunned from the second hit when the gun butt smashed the left side of his face. Clarence spoke up, "Fucking guy is crazy, Pete. We just came here to talk, that's all. We had some questions."

The sergeant looked over at Frank. Frank could tell he didn't want this to get messy, and he knew the security guys didn't want the Las Vegas Police involved. These guys were ex-cops, and cops didn't like ex-cops. The sergeant said, "So what do you want me to do, Frank?"

Frank said, "Witness."

"Okay, witness what?"

"I want you and these guys to witness. Pete, this is to let you know that there will be a fifty-thousand-dollar bounty on each of these guy's heads if I go missing or show up dead somewhere. Doesn't matter if I get hit by a car, have a heart attack, or slip in the tub. If I'm gone or dead, there will be a hundred grand to make these two disappear. The money will be held by my attorney. He will contact you tomorrow to confirm this arrangement."

Frank had never asked anything like this from the sergeant, and he was now out on a limb. He was putting Pete in a tough position. Maybe. But a hundred thousand was a lot of money, and if he were offered that when he was an MP in Vietnam, the person or persons would be as good as dead.

The sergeant said, "You heard the man." Then he added, "Frank, Clarence, Arnie, have a good evening." The sergeant walked out of the office and closed the door behind him.

————

Frank left the club just after three in the morning. He had his Head Bartender, Ed, take over for him and finish the night. He would try to get a few hours' sleep and then return early the next day to do the deposit. He wasn't tired, though, and needed a drink to wind down. The whole business with the two guys from the Westward Ho had shot adrenaline through his system. On his way home, he decided to stop at the Buffalo.

The gay bar was in a cinderblock strip mall on Swenson near the airport and, from the outside, looked like any other dive bar in Vegas. And it was a dive. The outside was windowless and painted yellow, with a green awning wrapped around the bar and the entire mall. A small Western-looking sign said simply, THE BUFFALO, in scrolly letters like some barbeque joint or Old-West saloon. He tried to imagine the tourists who stumbled into the place wanting smoked beef brisket and then getting an eyeful.

The place was packed at four in the morning with the younger after-dance crowd and the older chicken hawks chasing the youngsters. Toward the back was a second room that did have a Western theme but for the leather and S&M boys. The gay scene was big in Las Vegas, and the dance club just down the street, the Gypsy, was probably the hottest club in town, certainly bigger than Tramps. And every day, there were more and more out-of-town gay tourists, and they could certainly find the Buffalo or Gypsy just by asking any cab driver or concierge.

Frank stood by the bar and ordered a Tanqueray on the rocks with two olives. In the last few years, he'd seen more and more signaling with earrings, keys, bandanas, and leather. It was getting hard to follow, especially the back-pocket bandanas. He knew that the left side was dominant, the right was submissive, and then there were colors. He knew a light-blue bandana in the right-side back pocket meant that the kid liked to suck dick, and right then, he wanted a blow job in the front seat of his Mercedes. But he figured a kid with a blue bandana was in high demand and already cruising from car to car, and he'd have to stalk the parking lot to get what he wanted. He didn't know many of the other bandana colors, but he knew to stay away from yellow and brown. Last year, he'd hooked up with a guy from out of town who wore a brown bandana in his right pocket. Frank was drunk at the time and didn't ask or care. Back at the guy's hotel room, though, he pulled out a rubber boot from his luggage—the guy was traveling with just one rubber boot. He asked Frank to shit in it. He did. Then the guy put his bare foot into the boot. After that, with his toes twisting in shit, he gave Frank a blow job. Overall, the whole scat, urine fetish was not his thing.

He drank his Tanqueray and ordered another. It was getting close to five, and he'd need to be up at ten o'clock to do the deposit and get the club ramped up for Saturday. He finished the second Tanqueray in one long drink and then drove the two miles to his townhome for a few hours of sleep.

The blowjob would have to wait.

CHAPTER TWENTY

George Eiferman was a legend in the bodybuilding world, and every time Wood walked past his photos as Mr. America and Mr. Universe, he was awed. Then came the photos of Eiferman with Debbie Reynolds, Elvis, Stallone, Marilyn Monroe, and Rock Hudson, and the posters of his movies with Steve Reeves—*Hercules*, *Hercules Unchained*, and *Goliath and the Barbarians*. And Eiferman with the bodybuilding greats— Arnold Schwarzenegger, Franco Santoriello, Lou Ferrigno. Wood had seen him at the club once and shaken his hand. The man was small, only up to Wood's chin, but even at sixty, he was still colossal, sculpted, and tanned. Supposedly, the guy never took steroids.

Wood walked past the photos and movie posters and showed his membership card to a hot teenage girl with bright red lips who wrote his name and number down in some ledger. He tried to work out at Eiferman's at least twice a week, but with his dead-pet route, Tramps, and the Sally-Frankie thing, he'd missed almost a month. He started with a quick twenty-minute cardio workout on the stationary bike and then moved to the free weights. Wood was big, six-foot-two and two-hundred-twenty pounds, but he wanted to be bigger. The Hulk guy in the club wasn't much taller than him, but his body had been massive, weighing maybe two-eighty. Wood remembered that he couldn't physically pull the guy's arm around his back and figured his bicep was over twenty inches around. The Hulk was definitely doing steroids. Eiferman didn't allow steroids in his gym, and there was even a sign posted just above the power rack that said, STEROIDS ARE FOR DOPES. But the really big guys at the gym competed, and there wasn't a competitive bodybuilder who wasn't doing steroids—at least not since Eiferman last won Mr. Universe in 1962. But if you were like Wood, didn't compete, and didn't work out every day, these guys wouldn't talk to you. And you couldn't just start asking how to juice up. These guys had their sources, but they weren't sharing. From what Chris had said, the doctors were getting skittish about prescriptions, and steroid use for athletes would soon be outlawed. The whole industry was going underground. Wood spent another hour in the gym working on his upper body doing curls, presses, and rows.

Monday night, he hung out at Tramps looking for Chris. It was past one when he finally showed up, and Wood asked if they could talk. They took a booth farthest from the dance floor. Wood ordered a Stoli Cranberry. Chris had a Corona with a lime.

Chris was the kind of guy who knew specifications for cars, motorcycles, and stereos—things like ohms, watts, peak torque, flow rates, performance camshafts, and lifter kits. He could give you costs, model numbers, production years, and reviews. Chris had a great mind for details and probably spent his days memorizing magazine articles instead of watching soaps on TV. He would've been a great hi-fi technician, race car mechanic, or even a medical doctor if he hadn't taken up drug dealing. Wood asked him about steroids.

Wood heard a stream of jargon that he didn't understand: "Finajet, Primabolan Acetate, Sustanon preloads, Sten, Dianiabol, Syntex Anadrol 50, Winthrop Winstrol, Bolasterone, Testosterone Cypionate, Nolvadex…"

Wood said, "I thought they just took steroids, like testosterone."

Chris was in his element, excited, and his hands gestured Kung-Fu fast. "Basically, it is testosterone, but there are different kinds and different synthetics. Then, you can stack multiples together. There's also injectables and edibles." Then again came a stream of jargon, the list of unpronounceable drugs.

Wood spoke slowly, "Okay, so let's just say I'm not a competitive bodybuilder, and I just want to get big fast. It's not my life's work; I just want to get it done. What do I do?"

Chris smiled. The drinks had just come, and Chris shoved the lime into the beer bottle and held it upside down with his thumb over the top, mixing the juice and beer. He thought for a second and then took a sip of the Corona. "Finajet…Fina," he said.

"Fina?"

"Fina. Most of the other stuff is produced in Europe, and you'll need a doctor's prescription. You can probably get Dianiabol in Mexico, but that's an oral steroid and not as good. Oral steroids are mostly absorbed by your body before they produce muscle. It also fucks up your liver. Dianiabol is for pussies. What you want is injectable Fina. You want to put the testosterone directly into your muscle. Maybe twice a week, 500 milligrams each time."

"You inject it into muscle?"

Chris made a stabbing motion into his thigh. "You start with the quads."

"And I can get Fina in Mexico?" Wood asked.

"Sure, really, any *farmacia* in Mexico should carry it. What you'll ask for is horse steroids, but if you just ask for Fina by name, they'll take one look at you and know exactly what you want."

"Horse steroids?" Wood remembered Todd in LA, who'd said something about veterinary supplements. Not to look totally clueless, he added, "I guess I knew that."

"There will be a picture of a horse on the box. It comes in 50cc vials, one hundred doses. So, if it's just you, the vial would last six months. I've heard that around here, a 50cc of Fina goes for seventy-five bucks, but the price is going up. I don't know what the vial costs in Mexico."

"And it works?"

"You will gain thirty to fifty pounds of pure muscle in ninety days. I'm not kidding."

"Fuckin' A," Wood said.

———

Tuesday morning, he drove the six hours to Tijuana. His tank held nineteen gallons, and it took him almost two tankfuls. At a buck a gallon, he was already almost forty dollars into the venture. Money wasn't his problem, though. He still couldn't touch Sally's five thousand in savings, but he'd emptied the two thousand from her checking into his bank account. Now he had seed money. Plus, the dead-pet route was kicking in at least eight hundred a week, and there was no longer the two-hundred-dollar payoff to Lamar. And Tramps was keeping him in gas, food, and booze. Overall, he was doing pretty good.

Wood had been to Tijuana before and knew better than to drive his orange Chevy K10 with the lift kit over the border. If he left it on the street in Mexico, the whole truck would be gone or sitting there on cinderblocks with the extreme-country tires and rims missing. He parked his truck along with the other gringos in the lot just on the US side and then stood in line to go through customs. After crossing the border, he avoided the cab drivers he knew would take him on a scam ride halfway through Mexico. And he knew the walk into town was short. He took a right and crossed the wide walking bridge over the Tijuana River, really just a dry concrete spillway, like one big gutter to drain the whole filthy city. Where the bridge ended, the city opened up with all its cheap tourist stuff like ponchos, sombreros, toy guitars, leather belts and wallets, snakeskin cowboy boots, Mexican marionettes, noise makers, fireworks, and switchblade knives. *Farmacias* were everywhere, but he was looking for the one near the Club Oh. That's what Todd had said—near Club Oh.

He figured the club was on Avenue Revolucion, which was a few blocks down from the bridge. Revolucion was like the Fremont Street, the Glitter Gulch, of Tijuana, where most of the tourist bars and clubs did business. The sidewalks were wide, but the foot traffic spilled over into the street pitted with loose asphalt and axle-busting potholes. Wood was hungry but avoided the street food and even the restaurants. He avoided the hookers and an old man in a sombrero who offered to take his picture with a donkey covered with black zebra stripes. A sign said ZONKEY. The club was in the middle of the next block beneath a sign that stretched up and past the building's roof. Big red letters spelled out CLUB OH! and underneath in smaller letters, LASER DISCO.

Farmacias bookended the club, and a larger *Super Farmacia* was across the street. He noticed that all three advertised Fina and Dianiabol. In fact, he'd already passed countless *farmacias* with signs for steroids, like drugs were the new tourist tchotchkes, something for everyone: sombreros, switchblades, prostitutes, booze, and now drugs. And Wood liked that—the freedom. He chose the *Super Farmacia* across the street. Thirty minutes later, he was back out on Avenue Revolucion with a case of Fina, twenty 50cc vials, which the pharmacist had assured him was legal to cross the border with, "Just tell them that you are a rancher and that the Fina is for the horzzes." For Dianiabol, he was told he would need a US prescription that, given a day, the pharmacist could supply. Wood declined. The case discount for Fina was US$500, a bulk special that included twenty 1cc syringes and one hundred disposable needles. This was too easy, and Wood wondered who was buying all these cases of steroids. It seemed like Mexico was in on a conspiracy to make America stronger, one whole football team at a time.

The sun was setting and Wood was tired. He didn't feel like crossing the border and driving six or seven hours home. He found Hotel Caesars on Avenue Revolucion that looked clean and more American, with fresh, graffiti-free stucco and screened windows that weren't partially covered by leaky air conditioning units. Next door was a Carl's Jr. where he could get a commercially prepared hamburger. The room cost him twenty US dollars. A velvet painting of a bull and matador hung on the wall, and a clean towel was laid over the bedspread topped by a mini cake of soap. He ate at Carl's Jr., watched American TV, then slowly drifted into a nap.

When he woke past midnight, his window was open, and he could hear the sounds of the street: horns, laughing, a glass bottle breaking, and dance music. The case of Fina was on the dresser, next to the plastic bag that held the syringes and needles. He was curious to figure out how to inject Fina—what it felt like. He stood, crossed the room, and opened the case. The vials were lined up in cardboard separators like longneck beers, and he pulled out one vial. The stopper was rubber, and he knew from TV soaps like *General Hospital* how to fill the syringe and ensure no air bubbles were caught in the cylinder. He attached a disposable needle to the syringe and filled it half full of Fina, 500 milligrams or half a cc. He unbuckled his belt and let his jeans fall to his ankles. He sat on the bed and held the syringe like a knife with its blade down, his thumb on the depressor. The small pinprick and the heaviness of the Fina entering his muscle felt strangely good. He sat on the bed for a few minutes, waiting. Somehow, he thought he'd feel stronger. He laughed at the idea of his shirt busting at the seams like the Hulk, like Bill Bixby turning into Lou Ferrigno, all radioactive-green eyes and toothy snarl. He thought he did feel more awake, though, like he had more energy. He felt alert. He decided to check out Club OH!.

The two Mexican doormen out front nodded to Wood. They didn't seem to be checking IDs, mostly just stopping kids from taking drinks and beers onto the sidewalk. Inside, the place opened up, double the size of Tramps. Two horseshoe bars were on either side of a dance floor set off with brass railings, and even on a Tuesday night, the place was busy. The drinking age in Mexico was only sixteen, or non-existent, and most looked to be underage white kids probably down from San Diego. He might have been the oldest person there. The dance floor was packed, and they played the same music he was used to—Lisa Lisa, Michael Jackson, Bananarama's "Cool Summer," and Salt-N-Pepa's "Push It." The club did, in fact, have the advertised lasers. Different colored lines of light pulsed across the club, glowing brighter as the lines shot through the haze from a fog machine. Tramps had can lights with colored gels that flashed on and off, and the cans now seemed outdated, like all the train stuff.

At the bar, he ordered a Corona, then later did tequila shots from one of the hot Mexican girls who roamed the club with bottles of Jose Cuervo, fresh limes, and little shot glasses held in black leather bandoliers. He felt good, but he wanted to feel better, stronger. In the bathroom, he bought a quarter gram of coke in a folded white packet. He did a few hits in a stall using the edge of his driver's license. Then, leaving the bathroom, he had the sudden urge to shit. He knew it was from Mannitol, a baby laxative used to cut the coke. He turned around and closed himself back in a stall.

At two in the morning, he was on the street drunk and wired. He was also horny. Near the hotel, he walked around the block twice, checking out the prostitutes who roamed everywhere, seemingly three for every one tourist. Some called out to him, but most were on display, leaning against graffitied brick or smoking outside hotel doorways. Wood had his eye on two girls standing beside a *farmacia* still open. One was younger with long, straight black hair. She wore a black leather jacket zipped down to her navel with nothing underneath. The older one was probably his age. She wore a neon yellow bikini top and cutoff shorts. The older one looked up after Wood had passed twice. She said, "Two-for-one special."

He stepped toward them, stopping so close that he could see down the leather jacket. He asked quietly, "How much?"

"Forty dollars for two."

"That's not two-for-one," he said, "twenty dollars."

"Thirty dollars."

He'd never had two girls. "Okay. I've got a room."

They followed him around the block to the hotel. The front door was locked, and a security guy buzzed them in. He looked at Wood and the two girls and shook his head. He wore a blue uniform and a badge, and on his duty belt, he carried a sidearm, cuffs, and an old-time nightstick with a leather wrist strap. The black lacquer on the stick was worn in spots down to the white oak. Wood pulled a five from his wallet. The guy took the five and asked, "You need some protection, man?" He reached into his pocket and pulled out individually wrapped condoms, "One dollar for you." Wood shook his head, walked past the guard, and climbed the stairs. He heard, "Man, you'll be sorry." And that made him pause.

In the room, he counted out a twenty and a ten. He handed the two bills to the older one in the yellow bikini top.

The first thing he did was unzip the leather jacket. The girl's breasts stayed right there with nipples pointed and glowing with some neon-yellow makeup, like the club's disco lasers. The older one unbuckled his jeans and slid them from his waist. He was hard already, and she sucked his cock. He kissed the younger one and carefully tweaked her yellow nipples, spongy like mini marshmallows. He slid his hand down her shorts and felt for the crevasse that he was hoping was moist. It was more slippery than moist, and he figured the goo was some kind of lotion or lubricant. Then, the goo got him thinking about what the security guy had said, "You'll be sorry." And that thought, and the feel of her pussy ruined it for him, and he just wanted it to be done. He pulled his hand away, then pushed her head down to join the other. He came quickly, the older one using her hand towards the end, both watching as his cum dripped to the carpeted floor. And knowing that he was hardly the first to soil the carpet left him disgusted.

After they'd gone, Wood climbed into bed wearing his socks, t-shirt, and underwear. He kept his hands beneath the top sheet, careful not to touch the bedspread.

He woke up with a disorienting kind of hangover where he just didn't know where he was—no headache, no nausea, just lost. Then he saw his case of Fina and the velvet painting of the matador. Fucking Tijuana. His jeans were on the floor where the older one had left them. Underneath the jeans lay his wallet open, and he knew instantly he'd been robbed. He figured he'd had close to $200 in his wallet. Fucking stupid. Thankfully, he had his driver's license to get back across the border and his Wells Fargo bank card to access an ATM. He still had the steroids and box of needles.

———

Late afternoon, Wood finally reached Las Vegas. He had time on the long drive to think and was thinking about the Mega Slot money. He'd been through the house inside and out at least six times. He'd taken apart Sally's car, gone through the seats, the trunk, even looking behind the cavity of the dashboard—where Chris hid his stash—and still nothing. He tried to think of where the money could be if it wasn't in the house, her car, or the yard. He didn't think Sally would have trusted a friend with the money, not over thirty grand. And since Sally left, Frankie and his stuff were the only things removed from the house. He'd loaded the two garbage bags of Frankie's stuff and thought he would have seen bundles of dollar bills. But he hadn't checked Frankie himself. Could Sally have somehow stashed the money with him? Sally wasn't close to Claire, and they rarely talked, but they were still sisters. Could Sally have trusted Claire? It seemed a possibility. Maybe the only possibility he had.

Wood took the Tropicana exit and parked his truck at the Esso station one block over. He walked around the building across the street from the adobe house and watched. A Monte Carlo with blue Connecticut plates he'd never seen before was parked under the tree. He crossed the street to the post office and watched through the fence. He saw Frankie, and then he saw a fat guy with a red beard. It looked like they were working on a minibike—and talking. He'd only heard Frankie make the funny noises. He kept watching. The fat guy was doing most of the talking, but it looked like Frankie was responding. Sally always said he wasn't brain damaged, but Wood never believed her. Now Frankie was talking. And Frankie had seen Sally dead on the kitchen floor, Wood standing over her. And if Sally trusted anyone, it was probably Frankie. But how did that dimwit get out of the house with his money?

He'd find out.

Wood drove back to his and Sally's house and parked in the driveway. Right away, he saw that the front door jamb was splintered, and the doorknob was busted off and lay on the straw mat Wood had given Sally for a Christmas present. The mat was a joke that now seemed prophetic—it said THE NEIGHBORS HAVE BETTER STUFF. Someone had broken in, and it occurred to him that others might also be looking for his money—and they might still be inside. He decided not to find out. He slowly eased his truck out of the driveway and left.

He drove to John's apartment on Koval Lane. John was wearing pajama bottoms when he opened the door. He yawned and said, "What?"

"Dude, sorry to wake you. Okay, if I crash on your couch?" And then he lied, "Fucking bank foreclosed on Sally's house." The lie wasn't far off; he'd been getting foreclosure notices weekly.

John let him in, returned to his bedroom, and closed the door.

Wood sat on the couch and tried to call Mike The Mechanic at the Westward Ho. The operator transferred his call to Maintenance. The supervisor who answered said that Mike had not shown up for work in over two weeks. The guy added, "If you see Mike, let him know he's fired."

CHAPTER TWENTY-ONE

Claire did training rounds with an experienced phlebotomist, a medical tech who drew blood from patients. The girl's name tag read Carol Briggs. She was Claire's age, or close to it, and had been drawing blood for three years. She was shorter than Claire with a Kewpie doll face—plump, big eyes, and small mouth. They worked in General Admitting, checking charts, and then bouncing from room to room, poking arms and filling vials with blood. Between rooms, Carol was chatty and casual. She kept saying over and over, "It's not that bad," and "You'll get used to it," like Claire was squeamish around flesh and bodily fluids. In the rooms, Carol was all business and explained the procedure to Claire slow and loud like she was talking to a whole classroom, the patient almost non-existent—like a cadaver on a slab. And Claire just followed. She wasn't yet ready to do a procedure on her own that would come later after more practice on a dummy arm.

Later in the shift, they took a coffee break together in the cafeteria where Claire had worked just the previous week washing dishes. Claire now wore the green nurses' scrubs that the hospital provided and laundered. Carol explained the job, "It's not so bad. The tricky part is finding a stickable vein. You'll get used to it. Old people are the toughest because their veins get kind of ropy and move around like worms—you stick, and it slithers away. Then there are the needle-phobes who will scream and twitch before they even get poked. The trick with needle-phobes is distraction—start asking questions and get them to talk. Ask about their children or what TV shows they like. Then there are large people. Sometimes, the vein is buried in a blanket of fat, and you feel sorry for the discomfort as you dig around with the needle. And then you'll run into the pros. The pros are mostly patients with long-term conditions like heart disease or cancer. The pros often have partially collapsed veins that are really hard to poke, causing them lots of discomfort. The pros, though, will help you out and give you the trick. It's best to listen and not be a know-it-all. You'll get used to it." Claire noticed Carol and the others said "discomfort" when they really meant pain. She supposed it was like saying "dates" when she'd really been just turning tricks.

Claire sat and listened; she was interested and wanted to be good at the new job. And it felt like she was becoming part of a profession like being a lawyer, accountant, or doctor. "What happens if you can't find the vein?"

"It'll happen a lot when you first start. Over time, you get used to it and figure out the tricks. You get a feel for it. But when you start out and have trouble finding a patient's vein, just stop. Chances are you'll cause more harm and discomfort than it's worth. Find someone with more experience to do it. We ask for help around here, and it's not a sign that you're not doing your job.

"I'm good at finding the vein, but there's someone better than me. You'll run across Lovie Lopez. She's been doing this for like twenty years. She always finds the vein. What's weird is that you watch her work and ask her how she did it, like, 'Lovie, what's the trick,' and she's blank, nothing. She says, 'I don't know,' or 'I never thought about it.' And I don't think she does think about it. Some people are simply gifted—they do it, they do it well, they don't think about it, and they can't tell you how they did it."

It struck a nerve with Claire, and she thought about Frankie with engines. He was almost done with the minibike, and most of the time he was doing the work alone while Red sat in a folding lawn chair reading the *Review-Journal*.

Carol asked her, "What was your last job?"

It felt like another person who was the escort, the prostitute, and her name was Cher. It wasn't like Sally Fields in *Sybil,* with the different crazy personalities all jockeying for a piece of her mind. She wasn't psycho—she knew who she was and what she'd done. She could say it to herself, "I was an escort, a prostitute, a whore," but she chose to think of that person as someone in another lifetime, like reincarnation. It helped. "I worked here in the cafeteria. Then I went to Nevada Technical."

Carol said, "Well, good for you. I was a server at Carlos Murphy's. I made better money waiting tables, but I get more satisfaction with this job. I also get benefits and paid vacations. No such thing at my last job, just a free shift beer and fifty percent off on food—Carne Asada or Corn Beef and Cabbage." She laughed. "Get it? Carlos Murphy's, Mexican and Irish?"

Claire smiled and nodded her head. She got it—she'd been to the restaurant.

In the afternoon, they worked in the Emergency Room. Dr. Harold Meiser, Harry, was one of the physicians, and throughout the shift, they handled many of the same patients. Claire could see now he was rugged-handsome with his curly black hair and strong build, and she could see that the other females were suckers to his wide smile that showed twenty or more of this thirty-two straight white teeth. And he did the wink-thing when asking for a procedure, like, "Can I get a blood work-up on Exam Six," then wink, then, "Thanks." Claire remembered the wink right after he'd said, "That's the best I can do." Carol was nervous around Dr. Meiser and had trouble concentrating and doing her classroom lecture. She'd forget where she was, stammering until the doctor left the room.

Toward the end of the shift, he came up to Claire with a card. "I still feel bad about your nose. I'm no plastic surgeon, but this is a good one in town and connected to Sunrise." He handed her the card. One side had Dr. Meiser's name and information. The other side had the name of a plastic surgeon and phone number written in his almost-legible script. She read the name out loud to get it right, "Dr. Mark Fordham? 702-983-4477?"

"That's it." Dr. Meiser, Harry, looked at her, winked, and smiled. Then he looked closer, concentrating, and his smile relaxed. Claire knew he was staring at her nose again. He seemed professional, and she stood still. "Do you mind if I have a look inside? See how the nasal cavity has healed?"

"I guess."

"Let's go to exam room five, it's open."

Carol rolled her eyes at Claire, a gesture where the iris hit every edge of the socket. She said, "I'll be at the nurse's station."

Claire followed him to the room. He had her sit on the exam table and reached for the otoscope—the battery-powered nose flashlight. He told her to lift her head. He touched her hair and the back of her neck. Then he looked up into her nose. "Trouble breathing?"

"No."

"No nasally sound when you talk, like a whistling or hum?" He didn't wait for Claire but answered his own question. "Well, I guess I've heard you talk, and your voice is like an angel's."

"Boy angel or girl angel?"

He laughed, "Little cupid angel with wings and arrows."

She imagined the wink that punctuated the end of that line. She laughed also, and he told her to stay still.

"Looks like the passages healed fine. It's just cosmetic at this point. You might want to see Dr. Fordham."

"Maybe I will." And at that moment, she thought she might.

Harry put down the otoscope and stepped back from the table, "So it's great you're out of the cafeteria. You're one of us now."

"Well, not quite one of you. All I do is help out the nurses and take blood."

"It's important, and you'll be part of the team. You can move up from there—lots of opportunities in healthcare. We should have coffee or a drink sometime and talk about it." He was smiling again, teeth like glossy-white chicklets.

"Drink" sounded like a date, and Claire was flattered. Since her nose had been broken, she hadn't wanted to think of guys. Guys were part of that other life. And Red didn't really count. He was more like a forest troll. He was the landlord or, rather, slumlord. She said, "That would be nice."

At the end of their shift, Carol gave Claire a twelve-gauge needle, clamps, tubes, syringes, two IV bags, and a rubber training arm. The whole training kit came in a black case that might have also fit a trumpet. Claire was scheduled to start performing venipunctures on live patients the following week. Carol wanted her to get a feel for finding the vein, inserting the needle, and feeling the "pop" when the needle penetrated the vein. That afternoon, she sat out back practicing on the arm in a rusting lawn chair. At the same time, she watched Red and Frankie working outside on the minibike. Red was filling the tank with gas, and Claire looked up nervously to see what the man had in mind next.

Red straddled the minibike and then kicked over the engine. It took him a few tries, but the engine finally caught, and Red worked the throttle to keep it going. He had a screwdriver and tinkered with the carburetor until the engine idled. He handed the screwdriver to Frankie, who placed it carefully in the toolbox. Red then pulled in the clutch, kicked the bike into gear with his toe, and started riding. Red was too big for the minibike, like one of those circus clowns on a bicycle built for monkeys, and she laughed at that. She heard the bike's gears shift, and Red drove faster in a circle around the lot. She realized then that the minibike was more of a beginner's motorcycle. The tires were slightly larger, and the bike had suspension and gears. Red came to a stop in front of her lawn chair. Not a circus clown, not a forest troll, more a garden gnome.

"I think you're a little too big for that thing," she laughed.

"I think I'm a little too big for most things. Pretty amazing, though. Frankie rebuilt most of this himself. I can't believe it started right up. Really amazing."

"Well, you've been amazing with him. Who knew?"

Red cut the engine, then sat looking off in the distance. It was a way he had, maybe shyness, but it came off like some disconnect between his mouth and his mind. Finally, he looked at her, cupping his hand over his eyes to shield the sun. "Okay, if I teach Frankie how to ride it?"

The thought of Frankie on a motorcycle made her edgy. "I'm not sure that's a good idea."

"I understand. Maybe not such a good idea."

He looked off again and just sat there on the motorcycle. Claire didn't want the conversation to end like that. Part of her wanted Frankie to experience more things. Now, she wished Red would have tried harder. She asked, "Would it just be in the yard?"

"Well, yes. It's not like he has a license to drive on the street."

"Can he get hurt?"

He looked at her again with his hand cupped over his eyes. "No more than skinned knees, minor cuts, and scratches. Boy stuff. He won't be able to go too fast around the yard. And I'm not sure he'll even be able to figure it out."

"Sure, okay."

Red stepped off the bike and pushed it over to the shack where Frankie was standing. Red was giving him instructions, which Claire couldn't hear. Then Frankie sat on the bike. His feet easily touched the ground on each side, and he gripped the handlebars, his elbows up and out like stubby bird wings. He then leaned it to one side and kicked the starter. It revved up and then idled. Red was talking louder over the noise of the engine, and she heard the words "clutch," "gears," and "slowly." Red stepped back and watched. Frankie pulled in the clutch and kicked the shifter into gear. Frankie let go of the clutch, and the bike lurched forward out of control, then tipped over. Frankie fell over with it, and the engine died. Claire stood and ran toward the accident, the rubber arm falling into the dirt. Red was there first and pulled the bike upright and off Frankie. Frankie was silent.

"Frankie, you hurt?" Claire asked.

Frankie was looking at the bike and not at her. He didn't answer, but then she hadn't expected him to. Frankie stood and got back on the bike. He looked okay, and she didn't see any scrapes or blood. Frankie started the engine again. Red said loudly, "You need to release the clutch slowly and wait for the gears to engage. Slowly." Claire stood back and watched.

The second time, Frankie did the same thing, but he was able to keep the bike upright, and the engine just stopped. He kept trying over and over. Claire picked up the rubber arm and sat back down. Though now the arm made her think of injury, so she placed it back in the trumpet case and closed it. Red kept saying, "Slowly." Claire wasn't sure Frankie would ever get it, and then it occurred to her that he didn't even know how to ride a bicycle.

A half-hour later, Frankie figured out how to release the clutch slowly and get the bike to move forward without killing the engine. When he did, the bike went ten feet before it wobbled and crashed. Frankie's feet were out, and he kept upright and got off the bike before it tipped over. He picked it up and tried again, and again he rode ten feet before it crashed.

Finally, Frankie was able to go more than ten feet. He somehow figured out that if he accelerated after starting off, the bike would stay upright more easily. He did a loop around the yard in first gear, going maybe ten miles an hour. He did more loops, then shifted gears and went faster. He was doing it.

Red came over to Claire. He carried his folding lawn chair. "Fucking amazing," he said and then sat down next to her.

She agreed, "Fucking amazing. So what do you call that thing? A minibike? A motorcycle?"

"It's a Honda Mini Trail 70. It's a minibike with four gears that drives more like a motorcycle. It can go forty or fifty miles per hour. With me on, maybe just thirty." Red smiled.

They watched Frankie make another loop, and she figured he wouldn't stop soon. "You want a Bartles & Jaymes?"

"Sure, why not."

She went inside and took two bottles from the refrigerator. Back outside, she handed Red one. They drank the wine coolers and watched Frankie make lap after lap until the gas ran out and the engine sputtered, then quit. The sky was starting to darken. She thought about Red. He was a gnome all right and kind of funny. A happy gnome.

————

The following week, Dr. Meiser, Harry, asked Claire if she'd like to have a drink after work, and she thought, sure, why not. They both got off at eleven that night. She changed out of her green scrubs into designer jeans and a pink off-the-shoulder blouse—sexy like Jennifer Beals in *Flashdance*. She had makeup in her purse and applied reddish-pink lipstick, black eyeliner, and then powder to her face and nose. All in all, she thought she looked good—not a perfect Cher—but good.

Harry met her at the employee door with his car. He drove a red Porsche 924 like the one she'd owned months before in her other life, and for a moment, she was shocked and just stood still. Harry took it for a signal that she was waiting for him to open the door, and he opened it from inside, reaching across the passenger seat and pushing it out. He smiled, winked, and said, "Hey there, gorgeous."

They drove west on Desert Inn Road. He took a right at the Strip and then another quick right into the parking lot of the Peppermill Fireside Lounge. Claire knew the place well. The Peppermill, with its dark-blue mood lighting, was a popular date spot and a place to make out. The floors were blue carpet, and the booths were reddish pink like her lipstick. In the center was a fire pit three steps down, surrounded by brass rails and plush loveseats. The flame rose from a small pool of water and was fed by natural gas that bubbled up from below the surface. Two couples sat near the fire, both embraced and kissing like the pit was some public orgy. Harry led her to a more private area of couches nearby. The cocktail waitress knew Harry's name and asked if he wanted the regular, a Cuba Libre.

"Thanks, Angela, great. Claire, what would you like?" She'd been to the Peppermill to meet dates in the past. Some were conventioneers or tourists, but most were locals just cheating on their wives. They'd sit in the lounge and have a few drinks, then most of the time, it was sex in a car, too worried or too cheap to get a room. She didn't mind sex in a car—she knew it would be quick.

She'd also seen the cocktail waitress before but didn't get the sense she recognized her or Cher. She ordered a Long Island iced tea.

The drinks came—his small and dark with a lime, hers tall and tea-colored with a lemon. He toasted her new job and then drank. He talked about himself mostly, that he was from the East Bay near San Francisco, that he'd gone to the Reno School of Medicine because it was close and easy to get into, and that he'd been in Vegas for two years and loved it. He talked about a twin brother who was a United Airlines pilot and popular with the stewardesses. Before the Porsche, he'd had a Corvette, but he thought the Porsche handled better and was more fun to drive. He asked if she liked the red color. Claire's Porsche had been red, and now she almost missed it. The doctor had a nice smile, and she was glad he was doing all the talking and wasn't trying to ask about her. They ordered a second round of drinks.

Harry talked then about the emergency room and told funny stories about the weird things people stuck in their orifices. A kid had a Starlight mint stuck up his nose the week before. Rather than hurting him by trying to pull it out with forceps, Harry had the nurse irrigate the nose with warm water to dissolve it. Then, it was common for both women and men to come in with lacerations in their rectum, typically from broken bottles, glass dildos, and, one time, a broken lightbulb. He told her about a tourist with a travel-size toothbrush stuck in his urethra with just the bristles sticking out. Harry laughed while telling the stories, and Claire laughed along with him.

Then it was late, and Harry said he'd take Claire back to her car at the hospital. He paid the check and walked back to his Porsche. In the car, before turning the ignition, he looked at Claire and said her name, "Claire."

She looked at him, and then he leaned over and kissed her. She saw it coming, and in that split second, she could have turned away, done nothing, or turned to meet him. And in that split second, she turned to meet him. She didn't know why— her turn was instinctual, muscle memory like getting in a car and fastening the seatbelt. His kiss landed full on the mouth, and she just sat there somewhat startled and took in the tongue that followed. She could taste the syrupy coke and rum on his lips. She could smell in his hair the smoke from the lounge mixed with shampoo. And then he reached to cup her breast through the invitation of her off-the-shoulder blouse. The hand went in over the loose neckline and between her bra and flesh. Just that fast. And now, if there was a time to stop what was happening, that time had passed.

While they kissed and he fondled, she did think of her job. She was just starting off, and he was a doctor. She didn't want bad blood during her first weeks at work, and she wanted to be liked. She thought through what the doctor wanted. Already he had unzipped his pants and guided her hand to his cock. She leaned over without looking at his face or seeing his eyes, the wink. She took it in her mouth and, with her right hand, stroked the shaft. She was good at this—a pro—and in minutes, she could feel the pressure back up in his scrotum and feel the small quakes in his thighs. At the last moment, she pulled her head up and pointed his cock to the side. The white milky cum jumped out a few inches, landed on his jeans, and pooled in a wrinkle. She smiled at the doctor and said, "Oops, looks like you're done."

He looked at her and winked, "Wow, that was great." He zipped his pants, a dark spot growing in his crotch. He turned the ignition and then drove back along Desert Inn Road to the hospital on Maryland Parkway. He talked about his apartment near downtown with a hot tub on the roof and a view of Fremont Street. He was talking to fill the void of silence, and he did not ask her if she wanted to come see it.

She let him kiss her again before she left the car. It was a kiss that neither of them wanted, but she knew there'd be hard feelings otherwise. And as she left the Porsche, it occurred to her, in a twisted way, that she'd just done her first date since the beating at the Dunes. And it was just one more blow job in the parking lot of the Peppermill. But now she had no cash to show for it. She guessed that's what a real date was.

———

Claire had been trying to cut down on smoking, maybe quit, but in the car, she lit up a cigarette from a pack in her purse. She started the Ford Fairmont and pulled the knob that turned on the headlights. She heard somewhere that you could divine answers to life questions by closing your eyes and clearing your mind. Then the trick was to think about the question—*What should I do?* or *Who am I?* or *Should I do this?* —then quickly open your eyes and latch on to the first thing you see. And that thing would tell you the answer—like what your subconscious mind fell on was instinctively the metaphor for what you should do. She laid her cigarette in the ashtray and closed her eyes. She focused on the question—*What should I do?* —and cleared her mind of all the bullshit swirling. She opened her eyes quickly. The first thing she saw was a lit-up letter *C* in the word CARE on the side of the hospital. She thought *C* stood for Claire— not Cher—and the lit-up *C* was a beacon drawing her to it. It was a simple and obvious message—she needed to focus on herself and what *she,* Claire, wanted, and the rest would take care of itself. And what she wanted was a house, her dog Bud, and a regular job. And maybe she wanted someone else, but not some date like Harry—or Rod. Whoever that someone was would want the house and also Bud. And she thought she also wanted Frankie to be okay and maybe be part of her life.

She drove slowly back to the adobe house, taking a longer route that led her east toward the low mountain ridge that walled the city. Her open window let in cold desert air, and she left it open and turned on the heater. The combination felt good. The further east, the darker it got, with only a few streetlights at the base of the ridge. She turned south and then back west on Tropicana. She lit another cigarette. "C" also stood for "cigarette," and she decided that she really liked smoking.

The lights were off at the house and the shack behind. Red and Frankie were sleeping, but Bud would hear the car and be up to greet her with his tail wagging and mouth open and panting in a kind of dog smile. She'd need to be awake in four hours to take Frankie to school, but then she could go back to sleep if she wanted. Red would be reading his paper or off to eat at one of the cheap casino buffets. She had to work again the next afternoon but knew Frankie would be racing around the yard on his minibike until it ran out of gas, and Red would be watching.

It was good to be home.

CHAPTER TWENTY-TWO

Wood waited outside the adobe house until Claire went to work, and the fat guy drove off in his Monte Carlo. He opened the gate and walked to the back door. He heard the dog barking and worried what the black Lab might do. He lifted out his Buck knife and unfolded the blade. The door was locked but old and not very thick, more like a thin paneled closet door. He gave it an easy kick, and the strike plate ripped away without much damage to the doorjamb itself. Wood held the door slightly ajar. The Lab stopped barking, its nose sniffing through the crack like a vacuum nozzle, its tail wagging. Wood opened the door further, said, "Good dog," and patted its head. And Wood thought, *what a useless piece of shit*—better to have a German Shepherd or a Rottweiler, a dog with attitude. He pushed the Lab away and looked around.

He walked through the kitchen and found the two bedrooms. One was Frankie's, and Wood searched through the closet and then the dresser. He rummaged through the drawers, leaving them open. He pulled the sheets off the single mattress and flipped it over. He looked for a broken seam or zipper on the mattress, but there were none. He felt around for lumps. He imagined the size of the over thirty-thousand dollars to be like a wheel barrel full or even a bucketful, but then he knew the cash only added up to three and a half bundles, more like a beer mug full. There were no lumps in the mattress the size of a beer mug. He did the same in Claire's room. In the living room, he slashed open the couch cushions and upended a chair to look underneath. There were shelves with magazines, and on top was a black, odd-sized case. Inside was a weird fake rubber arm that must have come from her job at the hospital. He smashed the arm against the bookcase, but it seemed almost indestructible. He threw the arm to the Lab that seemed happy to take it up in his mouth. He destroyed the kitchen. The dog followed him through the house, wagging its tail and carrying the rubber arm.

Then he heard something outside or *thought* he heard something. He went out the back door and stepped carefully to the corner of the house with his back to the wall. He looked around the corner. There was nothing, but by then, he was spooked, and he decided to end his search.

Wood crossed the dirt yard and walked through the open gate. He stepped into his truck and sat for a moment. He thought the money had to be in the house somewhere. He shifted the truck into drive and drove slowly down Palo Verde. He drove east on Tropicana, angry and still thinking, *where?* At Maryland Parkway, he took a left and then, minutes later, a right into the parking lot of Reuben's. Before he went in, Wood took the solar-powered calculator from the dashboard and did the math. Sally had given him $17,500, so exactly $50,000 minus that was $32,500. That's what he was owed.

He sat at the bar in Reuben's, drinking a Coors. He knew

Claire or Frankie had his money. He'd find them and demand the thirty thousand five hundred. Give it back to him or else. He did two hits of coke in the bathroom stall and then left Reuben's with a fresh can of Coors. Wood drove back to the adobe house and waited.

———

Claire drove her car through the opened gate, parked, and walked to the back door. She pushed her key into the lock, and before she could turn it, the door just opened. She saw that the lock was broken, and inside, the kitchen was a mess. Food, broken glassware, and plates littered the floor. She backed out and ran toward her car.

She saw Wood walking from the street. Somehow, she'd missed his obnoxious orange pick-up. She stopped and stared at him. "You fucker, you did this. I haven't done anything to you."

"I need you to give me my money." He stood between her and the car door, not five feet away. His arms were folded across his chest, his hands buried behind biceps. He wore a yellow Tramps T-shirt, and Claire could see his fists clenched to push out muscle. What a meathead.

"What money?"

"The thirty-two thousand five-hundred bucks."

"You're insane. How is it I have your money? You drop Frankie off and then disappear. You leave me with nothing to help support *your* stepson? Now get off my property." She turned around and walked back toward the house.

Wood took a few steps and grabbed her by the arm. She tried to twist away and keep moving, but his grip pressed into her flesh. "I know you have it, or Frankie has it. You give it to me, I go away. You don't, well then, I don't go away."

Claire knew what he was capable of—beating a man or woman, slicing off an ear. "I have no idea what you're talking about. Does it look like I have thirty thousand dollars?" She looked back at the house, pointed toward it like a testament to her wealth—or poverty.

Wood held her arm and looked at the adobe house and surrounding scrub brush and dirt. He let go of her arm. "I'll give you some time to think on it. If you don't have the money, Frankie does. Get it from him and give it to me. If I don't have my money, I'll take this to the next level. Frankie can come back with me to his room in the basement. Frankie and I will have a conversation—man to boy. And the boy will tell me where my money is."

"I don't have it, and Frankie doesn't either. You lived with Frankie. You know he couldn't take anything or even hide anything. He's mentally disabled." She said it, though she no longer believed it.

"I've been watching the house. I've seen him talking, and I've seen him tinkering in back with the fat man. Frankie's smart enough to either have my money or give it to you. I want it back. And don't think the fat man's coming to your rescue. That would be his mistake."

Wood walked backward a few steps. He stared at her, and she could see his anger and desperation. He turned and walked toward the gate and then across the street. She saw his truck now parked in the gas station lot. He climbed in and started the engine. He put the pickup into gear and then sped down Tropicana.

Claire rubbed her arm where Wood had grabbed it and could almost feel the bruises coming on. She walked back to the house to clean up her ransacked kitchen. She had no idea what money the meathead was talking about but hoped he'd find it soon and leave her alone.

CHAPTER TWENTY-THREE

A week had passed since Frank's run-in with the Westward Ho security guys. Right afterward, he'd asked Sergeant Askoff to follow up and get the full story. Turned out Sally *had* won the Mega Slot jackpot that paid fifty grand. Then, a few days after the payout, the security guys found evidence of tampering. The mechanic who worked that night was on camera near the machine right before the jackpot hit. That mechanic was now nowhere to be found, and either he was hiding in Vegas, had split town, or was six feet under. Askoff had his bet on six feet under; the security guys were hard-dick, ex-cop assholes.

What Frank knew about Sally was that she was trustworthy and hardworking—no way Sally had come up with this scam by herself. She must have been tricked or coerced, and if she was, then Wood was involved. And if Clarence and Arnold hadn't gone after Wood yet, they soon might. He remembered a line in *The Godfather*: "Keep your friends close and your enemies closer." He had Wood come into his office later that night.

"Two guys were in here looking for Sally."

"Oh," Wood said.

"They say she was involved with a scam to rip off the Westward Ho casino. You know anything about this?" Frank was looking for the signs of lying he had learned in Vietnam—a pause in the response, a hand covering the face, throat clearing or swallowing, a grooming gesture.

Wood paused and stammered, then scratched his nose before adjusting his jacket. "The night before she left, she was out playing slots. I don't know where. For all I know she was with this Lamar guy."

Frank decided to step back and ask simple questions. "How is Frankie doing?"

"He's fine. He's with Claire. She has a house near the airport with plenty of room. She's working at a hospital now. As far as I know, she hasn't gone back to escorting."

"Where near the airport?"

"On Palo Verde just off Tropicana. An old house next to the post office."

"You been over to visit?"

"Yeah, two days ago. He's doing good. He's better off with Claire. I got these work hours, so it's better. I help her out with expenses." Wood cleared his throat and adjusted his pants.

"You still have the job with veterinarians, transporting pets?"

"Yeah, a few days a week, I have my route."

"What is it you do again?"

Wood looked at the office door, then the desk, and finally somewhere left of Frank's eyes. "I work for a crematorium in Barstow. It's medical disposal. The vets need to dispose of the dead pets whose owners didn't want them back. They have me take the pets to Barstow in my truck."

And Frank thought, *Who the fuck finds a job disposing of dead pets?* Fucking Wood. He changed the subject back to Sally. "So, who is this Lamar?"

"He used to hang out here, but I haven't seen him since Sally left me. He worked at Hugo's at the Four Queens, but I hear he hasn't been back to work."

"You have a last name for this Lamar?"

"No, just Lamar."

"Can you get a name? Maybe go down to Hugo's and ask around?"

"What for?" Wood asked.

"I'm worried about Sally. I don't think she would just run off like that. Maybe this Lamar knows something. Maybe if we find him, we can find Sally?"

"Okay, I'll ask around for you. For me, I might want a divorce. You understand…"

"I understand." Frank paused. "Have two guys been by your house? Security guys from the Westward Ho. One with glasses?"

"Someone broke into the place last Monday. I found the house upside down. Thought it was a burglary or something. Must be those guys. What do they want with me?"

"Their money. Presumably, they didn't find it."

"If there's money, Sally and Lamar have it." Wood touched his ear and then smoothed back his hair.

"Okay, look at me." Wood looked at Frank and met his eyes. Frank continued, "Those two guys are not fucking around. They won't stop until they have the casino's money and the people who stole it. Sooner or later, they will track you down, and you won't have John or Carl to save you. They'll assume you were involved and will fuck you up to get what they want. So tell me straight, did you know about this slot machine rip-off?"

Wood stared into Frank's eyes, "No, I don't know where their money is. You can assume that if I had the money, I'd be gone too."

Wood kept his eyes on Frank and sat still in the office chair, his hands on the armrests. Frank figured that part was true—Wood was still looking for the money. "Why don't you move in with me? I've got an extra bedroom in the townhouse and plenty of protection if you know what I mean."

Wood knew what he meant—lots of guns. He'd backed himself into a corner. "Thanks, Frank. That would be great."

CHAPTER TWENTY-FOUR

Wood walked into Eiferman's Gym for a workout and to see if he could move some Fina. He'd been doing the steroid himself for a week, three injections of 500 milligrams each, and thought he could feel the drug working. He felt good. His arms seemed tighter and larger, like right after a workout, and he hadn't worked out in weeks. He also thought the Fina gave him a head rush—an alertness and confidence, almost like coke. He hadn't felt this good in a long time even though shit was piling up—Sally, Claire, Frankie, the fat guy, the Westward Ho security guys, staying with Frank. It was getting hard to keep it all straight. And now he was sitting on twenty vials of Fina and needed to start moving some. Maybe he could quit the dead pet thing and just deal drugs.

He avoided the clique of competitors who'd taken over the dumbbells. He worked out on a bench press with free weights. He asked a guy nearby if he'd spot him and do some reps. The guy, a kid, was in his early twenties and wore a muscle shirt that read GOLD'S GYM. He was big but no competitor.

Wood asked, "You work out at Gold's in LA?"

The kid stood over him, waiting to see if he needed help with the bar. "No, just a shirt. My girlfriend gave it to me for Christmas."

"I was at Gold's in LA once and worked out on the beach at Venice. Those guys are fucking huge."

"There are some big guys here too," the kid said, jerking his head toward the competitors.

"It's the Fina that does it." Wood thought "Fina" sounded better than saying "steroids." More business-like.

But then the kid said, "You mean steroids?"

"Yeah, steroids." Wood held his breath and pushed. He was on his eighth rep and feeling it. He got the bar to the top. "I just started, and I feel great. You can gain thirty to sixty pounds of muscle in three months."

"My girlfriend says your dick gets small."

Wood had not heard that and, for a moment, didn't know what to say. He was at the end of his reps and struggled to get his tenth press to the top. The kid lifted the bar with one hand to remove just enough weight. Wood slid the bar back into the channels and sat up. "That's a misconception. Steroids make all muscles bigger, and there's muscle in your dick. It actually gets bigger too." He heard himself and it sounded good. Wood switched positions with the kid.

The kid said, "So you like it?"

"Yeah, I feel great." Wood waited a minute. "I've got more than I need if you're interested."

The kid started his reps. "No, my girlfriend would be pissed."

Wood backed off. "Yeah, I get it." Then for some reason, Wood couldn't fathom, he added, "My wife would be pissed too if she hadn't already left me." He knew instantly it sounded pathetic.

"Sorry, man," the kid said. And Wood was stuck doing two more sets.

Afterward, Wood thanked the kid and then looked around the gym to see if there were other potential customers. At that moment, thinking of the word "customers," it dawned on Wood that the whole drug-dealing thing was work. Somehow, he'd thought people would just approach him and buy; all he had to do was stand around, look good, and wait. That's what Chris did. He didn't realize he'd have to approach people, ask if they wanted the stuff, and overcome doubts. He realized that selling steroids wasn't going to be easy work. Actually, it was worse than work—it was sales.

After his workout, Wood drove the short distance back to the townhouse. Frank was at Tramps or somewhere, and the place was empty. And what he also noticed was that Frank moved his shit around. How come his clothes were folded and put away in his dresser? He thought for sure he'd left them in the dryer. He didn't like Frank going through his shit. Then, an antiseptic scent bugged him, on top of some smelly dried flowers left in glass bowls in the entryway, the living room, the dining room, and every bathroom.

CHAPTER TWENTY-FIVE

Wood was a slob. He'd moved into Frank's townhouse with a duffle bag of dirty clothes and a toothbrush. He used the washer, but a day later, the clothes hadn't been moved to the dryer, and Frank just did it for him. Frank folded his clean laundry and arranged the clothes in the guest bedroom drawers. He suspected Sally had done the same. Such a lazy piece of shit.

In the kitchen, Wood made frozen pizza or frozen dinners and ate in the living room in front of the TV. His idea of cleaning up was to put his dirty dishes in the sink. Wood borrowed Frank's shampoo and didn't return it. The final insult was that instead of using the bathroom in the guest room, Wood shit in the half bath on the first floor. A scrub brush in a chrome caddy stood next to the toilet, and a can of scented spray on top of the tank, but like a dog marking its domain, Wood left skid marks trailing in the bowl and his stench lingering in the air. Frank put out more bowls of potpourri.

Frank had followed up on Lamar himself. He called Hugo's and asked to speak with the manager. Frank said he wanted to complain about the service and that he had a very rude waiter named Lamar Smith. The manager said there was no Lamar Smith, only a Lamar Young, and *that* Lamar was no longer working there. Frank said, "Good riddance," and hung up. He then simply looked in the phone book. Lamar lived in an apartment complex on Flamingo Road near the Continental Hotel and Casino. At the complex, he found Lamar's name and rang the buzzer. There was no answer. Behind the complex were reserved parking spaces marked with unit numbers. Lamar's space was empty. Frank walked over to the shrubs surrounding the building and, with his cupped hands, carried back a small pile of dirt. He spread the dirt over an area of the parking space. He checked back for the next two days. Both times, still no answer to the buzzer, and the dirt remained undisturbed. It seemed Lamar was definitely gone.

He called Sergeant Askoff again and asked if he could find Lamar Young's emergency contact information from the HR department at the Four Queens. The sergeant called back within an hour with the name of Raelynn Young and a phone number with a southern Utah prefix. Frank called the number. The woman was Lamar's mother, and she was worried. She hadn't heard from him, and it wasn't like Lamar—he called faithfully every week. Frank told the woman he was the manager at Hugo's and that he had Lamar's last paycheck. He gave the woman his name and private office phone number should Lamar show up.

Frank checked on Sally's house. He parked in the driveway and checked the front door. It was locked. He walked around back and found the door that had been kicked open. It was still open. The stench inside was overpowering and reminded him of decaying bodies. A pound of ground beef was still in its wrapper on a countertop and covered with maggots that squirmed under the cellophane. Flies were everywhere. Rodents had gotten in and eaten much of the food and left feces. That they hadn't touched the ground beef was a wonder. He walked into the living room, where the furniture was tossed and the cushions ripped open. In the front hallway, the floor under the mail slot was littered with letters, magazines, catalogs, bills, and flyers. He opened a Countrywide statement and saw that the mortgage was behind by three months. A recent Wells Fargo statement showed that her checking account had been emptied, but over five thousand in savings remained. Frank knew that if Sally split with fifty thousand, she wouldn't leave the five grand behind.

He checked upstairs. Most of Sally's clothes were gone. What remained was a jewelry box filled with earrings, bracelets, and gold chains. In the bathroom, he found all of Sally's cosmetics. The few women Frank knew would never pack and leave without taking their makeup and jewelry.

———

Frank pulled his Mercedes in front of Claire's house. The last time he'd seen her was at Dominic's funeral, and then she was the same person he'd kicked out of his house years before. For that funeral, she wore a shiny gold dress with a ruffled hem that was maybe appropriate for nightclubbing but not for remembering a deceased relative. Her hair was spiky on top and long in the back, and with her heavy blue eye shadow, she looked like some weird David Bowie, Ziggy Stardust character. They didn't talk at the funeral; they hadn't talked at all since the day he found out she was escorting and called her a whore.

But the old adobe house didn't fit with that last impression. And neither did the Ford station wagon or the small black Lab wagging its tail and running out to greet him.

He walked through the gate and petted the dog, now tangled in his legs. The front door opened, and Claire stepped out. She wore a T-shirt, jeans, and sneakers. She wasn't wearing makeup, and her nose had definitely been broken—a far cry from Ziggy Stardust. He wasn't ready for her, for the unexpected daughter he was looking at, and didn't know what to say. She helped him out. "Hi, Frank," she said.

Frank stood ten feet from Claire. "Hi, Claire."

"You stopping by to see your grandson, your namesake?"

"I guess so. How's he doing?"

"You can see for yourself. Follow me."

Claire led him around the house to the back. He followed behind, keeping the same ten-foot distance. He saw a second car, a Monte Carlo, and another structure older than the adobe house. Frankie and a man he had never seen were in front, working on a minibike.

Claire spoke to the man. "Red, this is Frank, Frankie's grandfather." She turned to Frank and said, "Red's my landlord."

Frank nodded toward the man and then looked at his grandson. Frankie's back was to him. He was turning a wrench on the rear wheel, maybe adjusting the chain. Frank was used to Frankie not acknowledging or recognizing him. He'd tried over the years with presents at birthdays and Christmas. Sometimes, he liked the present but didn't seem to connect it with giving—he'd just start playing with the thing. He wanted to be a grandfather, but it seemed almost impossible with Frankie. He asked Claire, "So he's okay?"

The guy named Red spoke first. "The kid's good with

engines. He pretty much rebuilt this Honda by himself. You wouldn't guess it, but the kid has talents."

Frank walked over to Frankie and put his hand on the kid's back. Frankie flinched like it was a hot poker, and Frank stepped back. He said, "Hi, Frankie." There was no response.

"Wood just dropped him off a few months ago. Have you heard from Sally?" Claire asked.

"No, and I'm worried something's happened to her. Something isn't right."

"Wood was by here a few days ago. He's looking for some money he thinks we have. Thirty-two thousand five hundred is what he said. He threatened me."

Frank rubbed his forehead and winced. It just kept getting deeper and thicker, and for the first time, it crossed his mind that Wood could have killed Sally. He looked at Claire. "Sorry for that. Don't worry. I'll take care of Wood."

Frank turned back to Red. "Can he ride it?"

Red smiled. Red was a big man with a red beard, and when he smiled, his whole face lit up like a jack-o-lantern. "Just watch." Red turned to Frankie. "Go ahead, Frankie, show your granddad how you ride it."

Frankie took his time, finished adjusting the chain, and then placed the tools back. He sat on the seat and lifted the kickstand with his heel. He kicked the starter, and the engine came to life. Frank watched his grandson put the bike into gear and release the clutch. He took off on the bike, then shifted into second gear. A track of sorts went in an oval around the large city lot.

Red said, "Watch this. I built a small jump."

Frankie looped back toward the house and took the small mound of dirt standing up. The bike went a foot in the air. Frankie was focused, and Frank could see that the kid was consumed and that this was what he loved. Frank smiled and, for a second, thought he might cry. He looked over at Claire, who was smiling also. He said, "Thanks, Claire, for taking care of Frankie."

Claire didn't say anything.

Red held up his hand, and Frankie stopped.

Frank said, "That's great, Frankie. You look great." Then he added, "Thanks, Red. I appreciate your help."

Frank left and drove down Tropicana toward Boulder Highway, where he knew of a motorcycle dealer. He bought a gold helmet, size small, that matched the color of the Honda minibike. He drove back to Claire's house and dropped off the helmet. Claire thanked him. Before driving back to Tramps, he told Claire, "If you need anything, you know where to find me." He gave her a card with his phone numbers.

CHAPTER TWENTY-SIX

The next morning, a Saturday, Red stayed with Frankie while Claire went to work at the hospital. The kid was now obsessed with engines and wouldn't even stay in the house to watch Inspector Gadget. Frankie was talking more but in his own language with one-syllable words. "Bor" was a carburetor, "gin" was an engine, "die" was actually to ride, and "wer" was a mower. Frankie was saying, "wer," and Red figured he wanted to take apart the lawnmower again. It was the sixth or seventh time. Red said, "Sure, Frankie."

Then Red had an idea. He was getting fatter each day, and he knew that sooner or later, he would need to pull back on the buffets and maybe get a job. He could barely remember the last time he worked for someone else and thought he was probably unemployable. He wasn't comfortable taking instructions or doing things according to someone else's timetable. He also had no real skills—he'd hauled garbage for a living. But he was good with engines, and now Frankie was also good with them, maybe better. He wasn't sure Frankie knew exactly what was happening inside one, but he certainly knew how things connected. He figured the two of them could open a small engine-repair business on the property. It was already zoned for commercial use, and they could turn the shack into a shop. They could call it "Frankie and Red's Small Engine City." It was an idea as good as any.

Frankie still had his now tattered and grease-stained canvas tool bag and sometimes used his own adjustable wrench, but mostly he used Red's tools. He was meticulous about keeping them clean and in a precise order within the steel cabinet. Frankie started by removing the lawnmower's blade and then the carburetor's throttle cable. Within thirty minutes, he had the engine removed from the blade housing and on a table in the shack. It was still early, maybe nine o'clock, when Red heard a loud car in front and the gate opening. Red walked outside and around the adobe house to see who it was.

The guy stood over six feet tall. He had iron-pumping muscles and wore a yellow polo shirt with the Tramps logo. Claire had told him about her brother-in-law, Wood, and figured this was the guy. Claire had said Wood drove an obnoxious orange pickup truck, and Red could see it on the street like some overfed Hot Wheels toy. The guy looked tense and self-conscious as he walked, like maybe he'd been drinking and was just trying to keep it together. The dog, Bud, was running circles around the guy, wagging his tail.

Red smiled. "What can I do for you, pal?"

Wood stopped in front of him uncomfortably close. A pimple on his forehead was scabbed over and ringed by irritated red skin. He reeked of BO and cigarette smoke. His breath smelled like vodka. He said, "Where's Frankie?"

"What's Frankie to you?"

"I'm his stepfather. It's time for him to come along home

with me."

Red tried to slow him down. "Okay, let's start over. Hi, my name is Robert, but everyone calls me Red. You must be Wood?" He held out his hand to shake.

Wood folded his arms. "Listen, Red, I don't have time for this shit. I've come here to get my kid. So, if you don't mind, where is he?"

"He's out with Claire."

"Bullshit." Wood walked around Red straight to the adobe house. He opened the back door that was unlocked, and Red heard the footsteps moving from room to room. Within a minute, Wood was back outside. He walked toward Red. "Move out of the way, pig man."

Both heard the noise from Frankie inside the shack. Red thought it sounded like a far-off foghorn—mournful. Red said, "Not by the hair of my chinny-chin-chin."

Before Red could even finish his smile, Wood cocked his arm, then connected his fist to Red's chin. His face snapped to the side, and he went down hard. For seconds or minutes—a flash—everything went dark and blank.

Red came to slowly, his sight first, then a grogginess. He tried to remember what had happened, connecting the dots to the pain in his jaw. He heard Bud barking. Then he saw Wood dragging the kid toward the truck, and now it all made sense. Frankie's eyes were open, and he hung limp like a rag doll from Wood's grip. Red stood up and staggered forward. His mind started clearing, and he made his legs move faster. He reached Wood just as he turned. At the last moment, he saw the knife in Wood's hand. Wood did a slashing motion down and across. The knife caught Red deep in the forearm, and then he was down on his knees.

Red looked up to see Frankie come alive and jerk his arm

away from Wood. Frankie took off running across the lot. Wood ran after him, but awkward and sluggish like a drunk trying to walk a straight line. Seconds later, Frankie was over the four-foot chain-link fence, with Bud following and making the high leap. Wood just stopped. He walked back toward Red with his knife at his side. He stood above Red. "I'll be back, pig man, and next time, I will definitely huff and puff." Wood kicked him in the stomach. Red doubled over, gasping for air.

———

Claire drove her Ford Fairmont through the open gate and parked under the tree. Bud ran up to greet her. Behind the house, Red was sitting in his folding chair reading the *Review-Journal*. He wore a T-shirt and elastic-waist shorts with his reddish-white legs exposed. He dropped a corner of the newspaper and motioned her over. There was a towel wrapped around his left arm, splotchy with what looked to be blood. She assumed Frankie was in the shack working on engines.

Claire asked, "What the hell happened to you?"

Red was calm. He folded the paper back up and placed it on his lap. "Your brother-in-law, Wood, stopped by. Said he was taking Frankie back with him. I didn't think that was a good idea. Not at least until you got home."

"Is Frankie here? Is he okay?"

"Yeah, he's fine. He's inside working on that lawnmower again."

"So what happened?"

"Wood looked like he'd been up all night. I'm pretty sure he was drunk. Anyway, I told him Frankie was off with you. When Frankie heard Wood's voice, though, he made one of his sounds. Wood just knocked me out with a sucker punch.

He grabbed Frankie and started toward his truck. I tried to stop him, but he cut me." He held up his wrapped arm. "Then Frankie got loose and ran away. I found Frankie about a block down the street behind a dumpster with Bud."

"That fucking meathead." Claire imagined the scene. She knew Wood for what he was—a predator and psychopath. She should have seen it earlier when he threatened her. She should have done something back then. Now Claire had Red entangled in her fucked-up family. "Let me see that arm."

She led him into the kitchen and had him sit at the table. She unwrapped the towel that was coiled around his arm. With each turn of the towel, there was more blood in the fabric, and the blood was wet and fresh. Finally, she peeled away the last layer partially stuck to his skin. She tried to be careful. Red sat there looking at his arm as though he wasn't sure what to expect. The gash was still open and oozed blood. It was five or six inches long and stretched from his elbow toward his wrist. The knife had probably hit bone quickly, so it wasn't more than a quarter inch deep. Claire went to the bathroom, returned with a fresh towel, and started cleaning the wound.

They both looked at the cut. Claire said, "You're going to need stitches."

"Can't you fix it? I thought you were a nurse or something."

"I'm a nurse's assistant. I just help out and take blood."

"I'm sure you can fix it. Make some butterflies and wrap it up. I've done this before; it'll be fine."

Claire found her practice kit containing tape, scissors, gauze, antiseptic wipes, and the chewed rubber arm. Red showed her how to make a butterfly bandage. She took the first one and closed most of the cut. She started cleaning it with a wipe. She was making the next butterfly herself when Red asked, "So, what's up with your family?"

Claire didn't know how to answer, and for a while, she said nothing and just worked on the bandage. "It's complicated."

Red pushed through. "So, when did your father decide that he was gay?"

"What?" It had never occurred to Claire. "What makes you think Frank is gay?"

"Maybe he's not, but that's the vibe I got. The Mercedes, the loafers, the pressed clothes. And did you see that he has his nails done? What straight guy does his nails?"

Claire laughed. "It's a Vegas thing. Lots of guys." Then she added, "And I'm not sure Frank is my father." And without consciously meaning to, she'd opened a new, raw subject. Then, she just let go and started from the beginning. She talked about her mother, Deedee, who'd been a casino host and gone most of the time. She finally left altogether and was now possibly working at a brothel outside of town. She talked about Frank and Vietnam and her sister, Sally, who raised her.

Red asked, "Were you and your sister close?"

Claire then opened up all the way. She wasn't embarrassed about who she was and what she'd done. She told Red about doing escorts with Apple when she was seventeen. How Frank found out and made her leave the house. How Sally rarely spoke with her and didn't want Claire around her family. She told Red the story of Dominic, then of Wood. How Wood did security for her escort service before she was beaten up—before she left that work.

Red looked at her. She'd put eight butterflies along the cut and was now covering the wound with squares of gauze. He asked, "So, you were a prostitute?" He was smiling.

Claire looked up. For some silly reason, she didn't like that word and didn't like the word "whore" either. She'd described Deedee as a casino host but really knew she was a high-class hooker. Claire couldn't imagine what Deedee was now. Anyway, she didn't like hearing the word out of Red's mouth. She wanted to say, "I was an escort; there's a difference." But instead, she just said, "Fuck you."

Red's grin didn't change. Then he said, "You know we can't hang around here. It's probably best we find someplace to stay until this blows over. Probably out of town."

She knew Red was right, but what struck her the most was that he used the word "we."

———

Red came up with the idea. Move out to the desert, maybe find Deedee.

Claire said, "I haven't seen her since I was twelve. I'm not sure who she is anymore, and I'm not sure I ever did. I'm not even sure where she is."

"Well, guess." Red's arm was wrapped in strips of white T-shirt. It was sore when he moved it, but no blood soaked through the cloth. It felt okay.

"The closest legal brothels are in Pahrump, about an hour west of here. The others are further away, north toward Reno. The big one in Pahrump is the Chicken Ranch."

"Let's go to Pahrump then. If we can't find your mom, we can find a hotel. You'll be close enough to town so that you can still work at the hospital. I can talk to your dad, and maybe we can get past this in a week or so."

It was getting dark when they finished packing the station wagon and the Monte Carlo. Red took along his toolbox and the Honda Trail 70 that he'd lifted into the trunk of his car.

The front wheel and handlebars stuck out from the trunk lid tied down with a bungee cord. He had a map of Nevada in the car and quickly figured out the route—south on the Interstate to Route 160 and then straight west through the mountains and into the desert. He led the way, with Frankie and Bud riding with Claire in her Ford station wagon.

That night, they stayed at the Saddle West Hotel and Casino. Red paid sixty-seven dollars for one room with two full-sized beds. He had room service deliver a cot for Frankie. They ate at the Silver Spur restaurant at the hotel. It was a Saturday, and the buffet special featured prime rib for $9.99 and $4.99 for children under twelve. The cashier did not ask to see Frankie's ID. After dinner, they snuck Bud up through the back.

CHAPTER TWENTY-SEVEN

Deedee always had breakfast ready by noon. The girls usually worked until three or four in the morning and then slept. Some ate at noon, but she made breakfast all the way until three. It was her favorite part of the day, and she laid out six kinds of cereal, a variety of donuts, toast, English muffins, and several jars of jams and jellies. Deedee also played short-order cook and made omelets with cheese, fresh onions and peppers, waffles or sometimes pancakes with blueberries, bacon and sausage, eggs any-way-you-want-'em, and home fries or hash browns. Most of the girls wanted the hot food Deedee made.

She thought breakfast brought them closer together. Normally, there were no parties to work, and there wasn't the distraction of making money or looking good. The girls were expected to wash up and be presentable for breakfast, but they didn't need to apply makeup and could wear a nightie or pajamas. It was a time to talk about their other lives, gossip about the customers, and chat. She didn't have to be the madam, the boss at breakfast. She could just be casual and mother them a little. Her own mom was Christian and always said, "It's hard to remain enemies when you break bread together." Sometimes, she wondered if her parents were still alive. They had a small house in Henderson and would now be in their seventies. She thought if she'd taken one thing from her mom, it was the love of breakfast.

She was turning fifty in June, but in her mind, she was still in her twenties—in her body, too. She'd been waiting for the menopause symptoms, and sometimes she thought they were coming—hot flashes (but it could be 115 degrees in the desert), dryness (but she'd used lube forever), and mood swings (but she lived and worked with ten or fifteen girls and who wouldn't). The one thing she knew was that she still had her period at the end of each pill cycle. And she knew she still liked sex.

There was a new girl, Monica, from LA. She'd been a call girl in Hollywood. She was beautiful with short blond hair, bangs cut straight across, and a small mouth with plump lips colored black. She was in her mid-thirties and older than many of the girls. She came in cocky, like she knew it all, and hardly spoke to the others. During a line-up, while most of the girls wore nighties that the manager, Russ, sold out of a storeroom, Monica wore her own black miniskirt and red underwear. Her top was just a white bandana tied in the back. She looked exotic next to the others and right off did twice as many parties. The Japanese tourists who flew in on private junkets loved Monica. Then, not more than four days after she'd been at the Ranch, she came on to Deedee. It was no more than a touch on the arm and a nice word, but the intention was in her eyes.

She looked at Monica and said, "After you're done tonight, let me know if you'd like some special instruction." Deedee did her best, wicked smile with sexy, squinting eyes.

Deedee lived separately from the girls in her own Airstream out back, and that night, Monica opened the trailer door without knocking. She wore her miniskirt without the red underwear. Monica was the dominant one and did all the instructing. She had Deedee lie naked on the bed and tied just one wrist to the bedpost with her white bandana. She did all the nice stuff with her tongue, lips, hands, and nipples. But she also did naughty stuff with her teeth and nails. It wasn't so much how she did it—Deedee had seen and done everything—it was when she did it, the timing and alternation between naughty and nice. It was like a choreographed Vegas show—all synchronized legs, twirls, and feathers. It was the best sex Deedee'd had in years.

They'd done it a few times since, and the thought and anticipation were taking over her mind. She was having a hard time focusing on breakfast.

Sunday morning, just one hundred twenty-six days before her fiftieth birthday, she was making breakfast and thinking about the previous night with Monica. She heard the doorbell ring and thought it was probably a group of golfers up from Las Vegas to play the Lake View course. Golf seemed to be the only source of parties on a Sunday during the early afternoon. She put down her spatula and walked to the door. She looked through the peephole first and saw a younger woman and a larger man standing in the outer patio entrance. Not golfers. She opened the door. Sometimes couples wanted company.

Deedee said, "Welcome to the world-famous Chicken Ranch." It was a greeting Russ insisted on. "Ya'll come on in." "Ya'll" was also part of the act.

The two stepped into the large sitting room, where they did the line-ups. Immediately, she sensed the young woman staring at her and felt uncomfortable, like she was being judged. Normally, she would've had them sit down on the sofa and then round up a few girls who were ready to work, but she wasn't sure these two were here for a party. Deedee asked, "How can I help you?"

The man was quiet and looked over to the girl, who Deedee guessed would do all the talking.

"Deedee?" She asked.

Deedee looked at the girl, and the first thing she saw was the broken nose. Then she saw the straight black hair like hers, the large dark eyes, and the narrow face. The girl reminded Deedee of her own mother. Claire—it had to be Claire. A sadness came over her. She felt the edges of her mouth turn down and the beginning of tears. Then, it was as if her heart stopped. All the energy left her body, and for a moment, before she fainted, Deedee wondered if this woozy feeling was another symptom of menopause.

———

Deedee let Claire, Red, Frankie, and Bud take the trailer. She quickly moved clothes, makeup, toiletries, and jewelry into a spare room in the brothel. She told Russ she was taking the afternoon off and asked Claire if she wanted to go out for coffee. They drove Claire's car to a diner five minutes away. It was after lunch and before dinner, and the place was empty. Deedee had no car and rarely left the Ranch, so the waitress had no idea who she was.

They sat down on opposite sides of a booth. Deedee reached out across the table with both hands open, palms up. Claire sat still for a second. Then Deedee shook her outstretched hands, and Claire finally reached over and held them. Deedee smiled. A tear was making its way down the crevice of her cheek, and she could feel it tickle, like a sneeze coming on. She said, "How have you been, honey?"

Claire had only said they were in trouble and needed a place to stay. She said, "I'm fine," and then wondered what Deedee knew of her life and the lives of Frank and Sally. She decided to tell Sally's story with Dominic, then Wood, and Frankie. Somehow, Deedee knew some of it but needed the details. "What did Sally look like? Is Frank still as handsome as ever? Why is that boy Frankie so strange?" Claire talked about Frankie and his autism, Frank and Tramps, and Sally. Claire went on to say that Sally had supposedly left town with another guy. She told Deedee about how Wood was looking for some money that he thought she or Frankie had. Wood was crazy and had threatened her. He'd tried to take Frankie and had cut Red when he tried to stop him. Sally hadn't contacted anyone since she supposedly left, and she didn't think Sally would have abandoned Frankie. The word "abandon" hung in Claire's mind like a dull sinus headache.

Deedee said, "Claire, I'm sorry for everything. I truly am, and I wish things had been different. It was just all so crazy in Vegas."

"I was twelve years old when you left."

"I wasn't much of a mother to you or Sally. Not much of a wife either, I guess."

"I want to know what happened." Claire still held Deedee's hands and now squeezed them tighter. She wasn't looking for an explanation; she was looking for a connection. Deedee pulled away from Claire's hands and reached into her purse for a cigarette. She offered one to Claire and lit both with a disposable lighter.

Deedee began. "You know Frank was my first love. I was seventeen, and we were both working at the Sands. Las Vegas was exciting, and I met lots of the celebrities coming through town—Vic Damone, Frank Sinatra, Dean Martin, Jerry Lewis, and many more. I was a cocktail waitress and met them all. Frank was only a bartender, but he was one of the most handsome guys in town, and girls were falling all over themselves to get a date with him. But as far as I know, he didn't date. One night, I just cornered him and made him take me out. We dated, and I got knocked up with Sally. What I didn't know was that Frank had enlisted in the army. He was shipped out to Korea just after Sally was born.

"I was eighteen. I wasn't ready to be a mom and care for a kid. I was beautiful back then, and men asked me out all the time—guys with money and power. I didn't want to give all that up. And yes, I was selfish. I sent Sally to live with her grandparents in Henderson and sent my mom and dad money every month.

"When Frank returned four years later, he wanted to get married and do the family thing. I went along with it for a while. But by then I was sometimes making a thousand a week as a casino host. Frank was back bartending, pulling down maybe two hundred. And I liked my life. I wore the best clothes and had my hair done twice a week. I had real jewels. The casino bosses would call me and want me to show a high-roller a good time. I'd go to dinner and a show and then play the tables. I drank champagne. I was good luck, and the tips were unbelievable.

"But I wasn't much of a mother to Sally, or a wife to Frank. Not that Frank was much of a husband. He just never seemed interested, and sometimes, I think he was just fine with me going out each night. It wasn't like he complained."

Claire exhaled smoke. "Is he gay?"

"One morning, I was looking in his dresser for money. I

was light and just needed cab fare. I found his porn mags. I never said anything to him, and it wasn't like I could cast the first stone.

"Anyway, I got pregnant again. By then, I'd figured I could double the money I made by having sex with the guy. It's funny, it started slowly. Sometimes, I'd do a date and the guy would be good-looking and fun, and I'd just want to sleep with him. I'd always make a better tip and didn't have to ask. Then it just got easy to do, and I just fucked everyone. I used protection, but something happened."

Deedee paused, and Claire said, "So who is he?"

"Honey, I just don't know. It was either a Jewish guy from New York or a mobster from Kansas City. Or it could have been the casino boss I was dating—who's now either in prison or dead. After you were born, though, I knew it wasn't the Japanese guy or the Indian rajah."

Claire smiled.

Deedee went on. "So I had you. Frank obviously knew the baby wasn't his, but he went along. Then, three years later, Frank up and re-enlisted. I was furious, but he was already shipping out the next week by the time he told me. I sent you and your sister back to my mom and dad's in Henderson."

"My half-sister," Claire said.

"Right, your half-sister. It was the sixties then, and I was probably the highest-paid escort in Vegas. Every mob boss in America wanted me on their arm and in their bed. I got introduced to all the stars. For a while, I dated Bobby Darin, who was two years younger than me. I could tell you some stories."

Deedee paused and smoked and then resumed. "Frank didn't come back until around 1971. He stayed in Vietnam that long. By then, I hardly knew you girls, and I was not mother material. It just wasn't for me. Frank tried, though. He brought you both back to Vegas and hired that French girl, Beatrice, to help. I had some regular boyfriends off and on and was rarely home to see you girls. You might say I was disconnected.

"By the end of the seventies, I was a mess in every way. I was deep into coke and booze. I was no longer the champagne girl—more the Smirnoff girl. I was doing tricks just for drugs. I was still good-looking and escorted, but the guys I was going out with were, well, regular. Frank wouldn't let me near the two of you, probably for good reasons.

"The Ranch saved me in a way. About five years ago, a guy I know, Ken Green, bought the place. At the time, I was living in a motel on the Strip. I was messed up on booze and drugs, and I lived with a guy who was pimping me out. Ken knew I was out of control in Vegas—funny, he even called me "Vegas." Ken needed an older and experienced woman to help run the girls. He moved me up here with Russ, his manager. At the Ranch, I'm away from all the booze and drugs, and we're not normally allowed off the property. Ken and Russ are careful with the town and don't want us to mingle. So we work and have fun, and I've been mostly sober for all of these five years."

Claire asked, "Do you like the girls?"

"They come and go. The way it works is three weeks on, one week off. When they're here, they work seven days a week. The girls are all independent contractors and take fifty percent of whatever they bring in. It's good money; they can make two thousand a week. We've got rules, and Russ and I are the rule enforcers. If they don't like it, they can always leave. A few have been here as long as I have, and we're like family. We work, talk, have fun, cry, and help each other out. I make them breakfast every morning."

Deedee looked Claire in the eyes. "But it's not a place for you."

Claire leaned back in her seat. "What do you mean?"

"I heard you were escorting, that's all."

"How did you know?"

Deedee said, "The nose knows."

"Reuben?"

"Reuben was my coke dealer back in the day. I bought a lot of coke from him over the years. Now he's a customer of mine. He comes up here once every month or so to relax."

Claire said, "I'm done with all that. I work at Sunrise Hospital now."

"That's great you got out. So, who's this Red guy?"

"Actually, he's my landlord. He owns the house where Frankie and I are living. He lives in a smaller house out back. He's helped me with Frankie and now Wood. He's been great, but I'm sorry I got him wrapped up in our family's bullshit."

"Can you get him to lose some weight? He might not be half bad looking if he dropped fifty pounds."

Claire laughed. "It's not like that." She did think that Red was great with Frankie—and funny. He was relaxed in a way that she'd never been, like the world was just there and could do what it wanted, and he was going to do what *he* wanted— like he'd come to terms with the world. Claire was far from it. The world seemed like it was still chewing her up.

CHAPTER TWENTY-EIGHT

What had Red seen? The desert beyond the mountains was a moonscape of flat white sand and scrub brush in every direction. The single-lane highway went straight for miles, and Red steered with one thumb, his T-shirt stained with a dirt skid where his massive stomach sometimes touched the wheel. Right before the town of Pahrump, he saw the sign for the Chicken Ranch with red lettering on a white background. Underneath, in big block letters, BROTHEL. The Ranch was a few miles south and west of the highway, desolate and surrounded by more desert, some irrigated farmland, and the kind of junk farmers never threw out but seemingly never used. The driveway and parking lot were gravel with parking strips marked off by old tires painted white. The main building was a one-story ranch-style home. Attached was a string of narrow buildings like trailer homes stitched together. The whole compound was surrounded by an eight-foot-tall chain-link fence interspersed with gates. Behind the complex, he saw a gravel airplane runway with a windsock dragging east. An

Airstream trailer was outside the fence and near the runway.

A sign said, ENTER HERE. A gap in the fence led to the main building. Red parked the Monte Carlo and, with Claire, walked through the gap. Frankie and Bud stayed in the Ford with the windows rolled down. At the building's entrance, they pressed a red doorbell the size of a pinball plunger. A minute later, the lock on the front door buzzed, and they entered. Inside was a large living room decorated with acres of framed mirrors, gold-leaf-painted tables, and several white couches covered in clear plastic. Even the throw pillows were covered in plastic, which made Red think of bodily fluids.

Deedee had black hair just past her shoulders that was feathered and curled. She wore heavy black eyeliner and red lipstick. Her eyes were dark, and Red thought she looked like a combination of Liz Taylor and Raquel Welch, though where one ended and the other began, he couldn't fathom. He could see her age in the lines around her eyes and jaw, but her skin was creamy, and he felt like a schlub in her presence. When Deedee fainted, he paused for a split second and moved quickly to break her fall. He grabbed her by the waist, and as she slipped down, his fingers touched her breasts.

They didn't stay in the house long. Deedee led them outside to the Airstream, and he sat with Frankie and Bud on a picnic table under an awning while she and Claire moved things around inside. In the afternoon, he and Frankie moved the stuff from the cars into the trailer. The trailer was forty feet long and sat on three sets of wheels, but it still only had one bedroom. In the living room, a sofa folded out into a second bed, and the kitchen table could be converted into a third. He put Frankie and his stuff in the living room and Claire's in the bedroom. Afterward, he lifted the minibike from his trunk and looked around for a place Frankie could ride. The brothel was surrounded by desert, and it seemed there was no place he couldn't. Red crossed the road with Frankie, who was wearing his new helmet. He told Frankie to have fun but to not cross any roads. He took off on the Honda, and Red watched the cloud of desert dust move into the distance.

That evening, Deedee gave Red and Claire a tour of the brothel. The first thing Red saw was the movement of girls, all dressed in negligees and crisscrossing the brothel seemingly without purpose. Claire was introduced as "My daughter, Claire." They hugged and kissed her and then hugged her again. Red was "Claire's friend, Red." He received no hugs and kisses, just nods and polite smiles. The girls lived in one wing of the compound. In the compound's center was a large kitchen with a table that could seat a dozen or more. The girls lined up for customers in the front living room, and the opposite wing was where the girls did their business. Deedee showed them the Jacuzzi room with mirrors on the ceiling. Most of the other rooms were smaller, with just a queen-sized bed and nightstand. The final stop was the VIP room with its round bed, a ceiling mirror, and what she called "the passion chair." Deedee seemed proud of it and said it came all the way from Amsterdam. The red chair was a tangle of rubberized steel tubing with platforms for sitting or lying down and what looked like handlebars. She explained that three people could easily be intertwined on it in various positions, and she showed how the platforms could be adjusted up or down. It was a jungle gym for adults, and Red figured his weight would break it.

They were finishing the tour when they heard a plane descend and land on the runway outside. Deedee explained that it was turnaround time for the girls, that it was all hands on deck to service a junket of Japanese tourists and then turn the plane back around to Vegas. Deedee led them outside and through the gate to the Airstream. She said, "Unfortunately, that's all you get to see. The rules are, no friends or family, and I just made the one exception. I'll see you in the morning." Deedee looked at Claire and added, "Love you."

Red drove into town later and picked up a six-pack of Budweiser and a four-pack of Bartles and Jaymes. He stopped at a McDonald's and bought food for the three of them. When he returned to the Airstream, it was cooler outside, and Claire had set up the picnic table with plates, silverware, and napkins for two. It was Sunday and Frankie was inside watching *MacGyver* with Bud. Claire bought Frankie his dinner while Red unpacked the rest of the food. They sat down, ate, drank, and watched the airplane turn around on the tarmac and fly out in the dark. Cars came and went from the parking lot.

After dinner, Claire lit up a cigarette. Red hadn't smoked in years, but it looked good—relaxing—and he asked her for one. Claire passed over the pack and her lighter. Red lit up, inhaled, and it *was* good.

Red decided to tell a funny story he'd heard years before, changing the details some. "Did I tell you what happened last week? It was strange."

Claire looked over. "No, what?"

"Well, I was driving home late at night from the El Cortez, where I had their two ninety-nine steak-and-eggs breakfast that starts at midnight. Anyway, I was on a backstreet driving when a cat ran out in front of the car, and I hit it."

"You hit a cat? Did you kill it?"

"There was nothing I could do. I couldn't avoid it. The cat ran out fast and right under the car. I felt the bump and stopped. Yes, I killed it."

Claire said, "That's so sad."

"I tried to do the right thing. The cat was white, and I went door to door to find the owner. I was asking if they had a white cat or knew a neighbor who had one. It was late, and I was waking people up. I think someone called the police.

"Anyway, I found the owner—a nice lady who came out in her housecoat. I told her that her cat had died, that I had run it over, and that it was an accident. The lady started crying, and I didn't know what to do. At first, I offered to buy her another cat, but she said she didn't want another one; she wanted the one she had. I said again that I was sorry, and I offered her money. I pulled out two twenties. The lady looked at the bills for a second, then just took 'em. I left."

Claire said, "That *is* strange."

"Yeah, what's even stranger is that when I got back to my car, the police were there, and they asked what I was doing going door to door in the neighborhood. I told them the whole story. I told them about the lady who lost her cat—who I'd just given forty dollars. The cops stepped back and whispered to each other, and I couldn't hear what they were saying. Then they just walked past me and up to the lady's house. They rang the doorbell, and she answered. Now the cops told her she was under arrest, that she had to go downtown. They took her away in cuffs."

"That's horrible! Why'd they do that?"

Red looked at Claire and smiled. "I asked the cops that. The one just looked at me and said very slowly that she was under arrest...for selling her pussy!" He laughed, then stuck the cigarette into his mouth and inhaled. He had forgotten how good smoking was.

Claire looked at Red and didn't smile or laugh, and Red thought maybe he'd gone too far. Claire squinted at him and said, "That cigarette looks like a matchstick stuck in an asshole."

Red smiled and rolled his eyes. He left the cigarette in his mouth, blew out his cheeks, and puckered his lips.

Thankfully, Claire laughed.

CHAPTER TWENTY-NINE

Frankie liked shapes and the way certain shapes fit together. The most exciting shape was the disk on the Honda's rear sprocket with cogs that fit between the links of the drive chain. In his mind, the cogs and the chain made him feel like he belonged. The feeling made him want to ride the Honda forever.

Frankie drove with Red to the highway the next day and bought gas. The gas can was red and round with a round spout that screwed into curved pressed threads. Frankie liked round things, like the sprocket. The can held five gallons and could fill up the motorcycle exactly two times. He could go five hours on a tank of gas, 150 miles on the odometer.

They stopped at a store that sold food, and Red bought things they could eat for breakfast and lunch, like bread, cheese, ham, mayonnaise, potato chips, eggs, bacon, and Honeycombs cereal, Frankie's favorite. Each piece of cereal had seven round holes. There was an *O* in "Honey" and an *O* in "Comb."

After lunch, he drove his motorcycle around in the desert. Red had told him to stay within the roads. *Don't cross the roads.* He did a loop following the border and saw on the odometer that the roads were exactly one mile long before they hit another road going perpendicular. He could go through all four gears between roads, up to fifty miles per hour. He did three loops around the border and figured he could do at least thirty-five more laps on his tank of gas.

The motor sounded perfect to him—a hum that was comforting, that drove out other sounds like talking.

The desert was white, gravelly, and flat. There were grasses like dried spices and small bushes with short woody branches. He found one mound of dirt that he could use as a jump, and on each lap, he tried to take the jump just a little bit faster. He could see mountains in the distance.

Opposite the ranch, across the road a mile away, Frankie could see what looked like a dirt track through the desert. He crossed the road. He wasn't supposed to, but he did. The track seemed to be made for motorcycles—not quite wide enough for cars. He followed the track, which stayed within the next set of four roads and circled a lot littered with old rusting cars. He counted two jumps where he could get half his height off the ground. The corners had heaved edges where he could carry more speed through a turn. Another section of track had eight rows of mounded dirt that felt loopy like a carnival ride he once went on with his mother, Sally. And for a few minutes, he stopped and took his helmet off. It was hot. He remembered the last time he saw Sally. She lay still on the kitchen floor with Wood standing above her. He'd gone into the basement and never saw her again.

He heard Red yelling his name. Red's Monte Carlo was parked on the road he'd crossed. He wanted to yell back and say, "Red." He wanted to talk with Red, but what he thought and what his mouth did were disconnected. It was like seeing something that was just out of his reach. It was there, and if it were just a little closer, he'd be able to feel it. It would be real. He couldn't make his mouth and its words real.

He tried, and what he heard was a high-pitched, "Ahhh." More like a buzzer than a name.

CHAPTER THIRTY

Wood stopped in at Reuben's on Thursday before his shift at the club. He'd stayed up late Wednesday night, hanging out at Tramps and doing a few lines with Chris, before going home and watching a Betamax copy of Urban Cowboy on Frank's TV. He pretty much thought Travolta's character, Bud, was a pussy, and his leaving Pam, who was hot and rich for Sissy, who was not so hot and somewhat of a nag, seemed almost unimaginable. But who he really liked was Scott Glenn, Wes—one bad motherfucker—and Wood fell asleep thinking about that bitch at Wells Fargo and how he would love to shove a gun under her chin and say, "Hand it over, honey." After a few hours' sleep, he'd driven his dead-pet route through the city and out into the desert. Now, in an hour, he needed to clock in at the club. The Reuben's bartender came over and tossed a beverage napkin on the bar. "Wood, how you doin'?"

Wood could not remember his name again and simply said, "Hey."

"What can I get you?"

Wood ordered a Coors. Across the bar was the guy with the pink-tinted aviator glasses who'd sold him coke a month before. He also wore a black leather motorcycle jacket with a thin collar, and Wood figured the glasses were a functional thing and not a faggot thing, like yellow-tinted shooting glasses or glare-resistant driving glasses. And now Wood thought they looked cool. He nodded to the guy. Wood had about six hundred bucks in his pocket.

When the beer came, Wood motioned the bartender closer, "Can your guy hook me up with a gram?"

The bartender nodded and then went over and talked to the guy with the glasses. He stood up and Wood followed him into the bathroom. On the way, he reached over the bar and pinched a swizzle stick coke spoon from the cocktail waitress station. The guy locked the door to the bathroom. Up close, he had a trimmed blond beard like a five-o'clock shadow—like George Michael. Wood exchanged five twenties for a gram and then asked the guy, "Any interest in steroids? Fina?"

He dropped his head and looked over the top of his glasses like some old man with readers, "I don't fuck with that."

"Can you move some? I've got like a case of the shit."

"Sorry. No money in steroids. I just do the coke and some weed. I've got some weed on me if you want some." Now, he was looking straight at him, smiling.

Wood said, "No, I'm good." Weed made him turn inward, and he'd had enough crazy thoughts already. Also, he needed to be sharp to work the club. Coke, not weed.

The guy left. Wood locked the bathroom door again, stood over the sink, and did two hits in each nostril while watching himself in the mirror. He had an instant rush, euphoria, and the coke turned his whole being around, just that fast, like the first rum punch on a Mexican vacation. And he made a promise to himself that one day he would do that, take a vacation.

Wood sat back at hisbar stool and then just stared, spaced out, at the fish tank behind the bar. He fantasized about Mexico—Cabo or Cancun—and who he'd go with. He knew an older divorced woman at Tramps who'd been flirting with him. She drove a two-door Cadillac Eldorado with a convertible top. Wood knew the lady was kind of a slut and had already slept with both Big Tony and Little Tony. She'd go with him—she might even pay. Then Wood remembered seeing Apple at Reuben's and thought she'd be great on a vacation. He imagined her in a G-string bikini and then imagined her giving him head on a deserted beach under the hot sun. He could feel a stirring in his dick, a chubby. He motioned the bartender over. Wood asked, "You seen Apple?"

"Funny thing, I haven't seen her around in like a week." He paused. "You know Mae?"

"Her boss, yeah. I do work for Mae now and then."

"Well, Mae was in the other night looking for Apple too. Apparently, she hasn't called in. Mae got into her apartment, and all her stuff is still there. She just disappeared."

Wood said, "Weird." Then added, "I guess it's going around." People disappearing—Sally, Lamar—and he wondered why he fucking said that. Stupid, but the bartender left to make drinks for another customer.

The thought that Apple was gone soured his fantasy and left his dick limp. It changed his mood, made him bitter, and all he could think about were his problems. He didn't have his thirty-two thousand five hundred. He wasn't moving any Fina and didn't think he'd ever do another run to Tijuana. The pet route was good money but wasn't a business he could grow—

it was already getting crowded in the desert. And sooner or later, someone, like a cop, would start asking real questions about Sally—Frank was asking questions already. Only Frankie knew something. He was the only one who might say something, but Wood had only heard those strange noises coming from the kid's mouth. Then Wood remembered seeing Frankie with the fat man, and they seemed to be talking. What did the kid know? What could he say?

He'd gone back to the adobe house the day after he cut the fat man. The place was empty, and Wood figured they got scared and moved out. He'd find Claire and the kid and get his money. He'd keep Frankie from talking.

———

Wood did two more hits of coke in the Tramps parking lot and then unbuckled his pants to shoot 500 milligrams of Fina. Wood had weighed himself almost every day on the scale in Frank's bathroom. He thought he'd easily gained ten pounds of muscle and had only lifted at Eiferman's twice. He felt like Popeye after eating spinach. Wood buckled his pants and then changed into a Tramps polo shirt and embroidered Tramps yellow silk jacket.

At eleven, he was at the front door when DJ Dan D started the dance music. The club was busy by midnight, but not enough to start a line. Overall, he thought Thursdays weren't as busy as they used to be and wondered where everyone was going. Wood had heard a rumor that someone bought the old Jubilation on Harmon and was opening a new place called the Shark Club. Wood didn't know if it would be sports-themed around "Tark the Shark" Tarkanian at UNLV or shark-themed like, he guessed, with sharks. Anyway, if that was the next hot dance club, he would apply for a door position. Wood knew all the regulars and high rollers in Vegas. They'd need him, and Frank could go fuck himself.

Around one o'clock, Wood watched a guy and a girl scream at each other in front of a booth near the front door. The woman's hair was spread out all crazy like a dust mop, and her head recoiled back and forth with every sprayed word spoken. The guy just stood there solid and returned whatever words she fired. He was to-the-bone skinny and his eyes buggy, and Wood figured both for crystal-meth tweakers. Then the skinny guy lifted his arm back and slapped her so hard she fell to the ground. Instantly, she was up again, and now the two were at each other with non-stop dog-paddle slaps. Then, somehow, both tripped and fell. The guy then rolled over and pinned her to the floor, her dust-moppy hair spread out and, Wood imagined, collecting dust. People near cleared space and looked on like it was just part of the Tramps show.

He motioned Carl inside. Wood reached the two first, grabbed the skinny guy around the neck in a chokehold, and lifted him off the girl. He was light and couldn't have weighed more than a hundred pounds. Wood carried the guy by the neck toward the front door. Carl stayed behind and tried to help the girl to stand. He reached for her shoulder and arm, but she jumped up on her own and ran toward Wood. Carl held her back by the waist.

She screamed, "Let him go, you motherfucker, you're hurting him."

Wood continued carrying the guy through the doors and finally had him face-down on the pavement outside. Wood put his knee into the guy's back, then cuffed his wrists. Carl still held the girl by the waist, but now both were outside, and the girl was still screaming, "Motherfucker, cocksucker, let him go or I'll call the police." She spat at Wood, but the phlegm landed short. She made a deep retching sound and hawked up more phlegm. She spat again, this time with a higher trajectory, and the wad hit Wood on the cheek. And what went through his mind was, *you fucking cunt*, and he wiped off the phlegm by forcing the guy's cuffed arm to his face. She then violently twisted away from Carl. When she closed the four-step gap to Wood, he stood and landed a straight-on punch to her face. Her head was thrown backward, and Carl caught her before she hit the pavement. Carl turned her over, still knocked out and limp, and cuffed her wrists. He said to Wood, "Sorry, man."

When Wood looked around after hitting the girl, he saw Frank standing at the door. Frank didn't say anything or move to help.

Quickly, the girl came to, and before Carl picked her up off the pavement, he had Holt get him a bar towel from inside. Carl draped the towel over her head so she could no longer spit. Wood and Carl then walked the two behind the club, where they had a small storage room sometimes used like a holding cell. In the room, they pulled IDs and took photos, and Wood read the eighty-sixed speech. They closed the storage room door. Carl returned to the front of the club while Wood called the police from the office.

Wood sat in the office afterward and tried to calm himself. He knew it was a typical domestic dispute where you save the girl from the abusive boyfriend, and then she attacks *you* for somehow abusing *him*. But he couldn't get over it. His heart pounded in his chest, and his arms seemed ready to burst the seams of his shirt. His face felt red, and he wanted to toss the desk and smash the filing cabinet. He slammed his fists down onto his thighs and tried to breathe deeply.

He sat there until Frank walked in. He asked Wood, "Are you okay?"

"I'm fine. That cunt spit in my face, and I'm trying to get over it."

"Okay, take the time you need. I can watch the front door 'til you get back. And let's talk later. Maybe drive with me to do the deposit. I can show you how." Frank closed the door and left.

Wood sat there. Talking to Frank had already calmed him or distracted him. Now Frank wanted to meet later. What was that all about? Either he was actually going to show him the ropes and allow him to do drops in the future, or he was going chew him out for punching the girl. Either way, he wished he could just down a few drinks after work and go home.

CHAPTER THIRTY-ONE

Frank had met Craig in an empty church parking lot that couldn't be seen from the street. Craig had given him a blow job and then a cassette tape of a group called Wham! Driving to work the next day, Frank listened to the tape and turned up the volume. "Wake Me Up" was cute and very pop, but not a great dance song. "Careless Whisper" was a great slow song. But it was "Everything She Wants" that was danceable.

After the music at the club started, Frank walked back to the DJ booth with the cassette. DJ Dan D was spinning records on the two turntables— "Danny" to Frank because he thought the phony DJ Dan D name was, well, phony. He cupped one side of the headphones over an ear and matched beats by finger-tapping the vinyl to slow it down or speed it up. Then, he moved the slide control to fade one song into another. Couples kept dancing as though the two songs were just one long piece of music. Danny put the headphones down and looked at Frank. "Hey, Frank, what's up?"

Frank had a love-hate relationship with Danny. Frank

knew he was the best DJ in Las Vegas because everyone, including Craig, told him. Danny could mix, but he could also MC and talk. He understood the room's mood and could create energy, get people dancing, and then change the music to turn over the dance floor and get people buying drinks. Frank figured he'd invested over two hundred grand in audio equipment, lights, video, and vinyl. Danny took care of the stuff like it was his, and he probably thought it *was* his—which was the hate part. Danny did what he wanted in the booth, rarely taking customer requests or listening to Frank. He had even caught Danny doing coke. Anyone else would have been fired. But there were employees, and then there were *employees*. Frank knew he couldn't easily replace Danny.

Frank showed him the cassette tape. "Have you heard this? Great stuff. I like the song, 'Everything She Wants.'"

Danny gave him that stare and smirk that said, "You're a complete idiot." He looked away from Frank and picked through his records. He pulled up the Wham! album, *Make It Big,* and put it inches in front of Frank's face. "Came out in 1984, Frank. I've played that song every week for the past year." Danny pulled the record from the sleeve and looked closely at the grooves. "It's getting worn down; you might need to find me a new copy."

Frank said, "Fuck you, Danny," and walked away. He was halfway across the club when he heard the Wham! song fading in. He turned around and looked toward the booth. Danny had turned his overhead light on so that Frank could see him. He held up his middle finger and then, over the microphone, said, "Frank Welch, welcome to Tramps!" Frank forced a huge smile, showing his glowing, white-capped teeth.

By midnight, the club was crowded. Frank made his rounds every half hour, acknowledging regular customers, watching the tables and bar tops, and looking for empty glassware, a sign that the cocktail waitresses weren't keeping up. Frank was at the bar drinking coffee when the couple started fighting near the front door. He could see customers stepping back and making room for the two. He walked in that direction. Wood and Carl had already taken the two outside when he got there. He then saw the girl wrench herself away from Carl and lunge toward Wood. He saw Wood punch her and then saw her cuffed and dead-looking on the pavement. It was at that moment he thought of Sally. He knew Wood had killed her.

Nothing made sense. Sally wouldn't leave and not talk to him. She would never leave Frankie. She wouldn't leave her car and her house. And she wouldn't leave her makeup and bank savings behind. If there was a scam at the Westward Ho, she wasn't the type to think it up or even do it. But Wood *was* the type, and if Wood was looking for the money, it was because Sally didn't have it. He'd killed her trying to get it.

In that moment of clarity, Frank decided he would kill Wood. The decision was instantaneous and irrevocable, as simple as understanding from the acid bile souring your throat that you were going to vomit.

Frank asked Wood to go along with him to make the deposit. They'd drive to the bank, and there'd be an attempted robbery.

He walked out to his Mercedes and sat behind the wheel. His Remington .45 was under the seat. He took it out and first checked the clip. He then pulled back the slide and chambered a round. He flipped off the safety and placed the gun within easy reach in the open side compartment of the driver-side door.

CHAPTER THIRTY-TWO

Wood was off at three and waited for Frank to finish whatever he was doing in the office. He went out to his truck and fired up the engine just to listen to its low, throaty idle. He still had coke left and did two hits in each nostril with a swizzle-stick coke spoon. He sat still and felt the numbing in the back of his throat, then the energy hitting his brain. The earlier combination of coke and Fina had felt good, so he pulled a syringe, needle, and vial from his glove compartment and did another 500 milligrams in his left bicep. Rocket fuel. He did two more hits of coke and then turned off the engine. He walked back to the club and entered through the exit near the office.

Frank was just inside. He held a dark blue deposit sack with the embroidered name Tramps. The sack, the size of a lady's clutch, had a zipper pull pressed behind a key lock. Frank said, "Let's go." Wood followed him to the Mercedes. Frank got in first and then unlocked the passenger door. Wood stepped into the car. He felt low to the ground, and it was now that he'd either get chewed out for hitting the girl or get a lesson on how to run the business.

Frank started talking. "I usually do the deposit four times a week on my way home from work. After I get off working Thursday nights, I do the deposit from Tuesday and Wednesday. Since Sally's not around, I could use some help, so maybe you could do a few of the drops for me."

Wood was relieved to simply learn the business. "Sure, Frank," he said.

Frank pulled onto Flamingo Road and drove east toward the Strip. They passed the new Gold Coast casino, then the Interstate overpass, and went down toward Caesars. Frank drove slowly, cars passing him on the left. "So you still haven't heard from Sally?"

"No, Frank."

"How long has it been? Two months now?"

"Yeah, I guess so," Wood said.

"You know we had Sally before I went to Korea, and I didn't see her for four years. Then, in the sixties, I was gone again for another four years in Vietnam. I barely raised her. Mostly, her grandparents did. When I was finally back in the States, Sally was seventeen and almost an adult. After graduating high school, she and her sister moved in with me and their mom. When I started Tramps, she was right by my side. And while her mom was fucking everyone in town, Sally helped me go over design plans, figure out uniforms, hire employees, and do a million other things. I was good with the ideas, but Sally was good with the details. And she was reliable. Deedee and Claire went off to fuck their way through life, but Sally stayed close to the business and to me."

Wood couldn't remember the last time Frank had spoken so many words to him. He had trouble following, but what he clearly heard was the anger in Frank's voice. He didn't like where this was going. He felt the pounding in his chest again and the tension in his arms. He reached to his side and silently unsnapped the sheath looped on his belt. He touched the top of his folding Buck.

Frank continued. "Sally knew she was my only heir. The business would be hers, along with everything I own and everything I've saved. I don't believe she would just walk away from that. I believe she would walk away from you, maybe even trade you in for this Lamar guy. But she wouldn't just leave like she did—like you say she did."

"Frank, I don't know what you're saying. She left me. It's not my fault."

Frank pulled into the bank parking lot and stopped the car. "When I saw you hit that girl tonight and knock her out, I knew you were a bad man."

"Frank, she came at me. You saw her." Wood pulled the knife out of its sheath and, with his thumb and forefinger, lifted the blade up. He opened it the rest of the way by dragging its point against the seat's leather.

"Let me finish," Frank said. He reached into the side pocket and gripped the pistol with his left hand. He lifted it up and pointed the barrel across his lap at Wood. "I'm sure you killed my daughter, and now you're trying to rob me." Frank smiled, that smile.

Wood saw the gun and, at the same time, lifted his knife. The gun went off, but there was no jolt from a bullet entering his body. Wood plunged the knife deep into Frank's stomach. The motion knocked the gun loose, and it dropped to the car floor. Wood let go of the knife handle and reached for the gun. Frank looked down at the knife, stunned. Wood lifted the gun and pulled the trigger three times, hitting Frank in the chest with all three bullets. The jolt of the bullets pushed Frank against the car's window.

Wood quickly felt his stomach, checking to see if he'd been hit or grazed. He looked down and saw a tuft of white padding sticking out from a hole in his jacket. He found a second hole and realized that Frank had hit the jacket but barely missed his stomach.

He looked at Frank. His eyes were staring at him, and he was gasping. He touched the knife handle sticking out from his stomach. Frank said softly, "This can't happen to me." He was no longer smiling.

Wood saw Frank's breathing slow and then finally stop. His eyes stayed open, but the intensity was gone. Then Wood smelled the stench and thought Frank's bowels must've emptied. Wood waited a minute and calmed himself. He then reached over and pulled the knife from Frank's stomach. It came out easily. As almost an afterthought, Wood reached up and pulled Frank's left ear by the upper rim, then slit it off. He dropped the bloody ear onto Frank's lap.

He wiped the blade on Frank's pants, then folded it back into its handle. He put the gun in his coat pocket and then grabbed the deposit bag in the tray between the seats. He folded the bag around Frank's ear and put it in his other pocket. Wood opened the car door. When he stood up, he felt his boxers stick to the skin of his ass. He realized then that the stench had come from him.

———

Wood couldn't stay on Flamingo and be seen, so he walked up Koval Lane and through the maze of low-rent two and three-story cinderblock apartments. He crossed a street and entered the strip mall parking lot where Battista's Italian Restaurant advertised all-you-can-drink Chianti wine. Farther down was a small local casino called the Stage Door. Inside, he found the men's restroom and closed himself into a stall. He took off his shoes and then his pants. He peeled away his boxers from his ass and carefully stepped out of each leg. He threw the boxers into the toilet. He wiped the rest of the shit away with handfuls of toilet paper, piling the soiled paper on top of his boxers, now floating in the bowl. He put his pants and shoes back on and then flushed the toilet. The bowl quickly clogged, and the water inched up to the top. Wood fled the bathroom before the water crested and spilled onto the floor.

He walked next door to the Maxim Hotel and Casino. He remembered that he had gotten free tickets to a Maxim show a year earlier and had taken Sally. It was called *The Playboy Girls of Rock and Roll* and featured a foxy Playmate of the Month. There were plenty of bare breasts and lots of boob jobs, and Sally liked it just as much as he did. Both were turned on and drove home to have great sex. Then he wondered where it had all gone so fucking wrong. Why couldn't Sally have just been cool about the money? Why did she have to go screaming her head off like some tweaked-out club chick? He could be sitting in the Cabo sun with Sally instead of sneaking through the back streets of Vegas in foul, shit-stained pants.

Wood walked into the Maxim, then turned around and came out like he'd just finished gambling. He stood at the curb and had a valet signal for a cab. Inside the cab, he opened the window and hoped the driver didn't notice or mention the stench that still shrouded him. He had the cab stop in the parking lot behind Tramps and got out. Wood climbed into his pickup and drove off.

Sometimes, life, everything, gets so crazy that all you can

do is keep moving forward one step at a time. He imagined himself a shark swimming through Las Vegas, making smooth motions left and right, always looking for the twitchy motion of prey, tasting the waters for the tang of blood. Like a shark, he needed to keep moving and eating. That thought led him to remember that he still had coke left. He pulled the small vial from his pants pocket and opened the glove compartment to get another plastic swizzle-stick spoon. He drove with his knees while he did two hits in each nostril. He felt better, and in his shark mind, he swam through each step, each movement through the water: Open the deposit bag. Get his stuff at Franks. Get a room for the night. Show up at work like nothing had happened. Look surprised when he hears that Frank had been robbed and shot dead. Find Frankie and take care of a witness. Get his thirty-two five.

He took the first step.

Wood parked in front of Frank's townhome and removed the deposit bag from his coat pocket. The ear fell onto the floor of the truck. He left it there while he slit open the deposit bag with his knife. Inside were two deposit slips, one from each night. He added the two numbers together and figured around eight grand. In the stacks of hundreds and twenties, though, were personal checks. He left the checks and slips in the bag and stuffed the cash bundles back into his coat pocket. He reached behind his seat and pulled out the pickle jar. Inside, the ears were puckered and preserved. He picked up Frank's ear and added it to the collection.

He did not think anyone knew he was staying at Frank's, and he didn't think it was a good idea to let anyone find out. He undressed, stuffing his soiled clothes into the small bathroom garbage can, and took a shower. He dressed, then collected his other clothes and threw them in a pile. He went through Frank's closet to find a suitcase. Inside the closet was a safe, and Wood tried to think through how he could bust it open or take it with him. He figured it was the place he kept his gun collection and probably a stash of cash. He tried to lift it, but it was bolted to the floor. To bust it open, Wood figured he'd need dynamite or an atomic bomb. Next to the safe, he found Frank's army duffle. Inside were his old uniforms and assorted army stuff. He emptied the contents onto the closet floor. Wood stuffed his clothes into the duffle and left, leaving the safe behind.

Later, he paid cash for a room at the Holiday House near Bob Stupak's Vegas World casino.

CHAPTER THIRTY-THREE

News of Frank's death spread throughout the club. Ed, the Head Bartender, had worked for Frank for the past five years and had taken over from Frank's son-in-law, Dominic. On Frank's nights off, Ed had worked as the manager. He knew the combination to the safe and could do the counts at the end of the night. Frank usually did the drops, but bringing the bag to the bank wasn't hard. Everyone knew Frank just wanted to kill someone. He was bait for any thief who had the guts to try. Well, one had.

Ed was from Minneapolis originally and had learned his trade in the seventies at a disco called Scotty's. He'd started as a barback—restocking coolers, topping ice bins, cutting fruit, cleaning, and more cleaning—and then moved up to bartender. Scotty's had an antique deco interior and a classic mirrored ball over the dance floor that sent lasers of colored light throughout the club. It was packed every night of the week, and he made great money. Then *Saturday Night Fever* came out, and they were even more packed. But the movie spawned other discos further out in the suburbs, and business slowed. Then, the owner got busted for cocaine distribution, and the place closed.

Ed learned showmanship at Scotty's. He could juggle long-neck beer bottles, sending one behind his back or letting one fly to a barback who would snap off the cap for a waiting customer. He could pour a Long Island iced tea with four bottles at the same time, lifting two in each hand. For shooters, Ed would fill a shaker can, cover it with a liter beer glass, and tap it tight. He'd spin the joined can and glass in his palm and then give it a quick slap to break the seal and crack it like an egg into a line of shot glasses. People would order drinks just to see Ed perform.

Why had he moved to Las Vegas? He had a friend moving there to deal cards. That friend had another friend who was already dealing cards and making lots of money. Ed figured, why not tag along? He'd taken another bartending job at a live music club called the Caboose. The money there wasn't good—just young kids ordering Bud long necks and watching the musicians. Few mixed drinks, and instead of shooters, they ordered cheap shots of Old Crow whiskey. At the end of each night, his tip jar was filled with heavy change. So he quit and drove west with his friend. He picked up the bartending job at Tramps that first week. Then, the friend moved back to Minneapolis days later after discovering he'd need to pay for a casino school to learn how to deal cards. Ed stayed. So why had he *really* moved to Vegas? He had no clue, like wondering why he was even born.

That Friday night after Frank was shot, Ed covered his bartender shift and stepped in as manager. He wrote a sign with a black Sharpie that he posted above the time clock:

Fellow Employees,

Frank was found dead this morning in the parking lot of the bank. I think he would have liked us to continue with our jobs and continue making Tramps the success it is. I will work with Frank's bookkeeper to continue making payroll and ensuring all employees are taken care of. Please keep the thought of Frank in the back of your mind and how he would want you to do your job. As Frank would say, "No empty glassware, just full drinks!"
Thanks, Ed.

Wood came in later in the evening, and Ed saw him clock in and read the note. Ed walked over and touched his arm, "Sorry, Wood. I understand if you don't feel like working tonight."

Wood stared ahead and didn't make eye contact. "That's okay, I'd rather keep working. I wouldn't know what to do at home alone."

Ed patted him on the shoulder, "Anything you need."

Ed knew about Sally leaving town and wondered if she'd find out about Frank and return and how long that might take. He also wondered what connection Wood had to Frank and the club. Wood was Frank's relation, but just barely. He knew Frank didn't think much of Wood. He was incapable of doing anything but run the door and provide muscle.

Later that night, Wood approached him. "Ed, let's talk."

Ed walked to the office and opened it with his key. After Wood entered, he shut the door. "What's up, Wood?"

"Since I'm family, I think I should step in for Frank and run the place. I still need your help, and you definitely know what you're doing, but Frank always told me I would take over when the time came." Wood sat on the edge of the desk. Ed sat below him in a swivel office chair. Wood added, "Well, I think it's time."

Ed said, "Okay." He could tell Wood was coked up. His teeth were clamped tight, and the corners of his jaws were twitching. Ed had been around coke seemingly forever, and it didn't take much to tip him off. He'd noticed Wood doing a lot of coke lately and hanging out with Chris, the dealer. Wood also looked bigger and had pimples on his forehead like flea bites. Ed wondered about steroids.

Wood said, "I think you should give me a set of keys and the combination to the safe. Frank showed me how to do the deposit, and I want to make sure the money gets to the bank."

"Wood, I understand your concern, and I have the same concerns. I can try to get you a set of keys made tomorrow. As for the safe, I swore Frank that I'd never tell another soul, and I plan to keep that promise." Ed heard himself say the words, and it sounded plausible and sincere. But when Frank had given him the combination, there was no big ceremony, more like an afterthought on an evening after Dominic had left, and Frank desperately wanted a night off. Since then, Ed had been close to Frank, closer than Wood. He was sure Wood didn't even know Frank was gay.

"Ed, I'm the only family Frank has in town. You need to respect our family."

It was all such bullshit. "Wood, I'm doing what Frank asked me to do. I'm sure you're right, but let's talk to his lawyer. We can call him on Monday. I've got his number in the Rolodex."

"Fuck you, Ed. I'll remember this." Wood stood up, leaving him in the office, staring at the door.

Ed had heard about the new Shark Club opening in the old Jubilation on Harmon and thought he might apply for a bartending job. Or maybe a manager position, and for a moment, Ed wondered what he wanted to do with the rest of his life.

CHAPTER THIRTY-FOUR

Claire found out about Frank on Sunday when she arrived back at the Airstream from her shift at the hospital. Red was waiting outside at the picnic table. He had the *Review-Journal* out and folded open to the story. He gave her the paper. "You should read this."

The article was brief:

> *LAS VEGAS, NV. —Police are investigating a shooting and death that occurred early Sunday morning. Police were called to the Wells Fargo Bank parking lot on E. Flamingo Road and Howard Hughes Parkway at 6:25 a.m. by a passing motorist who noticed the open door of a Mercedes car and a man slumped to the pavement.*
>
> *The victim was later identified as Frank Welch of Las Vegas. Police on the scene were investigating a possible robbery, murder, and mutilation. In a follow-up interview, a police spokesman said that the deceased was missing a freshly severed ear. He said that any additional details would be released after*

an investigation.

Frank Welch is the owner of Tramps nightclub on W. Flamingo Road and S. Arville Street.

The police are requesting that anyone who saw something suspicious during the early hours of Sunday morning along E. Flamingo Road come forward.

After reading it, Claire stared at the article, watching the words go out of focus. She remembered the last time she'd seen him and remembered his smile. She was sad for Frank and sad for the years they hadn't spoken, the years when he could have meant something to her. Those years were gone, and now she retained only the distant memories of a father who came and went and tried. Her life was so fucked up, and she was sad for herself and sad for Frankie, only thirteen, who no longer had a grandfather. She felt tears on her cheek.

Red stood up and said, "I'm sorry, Claire." He entered the trailer and returned with a wine cooler and a beer. "Here," he said and twisted the top. She drank and wiped away the tears.

They sat silently for a while, and then Claire said, "I'd better go tell Deedee." She stood up from the table and walked toward the brothel. She left the half-finished wine cooler behind but took the article.

Deedee led her back to the room where she was staying. The walls were wood-paneled, and the floors covered with a thick, cream shag carpet. Across from the bed was an ornate vanity and mirror, like some knock-off furniture from a French emperor's palace, and Claire suddenly felt bad for taking her trailer. They sat on the bed, and Deedee read the article. She said, "Oh, Claire, I'm so sorry." She reached over and held Claire, and the tears were there again, filling her lids and then seeping down to soak into Deedee's shirt.

Minutes later, Deedee held Claire away from her and asked, "What do you think happened? Do you think he was robbed?"

Claire said, "Wood killed Frank. I know because he sliced off the ear of a guy in LA. I guess it's his thing now. And I know he killed Sally."

"How do you know?"

"I just know."

"If that's the case, you and Frankie are Frank's only living family. You're going to need an attorney, and you'll need to make arrangements for the funeral. You'll also need to figure out what's happening at Tramps."

Claire looked at Deedee and shook her head.

"Claire, honey, I'm sorry. You're going to have to step up. I can help. We have a great lawyer in Vegas who can assist you with the estate. You'll also need to go downtown to claim his body."

———

Deedee stood with Claire when she identified the body at the county coroner's office. She was with her three days later at the funeral and wake held at Tramps on a Thursday night. It had been eight or nine years since she'd been there, and nothing had changed. The same model train still ran in circles over the back bar near the DJ booth. The walls were still rough-cut wood made to look like the sides of old railroad cars. Deedee remembered Big Tony and Little Tony, who'd been bartenders from the beginning. She recognized no one else.

She walked with Claire to the casket that lay on a table in the middle of the dance floor. Frankie was between them, standing untouched. Claire was sobbing quietly. Deedee didn't cry until they were close to the body and saw his face.

Frank was fifty-one years old and still had a full head of dark hair, no balding or gray. His hair was longer than she remembered and combed back over his ears. A small forelock swept down and touched his eyebrows. His nose was narrow and perfect. His eyes were closed, but she remembered them as dark and squinty because he was always smiling. When she'd met him back at the Sands in the fifties, it was the eyes and smile that got her.

She touched his face and then his hands that overlapped his chest. She kissed him on the lips and touched his hair. She remembered getting married in Henderson when she was four months pregnant and starting to show. She remembered the few times before Frank left for Korea when they played house. She'd seen and done so much since then and had regrets. She was sorry that Sally wasn't standing beside her. She was sorry that the only family present were the two women who'd abandoned him and the one child who'd been hard for him to know.

CHAPTER THIRTY-FIVE

Wood learned about Frank's funeral from Ed's handwritten note above the time clock. He wouldn't have known about it at all if he hadn't stopped in on Tuesday to get his paycheck.

On Thursday, he showed up at five o'clock when the funeral started. The entire staff was there, along with some of the regulars who'd known Frank over the years. Wood recognized Frank's attorney, a short guy named Diamond. Others he didn't recognize. One middle-aged man was crying. Frank might've had a life outside Tramps, but Wood was clueless as to what it entailed.

He saw Claire and Frankie with another older woman. He saw the fat man with red hair at the buffet table. Wood did not want to speak with any of them or be seen. He planned to follow later and discover where they were hiding.

He did, though, want to meet with the attorney, Mr. Diamond. He was sipping wine and talking with Ed.

Wood interrupted, "Mr. Diamond, I'm Wood Harding, Frank's son-in-law. Can I speak with you?"

Ed walked away. He said to the attorney, "We'll talk later."

Mr. Diamond lit a cigarette and looked up to Wood. "Yes?"

Wood noticed his gold pinkie ring, heavy gold bracelet, and gold Rolex with its spin dial that had something to do with scuba diving. When the lawyer lifted his cigarette to smoke, he saw a diamond in the pinkie ring.

"Mr. Diamond, it seems I might be the only family Frank has left."

The man looked him up and down slowly, sending a message. He said, "Yes?"

Wood now felt self-conscious in his casual Zodiac boat shoes and a too-small short-sleeved shirt, but he pushed on. "It's important to me that I carry on Frank's business. Make sure his grandson, Frankie, is taken care of. Make sure things don't fall apart. I'm wondering if you could help me manage the place and stay on as the attorney?"

"I am aware of the situation. Frank told me everything about his family. I'm aware that Sally is missing and that there's no death certificate. Legally, she is the beneficiary of Frank's estate."

Wood realized then that he'd made a mistake. If there was a body, there'd be a death certificate. He thought about the five thousand still in Sally's savings account, money he couldn't get at so long as she was thought to still be alive.

Mr. Diamond went on. "There's also the sister, Claire, here with Frankie. It seems she's now taking care of the boy. So, here's the problem. Frank did have a will, but you and Claire are not in it. The estate is in probate until the judge assigned to the case can determine Sally's whereabouts. If Sally is deceased, the estate goes to Frank Barleto, Frankie."

"So, who's going to run the club?"

"Ed Gustafson. The judge has allowed him to be the administrator of the business until the estate can be resolved. So, you see, Woodrow, it's all been taken care of." Mr. Diamond looked past Wood's shoulder and spotted someone he knew. He said, "Excuse me," and left.

Wood stood there confused and pissed. And he hated it when anyone called him Woodrow. He wasn't sure what probate was, but he understood that if Sally never showed up to claim the estate, it would go to Frankie. If he had Frankie, he'd have the estate. He waited near the kitchen, hidden from most of the mourners assembled.

The funeral started. It wasn't a service with a real minister. DJ Dan D acted as the MC. He first played Elton John's "Funeral for a Friend" as everyone gathered around the dance floor and open coffin. Then "Careless Whisper" by Wham! Afterward, Danny invited people up to eulogize Frank. Mr. Diamond spoke, then Ed, and then a few others. One was the older lady with Claire. It turned out she was Frank's ex-wife, Deedee. She told a story about how she met Frank at the Sands and described Frank on the first night Tramps opened. She said that she'd never been so proud.

Wood was not asked to speak, nor did he volunteer.

He left when Claire, Frankie, Deedee, and the fat man left. He followed the station wagon down Flamingo, then onto the Interstate going south. At Highway 160, they turned toward Pahrump. Wood stayed back as far as he could and followed the glowing spot on the horizon as the setting sun reflected off the Ford's roof. Before they arrived, he knew that Claire, Frankie, and the fat man planned to hide out at the Chicken Ranch where Deedee worked.

CHAPTER THIRTY-SIX

Wood did his dead-pet route the following Tuesday. After dumping the carcasses at one of his spots east of Johnnie, he drove south to Pahrump. Near the Chicken Ranch brothel stood a neighbor's pole barn, and Wood parked his truck on the road behind the barn where it wouldn't be seen. He inched the cab out so that he could stay in the truck and watch cars entering or leaving the parking lot. It was over one hundred degrees, and he kept his engine running and the air conditioning on high. He wished he had a Mountain Dew or even a jug of water.

He saw a stretch limousine enter the parking lot. The capped chauffeur opened a back door, and four older men stepped out and walked into the brothel. They were dressed casually in tight tennis shorts and polo shirts. One wore black eyeglasses the size of drink coasters and led the way. Wood guessed he was the one with the money. Less than an hour later, they were back in the limousine. After they'd gone, a Toyota Celica pulled into the lot and skidded to a stop. Six boys piled out like it was some clown car, laughing and drunk. They were in and out in five minutes, turned away.

Then he saw Frankie on the minibike. The bike crossed the road and into a desert lot right in front of Wood. Frankie wore a gold helmet, and Wood saw the helmet turn and saw Frankie look at the truck. He kept going, throwing up a cloud of dust. He crossed another road into another lot. Wood put his truck into gear and followed the kid across the desert.

The next lot over was piled with rusted cars that went back years. The cars were half submerged in dirt like they'd melted under the hot sun. The cloud from the minibike passed to the other side of the pile, then stopped, the dust dissolving into the wind. Wood saw a track around the cars, like a speedway, and followed it. His truck was made for this shit, and in that moment, he realized the truck's true value. It was more than just cool; it was fast and functional. He sat high off the ground, his wheels like cat claws.

He hit a mound of dirt, a jump, and felt the truck leave the ground. It landed and bounced, and without his seat belt buckled, his head hit the roof. He took a corner, and the light bed of the truck swung out. The minibike was gone when he reached the other side of the rust pile. He saw the dust cloud moving around the track. He kept driving.

There were other jumps, and he had to slow so he wouldn't fly too high and lose control. He slowed for the axle-high rows of dirt that crossed the track like rumble strips. He took the turns as fast as he could, but the kid stayed ahead of him, and always on the opposite side of the pile. At one point, he stopped and thought he could pass through the littered cars, but he couold'nt see direct route, just a maze of slow alleys. He sped up to follow the track again. His windows became coated in dust, and he put on his wipers with a long squirt of fluid, which just turned the dust into smeared mud. He opened his window and stuck his head out to see where he was going. Then the mud cleared, and Wood was able to make up some ground. He got close to the kid, but in a series of curves, the minibike rode the berms of dirt faster than his truck, and Wood lost ground again. Then, in another straight section, Wood was very close and thought he could run the kid down. He accelerated into the cloud of dust. Then he hit a jump.

The orange truck went up slightly off-center and tilted away from Wood's seat. He was flying and felt motionless, weightless. And then the pickup hit the ground. The truck's right front tire hit first and collapsed. The bumper gouged into the ground, and then the truck rolled once and stopped on its side. Wood was still in the truck, but his head was pressed against the windshield, and his arm was pinned between the edge of the roof and the ground. He could see his hand out the windshield and, beyond that, the refrigeration box fifty feet away, crumpled like tin foil. He felt the weight of the truck on his broken arm before he felt the pain. He tried to move just one finger. It twitched. Minutes passed, and the pain came on stronger.

Then, next to his hand, he saw the fat man's white sneakers with Velcro straps.

CHAPTER THIRTY-SEVEN

Red saw what looked like a dust storm. He sat at the picnic bench for a few minutes and watched. He thought maybe Frankie was really tearing it up. He was getting good, and Red thought the kid was ready for a real dirt bike, a Honda or Suzuki 125. Then he saw Wood's orange pickup. He opened the trailer door. Claire was at the kitchen counter, slicing onions. He yelled, "Fucking Wood is after Frankie."

Claire held onto the knife and followed Red to his Monte Carlo.

Red drove the dirt road to the lot where Frankie was riding. The dust had started to clear, and Red saw Frankie on his minibike. His helmet was still on, but he had stopped and was just waiting. In the distance, on the other side of the lot, was the orange pickup, crashed and lying on its side. Red dropped Claire off near Frankie. She left the kitchen knife on the car seat next to him. He drove around the lot to the road nearest the pickup.

Red got out of the Monte Carlo with the kitchen knife and

walked slowly toward the truck. He didn't see movement, but when he got closer, he saw the hand pinned to the ground. He stood in front of the truck and just waited. The sun was high, and the heat was oppressive. Red was breathing hard. Sweat streamed off his brow, stinging his eyes, and he wiped it away with his shirt sleeve. He looked at the hand and saw one finger move. He covered his eyes from the glare of the truck's windshield and looked inside. He saw Wood looking back at him.

Wood said, "Get me out of this. Go call for help." His voice was strained, lurching, and muffled by the windshield. Red could tell he was in pain. He wiped again at the sweat in his eyes. Wood screamed, "You have to get me out."

Red wanted to kill the guy just to make him shut up.

He returned to the Monte Carlo, got in, and started the engine. He drove back around the lot and picked up Claire and Frankie.

He told Claire, "Wood's pinned under the truck; he's not going anywhere." They drove back to the trailer. After Frankie was safe inside, Red and Claire talked briefly. She said, "He knows where Sally is."

Red tilted his head and squinted. For a second, his mind strayed, and he thought about sunglasses—he'd lived in the desert now for months and didn't own a pair. He shook his head, wiping his thoughts clean. He needed to think clearly. Wood, fucking Wood. He said, "Okay, let's go."

———

Claire stepped from the Monte Carlo and walked toward the orange truck. She held the kitchen knife. She saw the hand positioned like he'd tried to pick something off the windshield when the car flipped. She knew, though, it was just dumb luck that the truck and the arm came down that way—and the fact that Wood wasn't wearing his seatbelt. She crouched and looked through the windshield. Wood looked back and pleaded, "Claire, get some help." His voice was breathy, and she could barely hear him through the thick glass.

Claire said, "Can you move your hand?"

"Yes." He moved his fingers.

"Good."

Red was beside her, and she asked him to break the back window. "So we can hear what he has to say."

Red found a rock the size of a grapefruit. His one arm was still bandaged from his encounter days before, and he held the rock like a bowling ball in the hand of his other good arm. He stepped back a few paces, then ran forward, hurling the rock underhand. Claire saw that he knew how to bowl, and under different circumstances, the motion would have made her laugh. The safety glass in the window splintered into thousands of small pieces and left a hole the size of the rock. Red started kicking the hole to make it bigger.

Claire watched on the other side and said, "Look out, Red, he's got that knife."

He stepped back and found another rock. This time, he bowled directly at the glass behind Wood's head. The glass smashed, and the rock kept going, grazing his ear.

Red said, "Wood, throw out your knife, or the next one goes right to your head." He didn't wait for an answer. He found another, smaller rock and threw it more sidearm like a baseball. The rock bounced off Wood's head.

"Goddamn it." Wood tossed the Buck knife backward into the bed of the truck, and Red picked it up.

"Let me have that," Claire said.

Red gave her the knife. She felt the Buck's razor-edged blade, then dropped the duller kitchen knife.

Claire told Red, "Keep his hand steady so it doesn't move."

Red walked to the front of the truck and stepped on the hand like a cornered cockroach. Wood screamed once in pain and then took quick, staccato breaths, hyperventilating. Claire knelt in front of the windshield where Wood could see her. She held out the knife and, without saying anything, used the point to find the artery just up from his wrist. She plunged the point in and felt the pop when the artery was punctured.

Wood screamed, "What the fuck are you doing? I need help." The blood pumped out and fell in squirts on the desert floor. It pooled at first and then soaked into the dirt.

She asked, "Where's Sally?"

"I don't know. She left me for some other guy."

"I don't think so." She had time to play this out, but not forever.

"His name's Lamar. He worked at the Four Queens. Find him and you'll find Sally."

Claire watched the blood flow. The punctured artery tried to clot and close. Claire used the knife to pick away the clotting and keep the blood flowing. She talked loudly to make sure he heard, "Here's the deal, Wood. You don't have much time. You've lost maybe a cup of blood so far. Your blood is flowing at about one pint every two or three minutes. There are two cups in a pint. So, you'll have lost a pint by the time I stop talking. You can lose that pint, no problem. If you lose two, you'll start shaking and getting cold. That's shock. You have a total of ten or twelve pints in your body, but you'll start dying when you lose half that. So now you have maybe ten minutes to tell me the truth. I'll be patient."

"Claire, I don't know."

"Okay, let's start with something simple. You mentioned thirty-two thousand five hundred dollars. Where did that money come from?"

"It was a deal I had with a guy at the Westward Ho. He rigged a slot machine. I put the deal together, but Sally won the money. She left with the money."

"If she left with the money, why were you looking for it at my place?"

Wood was silent.

"So Wood, you see, you're still telling me lies. And you're wasting time. Are you getting cold?"

No answer again.

"Okay, so Sally was gone, supposedly with the money, but you were still looking for it."

Red interrupted, "*I* know." He still had Wood's hand pinned with his foot. "I bet Sally had the money, and Wood killed her while trying to find out where it was hidden. Then he couldn't find it."

Claire looked into the window, "Wood, is that correct?" Claire picked at his wound again, and the blood continued to flow. Wood saw his own blood. "I'm guessing you're getting cold now and maybe shaking inside. I can stop the artery anytime if you tell me the truth. If not, I'm ready to let you die. So I'll ask again, did you kill Sally?"

Wood said softly, "Yes." Then he said louder, "It was an accident. We had a fight, and I pushed her back. She fell and hit her head on the kitchen floor. I didn't plan it."

Claire expected the answer, but now that she heard it, she wanted to cry.

"I told you I did it. Now, you need to get me help."

"Where's the body?" Claire picked away another clot.

"It's in the desert."

"Where?"

"Just north of here near a town called Johnnie. In the desert just east of Johnnie." Wood's words came out erratically, and Claire knew he was getting very cold. He was going into shock.

"What about Frank?"

"If you want me to say I killed Frank, then I did."

"I want you to say it."

"Okay, I killed Frank."

"How?"

There was a long silence, and Claire wondered if he was passed out. Then he spoke, "I shot him."

Red knelt down, his foot still on Wood's hand. He looked at Claire. She looked back at him. There were tears in her eyes, and she was shaking her head. She said to Red, "I can't ever see him again. I can't be reminded."

Red said, "Give me the knife."

Claire gave Red the knife and walked to the Monte Carlo. She looked back once and saw Red picking away at the artery. She sat in the car and leaned forward with her face in her hands, her eyes covered.

CHAPTER THIRTY-EIGHT

Red drove the orange pickup north to Johnnie. He had tipped it back over with a rope tied to the Monte Carlo's bumper, and then he pulled and pushed Wood's heavy body through the broken back window and onto the bed of the truck. Red changed the front flat tire with the spare bolted to the underside of the truck's bed. His T-shirt was now soaked with sweat, and he was relieved to have the AC on high, the vents pointed at his chest. Claire followed in her station wagon.

Johnnie was only fifteen miles north of Pahrump on a map Red found in the truck. He watched his odometer. At fifteen miles, there was no sign of the town, only a cluster of buildings off to the west with a line of mailboxes on the highway. Red figured it must be an old mining town, a ghost town. A staked sign said, NO TRESPASSING. On the east side was a cattle guard crossing and a single dirt road that led toward the open desert. Red took it, and right away, he could see tracks matching Wood's truck tires.

He drove slowly and watched Claire in the rear-view

mirror bouncing on the uneven road. In the distance were hills, and when he got close, there was a fork in the road. One was more traveled, and he could see the same tire tracks. He followed that road up a dry ravine. It was steep to his left, but the ravine opened up on his right with miles of flat desert. He saw where Wood had driven off the road. Red followed the tracks. Claire was still behind him.

He saw the birds first—ravens and vultures. Red knew birds and garbage, and he knew they wouldn't be out in the desert if there wasn't something to feed on. The tracks went off in different directions, but one set went toward the birds, and he followed those. He saw the pile of carcasses they were eating. He stopped the truck and got out. Claire walked up behind him. They stepped closer. Claire reached out and grabbed his hand. It crossed his mind that this was the first time they'd touched.

The wind blew from the west and carried most of the stench away, but not all of it. They backed off when it became overpowering. The smell was distinctive, like no other—a combination of shit, rotten eggs, and garlic—like baby shit and sulfur. He led Claire around to where the wind was at their back and the stench tolerable. They looked.

What they saw were dogs and cats that were decomposing and liquefying. The birds looked up but continued picking at the flesh. A cloud of flies surrounded the pile with a continual buzz, loud like a jet plane. Red looked for signs of a body, and he assumed Claire was doing the same. He knew the pile was too fresh for a four-month-old corpse. He wanted to look elsewhere but didn't want to let go of her hand. Then she did it for him; she let go of his hand and covered her mouth.

He walked west of the pile, staying upwind of the odor. Claire walked behind him. Minutes later, they found a second, older pile that was only dry bones and tufts of fur. He looked for a human skull. Claire circled the pile, staying clear of bones. She seemed calm and kept her eyes focused on the ground, looking. Her hair was loose and fell down each side of her face, covering it. Red could sense the tension in her locked and stiff arms, her hands in her pockets, afraid to touch. He was scared for her.

Red had been around garbage and landfills and knew what it was. He broke the silence with Claire, "Wood's been dumping dead pets up here. He probably gets paid to haul the carcasses to a crematorium but dumps them here instead and then pockets the difference. The desert here is probably littered with these piles." He didn't want to say it, but Sally's body was probably in one of the piles somewhere.

Claire nodded.

"It's going to get dark soon. We should leave. We'll need to get the police up here."

Claire nodded again.

Before they left, Red drove the orange truck through the ravine until he found a ledge eroded from a past flash flood. He stopped the truck at the top and set the parking brake. He left the engine idling and the transmission in drive. He stepped out of the truck, then reached inside, placing his hand on the brake-release handle. He stood ready to jump out of the way. Then he pulled. The truck lurched and slowly rolled over the ledge, then tumbled once before hitting the bottom of the ravine. It landed upside down. Wood's body was thrown twenty feet from the truck. Red walked back to Claire, who sat in the passenger seat of the Monte Carlo. They drove back to the Ranch in silence.

Deedee had a phone in the trailer, and Red anonymously called the police. Later that night, Red drank a beer alone at the picnic table. He went back over the details of the day to think of anything that could implicate him or Claire. He thought about the inevitable autopsy and wondered if the coroner would match the volume of blood missing from Wood's body with any blood on the desert floor. He thought it unlikely, not after the birds and coyotes gorged on him.

CHAPTER THIRTY-NINE

Frankie focused on the lawnmower in front of him and ignored the other lawnmower and rototiller next in line for repairs. He pulled the starter cord and felt the stiff resistance of good compression. He looked inside the gas tank and ran his finger under the opening. His finger came out with little crusts of varnish, and he knew the gas was old and had gone bad. He unscrewed the tank from the brackets that held it to the engine. He dropped it on a table that Red had set up for replacement parts (he'd put a part there, and the next day, Red would replace it). He took off the carburetor next and knew it would also be filled with slivers of gas turned to varnish. He took the carburetor completely apart, down to its casing, floats, jets, springs, and screws. He placed the parts into a wire basket that he dipped into a bucket of cleaning solution. He let them soak and let the varnish dissolve.

His grandmother, Deedee, sat in a folding lawn chair reading *People* magazine. She was there that day to watch him. Claire and Red had taken the Monte Carlo to spend the weekend somewhere else.

Deedee said to him, "Hi, Frankie, how are you?"

He looked down at his hands and made a noise. He thought the word "fine" and knew what it sounded like coming from other people's mouths. He knew the word rhymed with "pine," "shine," "mine," and even "sublime." But it wouldn't come out. The noise was more like, "nnnn," like the sound of electricity.

Then his grandmother said, "You know, Frankie, I used to call my grandmother Lita. She was Mexican, and Lita was short for *abuelita*, which is the Spanish word for grandmother. Try saying 'Leee.'"

Frankie looked at the ground, thought the word, then tried to say it, "Leee," and it sounded right.

She said, "Now try, 'Tahh.'" She sang it, "Tahhhh."

He tried it. "Tahhh."

"Now try, "'Leee,' then 'Tahhh.'"

He did it. "Leeetahhh."

"That's good, Frankie. You can call me Leeetahhh or Lita."

Frankie walked back into the shack. Red's bed was gone, and the place had more room for engines, parts, and tools. He grabbed his canvas tool bag that was now smeared with oil and grease and missing a handle. Red had given him a new steal toolbox filled with his own wrenches, screwdrivers, pliers, and more, so he only had a few old toy tools left in the canvas bag. There was one he wanted, a small screwdriver no bigger than a toothpick that was useful for the tiny carburetor screws. He felt around at the bottom, but it wasn't there. With his fingertips, he lifted up the cardboard bottom liner. Beneath the liner, he saw the three bundles of stiff greenish paper with wrappings like Band-Aids. He knew what money was and what it looked like but did not like the idea of Band-Aids that reminded him of hurts. He pushed the money aside, and found the screwdriver in the seam of the bag. He pinched it out and dropped it in one of the small drawers of his new toolbox. He closed the tattered canvas bag and handed it up to his grandmother. Lita would want the money.

She said, "Frankie, what would you like me to do with this old greasy thing?"

He wanted to say, "Take it." Just those two easy words, but what came out was the sound he'd made before, "Tahhh, tahhh, tahhh."

Lita held up the bag by its one remaining handle. "Trash? Is this trash?"

She asked a simple question that he could easily answer without words, with only a head nod or shake. But a shake, a *no*, would lead to a string of what-where questions, and he wanted to avoid trying to make more words.

Frankie nodded. *Yes, trash.*

EPILOGUE

Emmy stood behind the glass display case at the Gold Rush jewelry store. It was lunchtime, and he was eating a chicken salad sandwich his girlfriend had made him that morning. When the front door opened, triggering a buzzer, Emmy put his half-eaten sandwich in a drawer beneath the case. The guy who walked in was a petty thief and heroin addict who came in about twice a week with mostly junk. The thief's street name was Skinny, and Emmy wondered if the name was given to him after he became a junkie or if the guy had always been rail thin. He wore a surfer-dude outfit with a Billabong half-cap, long-sleeved Corona shirt, light-blue swimming shorts, and flip-flops. He was carrying a crumpled brown bag.

Right off, Skinny said, "I got something for you, man. Something g-e-n-u-i-n-e."

He opened the bag on top of the glass case and pulled out a ropy gold chain like something a hip-hop rapper would wear, like Run-D.M.C. They were called dookie chains or ropes. The nice ones were two grand or more; the plate ones were worthless. He could already see the base copper in places where the thin gold plate had worn off.

Emmy did not like Skinny or want his crap. Occasionally, he brought in a nice wedding ring or a broken gold necklace ripped from someone's neck. Emmy bought the stuff at a fraction of their worth, but he was now beginning to regret it. The Gold Rush was once owned by his cousin Tony Spilotro. It had been the center of operations for the Hole in the Wall Gang and a hub for fencing stolen jewelry. Emmy didn't have a gang, and his business was no gigantic criminal enterprise, so he didn't need the heat or the headaches. Sooner or later, someone was going to come in and identify a ring or a necklace, and then the cops would come. The cops wouldn't want the hassle, and they'd find a way to shut him down.

He said, "Get your shit off my counter and get the fuck out of my shop. I do not want to see your skinny ass in here again."

Skinny looked at him like he'd just insulted his mother. He said nothing, but Emmy could tell the kid was thinking of spitting in his face. If he spat in his face, Skinny's head was going through the glass cabinet top, and Emmy didn't care what the damage would cost. Skinny put the dookie chain back in the brown bag and walked out. Before he left the shop, he turned around and said, "Fuck you, Nuts."

"Nuts" was what everyone in the neighborhood had called him back in Chicago. His name was Emilio Nuzzarello. When he moved to Las Vegas in 1984, he dropped the name Nuts and told the new people he met to call him Emmy. Nuts was not someone you wanted to buy jewelry from. The name Emmy, though, was *very* Vegas. You could buy a five-thousand-dollar diamond pinkie ring from a guy named Emmy. But when he registered for a Sheriff's Card downtown, his name came up as a felon from Chicago, an Outfit guy. The cops were on him the next day, asking what he was doing in town. He told them he was taking over his cousin's business, that he owned it now. They'd done their research and called him Nuts. The name somehow got around so that even some street punks like Skinny would call him Nuts. They knew he didn't like it.

Minutes after Skinny left, Sergeant Askoff walked in. He was in plain clothes, wearing a Members Only jacket even though it was a hundred degrees outside. Emmy supposed it was to hide his piece. Sergeant Askoff was one of the first cops to visit him at the Gold Rush after he opened. He made it clear that the Gold Rush was only doing business because he, Sergeant Pete Askoff, had deemed it necessary that it should be. Since then, Emmy had done Pete favors. Sometimes, it was just information about who was selling what, but favors could also include hurting someone that the cops didn't want to directly hurt themselves. When he was Pete's muscle, he was paid. And the pay was usually good, better than the rates in Chicago. Pete called him Nuts, and Emmy figured it was his way of saying, "I know who you are, and I own you." Pete said, "How's it going, Nuts?"

Emmy said, "Pete."

Pete walked into the back room, where there weren't any cameras. Emmy locked the front door and put up a sign with a clock that said, "Will Return." He set the hands of the clock a half hour ahead.

Pete was already sitting at his desk when Emmy came in. He sat across from Pete in one of the two stuffed chairs. He said, "I have a job I need done. This one is special."

Emmy shrugged his shoulders. "What?"

"Two guys I need gone. There's ten grand in it for you.

Each."

"Okay." This was the first time Pete had asked him to off someone. He was sure Pete had done his research and contacted the Chicago police to ask them about Emilio "Nuts" Nuzzarello. His felony conviction was for robbery. It was a class-4 felony because he hadn't carried a weapon, and he'd only served six months in the Cook County jail. But the detectives would have told the Vegas cops the crimes he had *supposedly* committed. He was good with explosives, and people had died in car bombs. In Chicago, the going rate for a hit was five thousand, so ten thousand each was a good number. And it wouldn't be easy to say no to Pete.

"Their names are Clarence Farmer and Arnold Ramirez— two security guys at the Westward Ho." Pete handed Emmy a manila folder with a string tie. Emmy didn't need to open it; he knew it contained photocopies of driver's licenses and other personal details.

Emmy put the envelope on his desk. "I'll need supplies. I got no connections in Vegas."

"Just tell me what you need."

Emmy was a bomb guy—he wasn't a sharpshooter and didn't work close with a knife or a garrote. There were only two things he would need. "Six one-pound blocks of C-4 and two electronic detonators."

"Okay."

"And, Pete, you better know where the detonators came from. They'll have a signature, an ID, and someone in your office will trace them back."

"Understood," Pete said.

"What's your timing?"

"As soon as possible. Yesterday."

Emmy wondered why he even asked. "I'll need time to

eliminate risk."

He'd learned how to handle C-4 from a military explosives expert that had blown shit up in World War II. The guy was then working for a demolition company in Chicago and still blowing shit up, mostly buildings. He always talked about eliminating risk. Risk was all about what could go wrong: getting caught setting the charge, placement of the charge and making sure it stayed where you placed it, anticipating anything that could deaden or divert the explosion, bad batteries triggering the detonator, poor detonator connections, range of signal devices, getting blown up by the detonation, and being seen blowing something up. You could never eliminate the risk altogether, but you could make getting caught a remote possibility. And Emmy was still alive with working toes and fingers. He'd never been caught.

———

Emmy watched the employee entrance to the Westward Ho while reading the *Review-Journal*. The lead story in the local section was about the possibility of a serial pet killer in Las Vegas. He'd read a paragraph and then look up to see if the two security guys were leaving the building. The headline was "Remains of Pets Found in the Desert Tied to Serial Killer."

> *PAHRUMP, NV. —The remains of pets have been found in a remote area just outside the city of Pahrump that Nye County Sheriff Burl Carver described as a dumping ground for a suspected pet serial killer. The exact number of pets is unknown, but Sheriff Carver said, "There may be hundreds."*
>
> *In the same area where the skeletons of pets were found,*

police also found the remains of a man in his late twenties. The Nye County Sheriff said that they believe the man could have stumbled upon the killer in the process of disposing of carcasses.

"This is certainly a burial site," Sheriff Carver said.

The name of the deceased man will be released upon notification of next of kin.

Sheriff Carver cautioned Pahrump and Las Vegas residents, "Until we apprehend the person responsible for this crime, we recommend that all pet owners in Nye and Clark counties watch their pets. Watch over your cat or dog in the yard or keep them on a leash."

Sheriff Carver added that anyone missing a pet or knows information regarding the dumping of pets should call the Nye County Sheriff's Department.

Emmy had never heard of anything like that in Chicago and wondered if it was a Nevada thing to kill dogs and cats.

He sat in his car and watched the entrance for more than three hours before Clarence and Arnold finally walked out of the casino and into a dark gray Dodge four-door sedan. He followed them down the backstreet and across Sahara Avenue to the Crazy Horse Too strip club. He waited there for another hour until his bladder was ready to burst. He walked into the strip club and used the restroom. Clarence and Arnold were at a table drinking beer and watching the girls. Thirty minutes later, they came out and drove back to the Westward Ho. Emmy watched again from his car. Two hours later, he was hungry and left to get a McDonald's. The Dodge was still in the parking lot when he returned with his food. At three in the morning, the two left the casino again. He followed the car to an apartment off Desert Inn. It seemed as though the two both worked together and lived together. Emmy figured maybe one was divorced, the other single. That or they were queer, but then the strip joint didn't fit. Anyway, killing these two was going to be easy.

Afterward, he drove home. He was now living with his girlfriend, Vivian, who had a small house in a new development on East Flamingo past McLeod. The house was Spanish-style, with roofing tiles that looked like terracotta and a double door that arched in the center. They had trees and a small, irrigated lawn.

Emmy was also divorced, a quick settlement after his wife said she was in love with another man. They didn't have kids, so moving west and starting over was a no-brainer. Now, things were different. Vivian came with a thirteen-year-old daughter, Tanya—a real handful—and a crazy job dealing cards where she was gone at seven and didn't return until three in the morning.

When he got home, Vivian had just gotten off work. She was eating Stouffer's lasagna and offered him some. He said that he'd already eaten. They talked about Tanya's homework. The assignments were easy, but she'd gone through a phase where she wasn't turning anything in. Emmy thought she was caught up now, but Vivian wasn't convinced. They both went to bed at four-thirty. Emmy turned the air conditioning up and the fan on high. In the cool room with the muffling noise, they had sex. Afterward, Emmy sat up and smoked a cigarette while Vivian slept.

He was nearly forty and had grown up tough on the northwest side of Chicago. Emmy, then Nuts, had been a soldier in Chuckie English's crew along with his cousin Tony. Now, he was in Las Vegas selling jewelry and checking homework. He marveled at how his different worlds collided and danced around each other like opposing magnets.

Emmy followed the two guys for another three days. They lived together, worked together, and always drove in the same Dodge car. They changed clothes, but one day, one would wear a blue Madras shirt, and the next day, the other would wear the same or similar shirt. It got to be that he didn't know which was Clarence and which was Arnold until he remembered that Arnold wore the glasses. It didn't matter. The two didn't leave the casino until late at night, three hours before their shift ended when they'd have their break at the Crazy Horse Too. That's when he'd set the charge.

While he waited and watched, he read the *Review-Journal* cover to cover. Each day, there was more information about the pet serial killer. Two more dead bodies were found, human bodies this time, and the story jumped to the front page. Now, the serial killer went after anything on two or four legs. Emmy didn't see anyone walking their dog, though not many would in the 110-degree heat. But then feral cats roamed the streets seemingly everywhere, and Emmy figured the killer could take their pick.

Then, the story changed again. The Las Vegas police tracked down the pets and found that all of them had died of natural causes or been euthanized by a veterinarian. Someone was taking all the dead pets and dumping them in the desert. But that, of course, didn't explain the dead bodies. He'd have to wait another day to find out more.

Pete dropped off the C-4 and detonators in a banker's box. He didn't say anything or ask any questions. He dropped the box on top of the glass cabinet and walked out. He didn't even smile.

Initially, Emmy had thought, two guys, two bombs. Now he had extra C-4 and an extra detonator. Three pounds would have been enough to blow one car to kingdom come. He'd use four pounds on the Dodge to make sure the job was done right. The chances of collateral damage in the parking lot at three in the morning would be minimal—not that he didn't allow for some damage if it came to that.

He rigged the detonator to a small square nine-volt battery and the kind of beeper every doctor, lawyer, detective, hooker, and drug dealer in Vegas used. He wired the guts of the beeper so that when he called the number, it would open a switch from the battery to the detonator. He had long zip ties to connect the bomb to the car's undercarriage. He'd plunge the detonator into the putty-like C-4 at the last moment.

The day before, Emmy rented a portable cellular phone from Radio Shack. He had wanted to own one, and so did almost everyone else in Las Vegas, but they cost around four grand and maybe two or three hundred a month for the minutes. Only lawyers and millionaires had cell phones. The one he rented came in a nylon carrying case the size of a lunch box and plugged into the lighter of his car. It rented for a hundred a day and included ten minutes of talking time. He'd use ten seconds.

On the night Emmy planned the bombing, he sat waiting in the parking lot reading the *Review-Journal*. The guy the sheriff had initially found dead at the scene was now their prime suspect. The veterinarians had identified him as the man hired to dispose of the carcasses. One human body was identified as the man's wife, the other a known acquaintance. A weird twist was that the guy, Woodrow Harding, had collected four ears from his victims and kept them pickled in a jar. The sheriff's department matched two ears to the two victims and the third to Woodrow's' boss and stepfather, who'd been gunned down just weeks before in a Wells Fargo parking lot. But they had yet to find the owner of the fourth ear, and they assumed there was at least one other body somewhere out in the desert. The headline was "Trophy Ears Linked to Human Bodies," and Emmy thought the headline didn't really capture the whole strange story.

Emmy dialed the beeper number just as the two entered the Dodge sedan. The explosion destroyed nine more cars in the parking lot, but no one else was hurt. He drove home afterward, thinking that he'd finally get some sleep.

———

Emmy remembered the night he drove into Las Vegas. He'd been driving for two days, renting a motel room once in Denver. He was listening to a cassette, *Only the Lonely*, Sinatra's best album, he thought. The sky was clear, with more stars than he'd ever seen in Chicago. He had his window down because it was cool and kept him alert. At times, it smelled like the creosote and diesel of a train yard, and at other times, it smelled like rain. He first saw a glow on the horizon just to his left. Then, the glow radiated higher above the horizon like a rising sun. As he got closer, the light had definition, and it sparkled. It was exciting. Vegas.

The Interstate went close enough to Glitter Gulch that he could see the neon cowboy, Vegas Vic, waving his arm and giving him a wink. The Interstate ran parallel to the Strip, and he had glimpses of Circus Circus, the Stardust, the Riviera, and the Desert Inn before he pulled off on Flamingo and saw the fountain at Caesars Palace that Evel Knievel had jumped. The Dunes was across the street, and the MGM Grand was catty-corner where the marquee advertised "Dean Martin and the Golddiggers." He took a right down the Strip and stayed at the Tropicana, where he knew someone who knew someone. He was comped a room and champagne. Later that night, a girl showed up.

Since then, he'd been on his own. The people he knew or thought he knew were gone within a year. No one from the Outfit still worked in the casinos, and the few guys working off the Strip were dead or gone. The Gold Rush was in his name legally, and he was supposed to kick up to his crew in Chicago. But Chuckie English had been demoted from capo to soldier, then finally gunned down in '85. Now, there was no one left to pay.

A few days after the hit on the two guys, he was paid his twenty grand. It was a nice score and would help him move up. The Gold Rush was a dump on Sahara, and no self-respecting whale from out of town would go there to buy jewelry—he was strictly chains, bracelets, and rings for local Vegas guys trying to reach big-shot status. Women didn't come in the store, ever, and only a loser in a hurry for a quickie marriage would buy a stone. He wanted a better location, a nicer store.

Not far down the Strip, they were demolishing the old Castaways for a new casino Steve Wynn was building. The name was The Mirage, and it would be the biggest and swankiest place in Vegas. Emmy thought he'd like to have a shop there and deal strictly with high-rollers. He wondered who he needed to know, who he needed to contact. Maybe Pete would know. Then he wondered if it was even possible.

Emmy read the *Review-Journal* when he got home after closing the shop. Tanya was back from school and doing her homework. Vivian was off at the Riviera dealing cards. The pet serial killer story was still on the front page of the local section.

They were now linking the killer, Woodrow, to the robbery and murder of his father-in-law, the owner of the third ear.

And the owner of the fourth and final ear? The Nye County Sheriff's Department was still searching the desert.

FIND MORE FROM AUTHOR
KURT JOHNSON

www.KurtJohnsonBooks.com

KurtJohnsonBooks.substack.com

* 9 7 9 8 2 1 8 3 4 7 1 8 5 *